Orion

by
A. S. Johnson

Strategic Book Group

Strategic Book Group
P.O. Box 333
Durham, CT 06422
www.StrategicBookClub.com

ISBN: 978-1-60976-545-3

Printed in the United States of America

Cover Design:

Book Design: Arlinda Van, Dedicated Business Solutions, Inc.

DEDICATION

*For my mom, Daisy, you showed us what true love
really is. To all those who serve our great nation and
the world past and present who sacrificed their blood,
sweat, tears, and their own lives all in the name of
science and space exploration.*

I Thank You!

CONTENTS

FOREWORD

The One

> You, Chance are the one I've dreamt of
> practically all of my life;
> you make me feel so loved,
> in this world of grief and strife.
>
> The feelings I have for you
> are so magically intense;
> you've swept me off my feet,
> leaving me in sweet suspense.
>
> Our love has grown into something
> provocative, strong, and true;
> my nights are no longer spent lonely,
> now filled with dreams of me and you.

by Stacy Lyn Cornish

PREFACE

My lips found his, slower deeper than any kiss in my life, I surrendered into his arms. I couldn't stop myself any more. I kissed back deeper, stronger, and with more passion than I ever knew existed. He was all I wanted and nothing else mattered. It was more than before, with intensity and an urgency to let him know exactly where he stood. I held nothing back and he did the same in return. I knew in that moment that every word, every kiss, and every touch that he gave me was the truth. The realization that I loved him was the only truth I knew. Yes, I loved him.

Chapter I

Dream

We were walking slowly, hand in hand making our moment together last as long as possible. The sand was beneath our toes cooling our feet as we strolled along the beach watching boats motor by stirring waves as they pass by. The lake was always our favorite place to be, where nothing else in the world mattered, but the two of us. As we took in the beauty of the lake, the sun reflected off rippling waves making its way down the horizon and into the sunset. I looked to his face allowing myself to drink in his image this would be our last day together.

Tomorrow, he'd be off to basic training and I would face the upcoming year of high school without him by my side. As I caught a glimpse of his sky blue eyes and his soft tan skin, I couldn't help but smile.

"What?" He asked as he caught me glancing.

"Nothing really," I lied trying to hide the pain, "I just wish this day wouldn't end."

He gripped my hand more firmly and stopped in place turning to face me. As he released my hand and moved me into his arms pulling me dangerously closer and my eyes fixed on him never breaking from his trance. He was breathtaking and I wanted nothing more than to be completely consumed by his presence. Before I could speak, he took my face into his hands, caressing it. His lips meet mine with a deep urgency. I instinctively pulled myself closer feeling the warmth of his embrace as his kiss answered my statement without speaking. He was all I longed for, all my dreams, all my hopes, all my soul wanted, and he made my heart sing while making my mind spin, I was lost in the moment.

* * *

"Beep, Beep, Beep." I slowly opened one eye. I could see them all staring at me, smirks, giggles, and puzzled. Trying to ignore them I closed my eye and tried to drift back into my moment of bliss and my dream of elation.

"Susan, Earth to Susan!" Ty snickered.

"What?" I snapped back slowly opening both eyes now to get a good look at him and growled.

"Hey don't get all bent out of shape," Ty replied as he tried miserably to hold back his amusement.

"The preliminary reports are ready, time to transmit data back to Houston," Abe said.

"Yea, okay give me a second!" I scoffed knowing there was no way I was going to get an extra second of sleep.

My eyes closed and I stretched out my arms hoping to pop the closest victim. They had backed away, darn. I opened my eyes back up and unzipped myself from my cocoon letting my body float out of its place of hibernation and making my way to the control room.

"Alright," I said while taking my seat and strapping in. "Is everything ready to go?"

"Yes, everything is a go," Chance confirmed. "By the way, who is Brian?"

His question threw me off. I'd never told anyone who Brian was or ever recalled speaking his name so I tried to ignore Chance. I shook my head clearing the thought and continued with protocol.

"Good morning Houston, space shuttle Orion ready for status update," I firmly spoke allowing myself to transform back into command mode and the business at hand.

"Good morning Orion flight crew," a voice from Earth spoke, "copy, status update confirmed, go when ready."

Our briefing of system checks, crew status, and weather for reentry topped our conversation with ground control.

Once protocol was finished then it was time to ready the shuttle for its trip back to Earth.

"Houston, we'll be back in two hours for the space-walk checklist and systems reports," I replied as I turned off the communication link once Houston signed off.

Ty and Chance would be the crew members going out today for the final space-walk to assess our shuttle condition prior to reentry.

We made the best of the next two hours. One by one each crew member sent off e-mail back to Earth to update family and friends.

We'd been in space almost six days doing experiments on each other all in the name of science. Doctor Jeff Brady kept a strict routine of testing blood, urine, and vitals of each crew member and himself along with other bio-oriented experiments in space.

Our mind and bodies were always at odds with the zero gravity of space. Jeff was working on better ways to treat crew members in hopes of advancing the health of astronauts for upcoming space travel to the Moon and Mars. We were his "guinea pigs." So far so good and nobody got too sick or even passed out. He was involved with bettering space medicine and he enjoyed being on the cutting edge of medical technology. Jeff was a longtime friend and I trusted his knowledge of medicine completely as well as his own judgment. He liked to push the envelope at times, but all for a good cause and all in the name of space travel.

"Hey Susan, are you going to e-mail home?" Christina the only other female aboard asked.

"Maybe one or two, you go-ahead and I'll get to it after you're all done," I quickly replied.

Christina had plenty of pen pals from around the world that kept up with her travels to space.

It was nice having another female on board to talk with someone whose life didn't revolve around baseball, football, or hockey.

I was looking out one of the portal windows gazing back to our Earth. I was admiring the vivid colors of the ocean below as the clouds swirled around making me feel calm at the thought that we'd all be home safely soon enough.

"Who is Brian?" Christina asked breaking my trance and interrupting my quiet reflection of Earth.

"What?" I asked acting like I was clueless to her question.

"You spoke his name while you were in la-la land, Brian," Christina mocked me as she giggled. "Who is he?"

"Why didn't you wake me up," I responded to her questioning, "you let me blab in my sleep. That's great now I'll never hear the end of it!"

I looked back at Ty and Chance who tried to act like they weren't listening, but I knew better with the smirks and childish giggling going on over in the corner.

"I don't think so girlfriend and miss out on all the fun," Christina teased as she continued with her inquisition.

"Who is Brian?" She was demanding an answer.

"Just a guy I use to know back in high school, nobody you need to be concern with," I replied as I nodded my head.

"Yea, well I figured that much. So, was he a lost love?" She asked not letting up.

"Sure," I replied curtly hoping to kill her curiosity and trying to end the issue so she could move on.

"I knew it! I knew it! You've been holding out on us haven't you?" Chance took up where Christina left off. "I'm crushed!"

Chance teased as he and Ty began to laugh again.

"As you recall I can only handle one man at a time. So, don't go worrying your pretty little self over a guy from my past," I snickered in response in hopes to turn the attention off of me, "besides Chance, you know I have only enough room in my heart for you."

Everyone had been listening and started to join in on roughing Chance up.

I was feeling relief as the attention shifted from my dream to teasing Chance.

"No way Chance, sounds like Brian was more than a guy from her past just oddly popping up in her dream," Ty put his two cents worth in.

"Yes Chance, I thought you said you liked brunettes, not to mention Susan is older than you, and as I recall you like them young," Jeff chimed in.

The entire crew erupted with laughter as the joke fell back on Chance.

He turned and went back to his e-mail pretending to sulk and Ty whispering in his ear and started to laugh all over again milking the joke as much as he could.

"Okay, enough picking on Chance. You guys best get ready for your space-walk," I spoke trying to pull everyone back into work mode.

"Ty, did you double check the camera batteries so ground control can view the space-walk in virtual time?" I asked firmly so he'd leave Chance alone and to give Chance a break from Ty's teasing.

"Yep, got it done an hour ago," Ty replied.

I knew Ty and Chance were best friends, almost like brothers, but sometimes Ty just took things too far and I had learned to read Chance's expressions over the past five years enough to know when he needed backup.

Ty and Chance had suited up for the space-walk and I got back to the control center to open our link back up with ground control. They needed to monitor the entire space-walk so experts on the ground could view what the guys were doing and maybe see anything our crew might miss.

"Space shuttle Orion to Houston, confirming our communication link, all systems go for space-walk," I began our transmission.

"Orion, you are go for space-walk all systems go, communication link and video are up and running Banks over," Chief Banks from ground control responded.

For the next hour standard procedure was followed for the final space-walk, everything went smoothly, and our space-walk was a success. Ty and Chance had the most experience of any astronaut for space-walks and were top mechanics as well. I've never questioned either one's ability or knowledge when it comes to the safety of the shuttle and crew, they both brought a sense of pride and confidence to each mission they were involved with. I enjoyed both men as part of my crew on previous missions and always found relief when one or both were named to my crew. Ty was a California native who had always loved adventure. Chance was the true Texas southern gentleman. Not only were they part of the crew, but friends I could count on.

"Space shuttle Orion, you are a go for reentry in nine hours. Get some rest and we'll be back to brief you in six," Chief Banks replied.

"Roger Houston, space shuttle is a go for reentry in nine hours confirmed," I responded.

I finished our link and turned the shuttle controls over to Abe for standby.

"Ty, Chance, and Christina you three are off to sleeping quarters I'll wake you up in five hours, Abe's got controls," I said returning myself to command mode, "Jeff, you and I can go over to the medical bay and get everything there packed up and ready for reentry."

"That sounds good to me," Jeff replied as he floated off first to get his checklist ready.

The rest of the crew headed off to sleeping quarters as I finished up protocol with ground control along with Abe and started our checklists going over procedures for reentry.

Home finally. My body and my mind were both exhausted from the deep space routine.

The shuttle activity had calmed down. Houston played some of our music list requests over the communication link with more subdued than our normal morning jam session since we were scheduled for a night time reentry this time around. I pulled down the blinds over each window to help shut out the Earth and Sun.

Abe, Jeff, and I had already had our five hours of slumber earlier while the others did their part of the checklists and reports.

I made it back to the medical bay to find Jeff had already begun strapping things down and returning the scientific studies back to the lockers. He'd done a lot of testing on germ culturing this mission and I was excited to learn his results.

"So Doc, how did everything go?" I asked.

"Our results thus far show everyone reacted within limits to the various strains, I exposed them to and the blood work came out well. We're lucky to have so many healthy people on board anyone else may have been sick due to exposure. The cultures did really good," Doc held them up as he spoke and placed a few up to my face. I pulled away feeling nauseous and sick.

"Doc, that's gross!" I replied not sure if that was the reaction he wanted as I made a frown.

"Yea I know, but I get a kick out of everyone's reaction. I wish I had a photo of Ty and your expressions," he said as he chuckled.

"I am so glad I could amuse you," I smirked then picked up some of the test tubes. "What's this?"

"Seeds," he replied, "carrot, bean, and red beets."

"Yuck!" I commented as I stuck my tongue out when he said red beets. The thought made me shiver. Beets are the one vegetable I could live without on Earth or in space for that matter.

"What you don't like beets?" Doc asked teasing me because he already knew the answer.

"No, you let me know when you get to steak and potatoes and I'll be more than happy to help," I replied.

"Thanks now you got my stomach growling," Doc informed me as it growled again.

"Maybe after you finish up I'll get you some dehydrated mush from the food locker," I said teasing him as I floated out of medical bay heading back to controls.

"Thanks," I heard him snicker from behind.

"Abe, you best go eat, then help Doc lock down the food lockers, and bring me back a dehydrated ice cream?" I asked.

"Ice cream that sounds good now if it were only Ben and Jerry's," Abe replied turning back to me, "monitors are all up and running, the control checklist is finished, and I just need you to sign off."

"Sure I'll get right on it. Thanks Abe," I replied as I settled in.

Abe came back to controls after an hour to report things had been locked down.

I went to the laptop and sent off my e-mail to my mom, sisters, nephew, nieces, and a few elementary school pen pals. After another two hours had passed, I went back to the sleeping quarters to wake the rest of the crew and do check-list of the rest of the shuttle.

"Okay sleepy heads, time to rise and shine!" I shouted as I entered.

Ty was already awake and had started strapping things down and putting items away in their assigned lockers. Christina was next to awake, she floated off to get the latrine and wash station prepped.

"What does he think he's special?" I asked to Ty pointing at Chance.

"No he knows he's special," Ty joked as he burst into laughter.

I couldn't resist and joined in laughing so hard we both were in tears and finally sleeping beauty awoke.

"Hey what are you two jokers laughing at?" Chance asked as he looked over at us and snarled.

"You!" Ty and I jointly replied followed by more laughter.

"Now Chance, from the expression on your face I'd say I wasn't the only one on this ship having lofty dreams," I said as I giggled.

"Yea Chance, it looked like you were enjoying something good. You care to share?" Ty asked as he followed along with his tease of his best friend. "Aren't holding out on us again are you old buddy?"

"Yea, I am," Chance snapped back as he cocked one eye brow, "you know me always got my head and heart in the clouds."

"Oh Chance, I thought I was the only one you dreamed of!" I joked along returning the favor from earlier when he joked about my dreams.

He was almost in shock as he glared cruelly at Ty.

"What the hell," Chance trailed off.

"Hey man, don't look at me I have no clue," Ty replied and turned quickly away from me facing Chance so I couldn't see what he was mouthing.

"What did I say? I was only kidding Chance. Don't be upset with us, we were just roughing you up, you know, like you did earlier," I reminded him.

Ty shook his head in agreement and the expression on Chance's face turned from one of pain back to his playful happy go lucky look.

"Yea, you know I love you," Chance replied with a grin and wink.

"Thanks," I quietly replied as I patted Ty on the shoulder then headed back to control not giving their exchange a second thought.

The crew finished with their checklist and returned one by one to control to get ready for our reentry systems check.

"Everyone got their reports ready, we're live in fifteen," I informed the crew.

Each responded with a muted yes.

"Houston, this is space shuttle Orion," Abe spoke.

"Orion, you are confirmed and ready for reentry in one hour, weather is good, and all stations are a go," Chief Banks replied.

"Roger Houston," Abe responded taking over communications as I went over my final checklist.

"I am up linking data now," I said.

"Roger Orion, we're preparing for the up-link," Chief Banks spoke, "your up-link was successful and complete."

Chief Banks continued with his ground control checklist as each crew member reported status of their assigned protocol.

"Orion you are a go for reentry in twenty-five minutes," a female voice from ground control stated.

"Roger Houston, Orion is a go for reentry in twenty-five," Abe replied.

I turned to my crew making sure everyone was seated, helmets on, and locked in.

Everyone was happy about our mission ending. Jeff would return home to his wife Patti and two adorable boys. Abe would get time off to go see his family back in Australia. Christina would return for a week to see her family and attend her sister's wedding in Colorado. Ty's girlfriend Stephanie would be happy to have her man back. Chance's parents would be attending for the first time to see his return from space.

I would just be happy regardless. My mom and sisters had already attended shuttle launches and returns prior. My nephew was on tour with his band and my nieces were all off to college.

I'd make it back safely, but nobody would be waiting on the tarmac to greet me like the others. I'd had that experience when Mike was alive. It felt good knowing my crew had done a great job and would experience that kind of joy back on Earth soon and that was comfort enough for me.

I didn't dwell on it for very long I was concerned that my mind would start to remember and I'd become too distracted to do my job safely. I looked around to each of them to see what expressions each had as they put on their helmet and everyone looked happy. I turned to see Jeff and share our ritual wink and nod that all was good. Jeff wasn't looking towards me so I shouted his name trying to get his attention.

"Jeff, Earth to Jeff," I said as I waved my hand to draw his attention and then I saw his face, "Abe, take control get Houston on the horn," I said. "Now!"

Ty jumped up seeing what I had seen and pulled Jeff's helmet off.

Chance grabbed Jeff's arm helping Ty take Doc back to the medical bay.

Christina grabbed the floating helmet and secured it and Abe contacted Houston.

"Houston we are declaring a medical emergency," Abe reported, "we are negative for reentry at this time."

"Roger Orion, confirm emergency," Banks spoke without haste.

"Banks, its Doc he's passed out and bleeding from the nose," I shouted back as I moved from the cabin to the medical bay.

"Roger Orion, Doctor Johnson is live when you are ready to proceed," Banks responded as he alerted the rest of ground control to our medical situation.

"Abe, get the link to the medical bay up and ready and abort reentry codes," I commanded as I quickly locked my helmet down and floated out.

"Ty, I need a status on Doc. Chance, I need you to get that monitor up," I said as I assessed Jeff's condition.

"Abe, do we have a link?" I asked.

"The link with Houston is ready," Abe shouted back.

"Okay Banks, you got Doc Johnson ready?" I asked as I felt almost out of breath due to the emotional rush.

"Roger Orion, Doc Johnson is now live. Proceed with assessment," Banks curtly spoke.

"Ty, I'm going to need you to assess and take over this part," I said as I looked at him.

"I'm on it," Ty said.

"Houston, this is Captain Lowery I'm ready to go when you are," Ty spoke up.

For the next half hour Ty and Doc Johnson continued with the health assessment of Jeff and went step by step to stabilize him while Chance and I took readings from monitors and tried to stay out of Ty's way. Ty was the next in line for medical emergencies, he had more training than us, we helped when we could, and allowing him to go with the knowledge Doc Johnson shared.

I was glad to have Ty aboard and Chance as well. They both knew how to keep me grounded and calm.

Jeff wasn't just a fellow crew member, he was a dear friend for almost fifteen years, and I had been his wife Patti's roommate in college. I had to force myself to keep calm and remember I was in command.

"He's responding, pressure is stable, eyes responsive, and vitals stable," Ty said almost monotone making sure Doc Johnson and ground control had all the correct information they needed on their end.

"Doc," Ty spoke as he patted Jeff's chest. "Jeff, are you okay?"

All eyes were glued on Jeff, finally he blinked.

"Houston, Doc's awake," Ty's voice filled with happiness and relief.

"Jeff, don't do that to us again," Chance added as he patted Jeff's leg.

The tension broke and relief was in the air as Jeff became more coherent.

We could hear Christina and Abe cheering from control as I looked up to see Jeff.

"Thanks Chance and Ty. I don't know what I would've done without the two of you," I softly spoke as my hand rested on Chance's back and his arm found its way around my waist.

"Anytime," Ty replied.

"Sure anytime," Chance agreed with a wink.

"Jeff, don't you ever scare us like that again. Do you hear me?" I scolded, then leaned over and kissed his forehead. "Patti's going to kill me enough as it is."

Abe and Christina took over control and relayed Jeff's health updates to Doc Johnson and Chief Banks while the rest of us took shifts watching over Jeff for the next six hours.

"I'm sorry guys. I don't know what happened, one minute I was looking at Susan and the next I was out cold," Jeff shared what he remembered.

"It's okay. What's twenty-four more hours right," I teased, "all is good. You just stay here and rest."

"Thank you all," Jeff softly spoke as he allowed Ty to strap him down.

With Jeff stable, we all took two hour shifts monitoring him, and sitting with him as he rested.

I had Ty take first watch. I had Abe and Christina get some rest it was going to be a long night.

I made my way back to control and found Chance there looking out the window back towards Earth. The sky below had started to turn dark, night had fallen over the landscape, and the lights from the larger populated cities lit up the night like beckons.

"You did the right thing Susan," Chance spoke up as he continued his gaze at Earth below.

"Thank you for being there and helping out," I replied while watching him in his moment of reflection.

I allowed my thoughts to drift. Chance was incredible I thought to myself as I studied his features. He was six feet tall, a muscular athletic build, short light brown hair, green eyes, handsome, and a smile that could melt a glacier.

He pulled back from the port window. "You want to take a look? It's beautiful tonight," Chance spoke almost in a whisper as I moved towards him.

Something had changed or maybe I had changed. He looked different tonight. I couldn't figure it out. Maybe I was just so relieved the crisis was over I had let my stern guard down and looked at Chance, my friend, briefly like there was something more than friendship between us, instead of Chance Walker part of the crew. Either way it was nice to have his company. I always felt at ease when he was around, and I liked that. I smiled at him as I turned to look at Earth below.

"Yes it is beautiful tonight," I replied.

I began to feel a strange urge to feel him closer to me as my non-friendship feelings for him crept up again. I dug deep and backed off while trying to block this present urge and forced myself to return my thoughts to making sure Jeff was okay.

I turned and made my way back to Jeff, who was stable and resting. There was no way I would've done anything differently. I would not risk anyone's life for reentry.

The anxiety had subdued itself and everyone went about their business more composed and keeping busy.

I took the next shift over Jeff. Ty went to rest up and wake up Abe and Christina, so they could take over controls while Chance went to find something to eat.

I was happy to see Jeff stabilized and resting well. I strapped myself down so I could sit by his side while holding his hand and thinking how blessed we all were to have such a great friend like Jeff in our lives. He had been there for me three years ago in my darkest hour, even sacrificing his own time with his family to be there. I looked over his stern worn face recalling how stubborn he was and how he never complained about anything, even today. Jeff was truly amazing. I recalled how he brought me back from a deep level of mourning to live again and go on. I wasn't about to give up on him either, I owed him that much.

I found myself gazing out the shuttle window back to Earth thinking how I was grateful to this man who wouldn't let me curl up and die. It was a beautiful night sky and had I allowed my sorrow and depression to overcome me I would be missing this right now, I thought to myself.

"Susan, how's Doc?" His voice pulled me back and I had to work to refocus.

It was Chance holding himself in place next to me. "How are you? Is everything okay with you?" He asked watching me and trying to read my expression or thoughts.

"I'm okay I'm hanging in there," I replied softly back. "How about you?"

"I'm good. I got some granola in me and I'm ready to baby-sit," he replied as he held his hand out offering me a bar.

"Thank you. I could use a short break," I said.

"Take all the time you need, I'll be right here," Chance said.

"Are you sure? I'll be quick."

"Yes, take your time, I got you covered," he replied as he smiled.

"Alright I'll be back in a few minutes. You need anything?" I asked.

"No, I have everything I need," Chance paused looking down, "no, I'm good."

I opened the granola and ate it as I floated along. Realizing I hadn't eaten anything in many hours, I went to the food lockers to see what was left to eat before my stomach alerted the crew.

I finished up eating and figured I'd go check on everyone else to make sure no one else had fallen sick. The crew seemed in good health and everyone was keeping busy. Abe was writing another e-mail to send back home.

"Hi Abe, it's a nice night isn't it? Did you get a chance to see Australia as we passed over her earlier?" I asked.

"Yep, sure did. I already have the pictures downloaded and ready to send off," Abe replied with a chipper tone.

"You need anything?" I asked.

"No I'm good," Abe replied. "How is Doc?"

"So far so good, I'm about to go and check on him and Chance. I'll get the update on Doc's monitors," I said. "Are you ready to take over for Chance in thirty?"

"Yes sure no problem, just give me a holler," Abe replied.

Ty and Christina were still sleeping.

I headed back to the medical bay to sit with Doc.

"Hi," Chance said. "Back so soon?"

"Yes, I went and checked on everyone and all is good, so I figured I'd come back here and check on you and Doc."

"Cool!"

I didn't push I figured he was off dreaming about some young brunette back home and feeling lonely, so I left him alone and seated myself back near Jeff while I began looking over the charts and filling out paper work.

"Abe will be into release you in about fifteen minutes," I stated.

"Sure," Chance replied.

He was back to one word replies, great. I didn't impose and just let him be.

"How is Doc? Are you two ready for some shut eye?" Abe asked as he floated in.

"I'm okay. Chance, you should go and get some rest you look like you need a break," I told him.

"Sure," Chance spoke looking back at me, then a smile crossed his face, and he was off.

I sat with Abe for a few minutes going over the standard medical checklist, showing him how to read the monitor, and what to fill out then figured I'd go rest as well.

Tomorrow is going to be stressful enough, and if we were to be a go for reentry, then I needed to be rested and ready to go.

Chance was already tucked in as a look of surprise came across his face as I entered the sleeping quarters.

"I figured I'd best get some rest too," I quietly spoke. "That is if you don't mind me sleeping in here with you?"

"No that's good, always enjoy the company of a pretty woman," he replied edgy then looked down in embarrassment that it slipped out.

"Well thank you," I replied along with a childish giggle.

I got in the cocoon next to him hoping to take a private moment to chat with him.

"I'm glad you're here," I told him, "I'd like to talk if you can spare a few minutes."

"Sure, is everything okay?"

"I think so," I trailed off, "it's just Chance I've known you for nearly five years and up until last year you were well kind of my best friend," I continued as I watched his eyes and his expression, "maybe it's me, I don't know, maybe it's you, but we use to talk, hang out, be buddies, and then all the sudden nothing you know. It bothers me, I care about you, and I feel like you are hiding something from me, or maybe you hate me now or something, who knows. I just know I miss being around you," I paused to study his reaction.

"I'm sorry Susan, it's hard to explain. It's not you, really," Chance replied looking down refraining from facing me. "It's me!"

"Well I'm here, no place to hide, and I'm listening," I responded.

"It's difficult to tell you what's going on with me," he spoke as he looked up to meet my eyes with his as sadness filled them.

"I do care what's going on Chance, I miss my friend," I declared.

"I know and I miss you too," he paused, "when we get back, I promise to work on it, okay."

"Good, because it's been really upsetting me lately and I don't know what to think."

"I'm sorry. I just have something I need to work out," Chance softly replied.

I looked at him and I could see something was torturing him. I did care about him deeply. I didn't understand, maybe I was the one who wasn't as good as of a friend as I should be. He is suffering and I haven't been there for him.

I held my hand out toward Chance and he took it into his and smiled back.

"Thank you," I whispered to him as he held my hand caressing it with his thumb.

"Susan, I promise when we get back things will be better between us, seriously," Chance said.

"That would make me very happy Chance. I miss you being around."

It was at that moment, I saw him vulnerable again, letting his guard down as I looked into his beautiful green eyes. How could I ever be upset at a face like that? I'd have to be insane.

"You know I will try, I haven't exactly been the greatest friend to you either lately. I promise to be a better friend to you," I declared to him quietly as I allowed myself to drift off to sleep while he held my hand.

Chapter II

Earth

"Nap time is over," Abe quietly spoke as he woke me.

"Thanks," I replied opening my eyes to see what time it was.

"No, let Chance sleep, he opted to hang out with me during my watch over Doc, and he could use an extra hour."

"Sure, Ty's at control and has ground control back online going over the system again," Abe said.

"Sounds good, I'll go relieve Ty and he can take over for Christina," I said as I floated out of my cocoon.

It had been a long night. I headed back to the medical bay to check on Jeff's condition.

"Hey there's my girl," Jeff spoke full of energy as he floated through the room.

"You're awake," I replied. "Why didn't someone wake me?"

I was surprised to see Ty in the bay holding up a hand of cards playing blackjack with Jeff.

"He told me not to wake you," Ty accused as he pointed teasing Jeff. "Blame him!"

"So you are up and running better today Doc?" I asked as I looked over the medical charts.

"Me? Yea I'm good never better I'm beating the kid two hands out of three," Jeff said.

"Good then you two back to get back to work, we have a date with Earth," I said as I turned to head back to control, "get this place locked up and ready to go."

I was relieved to see Jeff back to his old self and Ty there once again to help out.

Never a dull moment on this shuttle, I thought to myself as I reflected on yesterday's medical scare and my talk with Chance.

Back at the control station, I saw Christina on the laptop chatting online with one of her sisters in Ohio and was reminded of a story she told me about how she was the first African American in her entire family to earn a college degree. I was so proud of her and all her accomplishments.

"Chris, you need to finish up your fan mail and go get some rest we still have a few more hours before we make contact with Houston and I want everyone rested before reentry."

"Did you see Doc? He's doing great today we're not sure what happened, but he claims he feels great," Christina replied.

"Yes, I stopped in on the way up here. It was good to see him up and about," I said.

Once again, I sat alone going over charts, reports, checklists, and protocol trying to keep my brain busy as my eye lids fought to stay alert.

"Beep, beep, beep, beep."

"Are you going to get that?" I heard his voice ask.

"Yes," I replied as I stretched out my back pausing as I worked out some stiffness, opened my eyes to focus, and answer the beep.

"Why did you allow me to fall asleep at control again?" I quizzed turning to see him sitting next to me with a big grin on his face. "Chance, why didn't you answer ground control?"

"Sorry, I didn't realize you were in La-La land again," he said as he snickered. "I'll get it!"

"Hello, Houston," Chance curtly replied to the beeping.

"Roger Orion, how's our crew today?" Banks replied back.

"Houston, Doc is doing better and feeling ready to go home," I said as I took over.

"Roger Orion, that sounds great and the weather here is looking great for reentry in four hours," Banks replied.

"Roger Houston, four hours, all systems are online, and a go," I continued to respond going over Jeff's medical chart so Doc Johnson and ground control would be up to date on his progress and then reporting back on systems checklist.

I finished my duties and then turned back to Chance to snap at him some more, I recalled my promise I made him to be a better friend.

"Chance, we need to get Abe up and the two of you can get your inspections of storage bay going soon. You might send Christina to rest for another hour."

"Okay I'll get right on it," he replied with a smile as he floated away.

* * *

Chance made his way through the cabin to get Abe up and then he headed over to the medical bay to check on Doc and Ty.

"Well speak of the devil!" Jeff spoke loudly as Chance floated into the bay.

"Hey Doc, how are you doing?" Chance asked.

"Good I actually don't know what happened yesterday, but today I feel great," Doc replied.

"Hey Ty, take a break man get some food, I think Doc can handle things from here," Chance said.

"Sure thanks," Ty replied.

"Doc, you got to let us know when you're feeling sick man," Chance continued, "you really had us all pretty scared and you should have seen Susan's face she was white as a sheet."

"Thanks for the watchful eye and all the care," Doc replied.

"Ty, dude you got to lay off the teasing when she's around it is hard enough on me the way things are now you don't need to go and make them worse," Chance said.

"Hey Chance, I'm sorry man. I just got caught up in the moment and sort of forgot," Ty replied as he looked down.

"So what is up with you two anyway?" Jeff asked as he chimed in.

"Nothing is up. Why?" Chance replied as he was intent on seeing if anyone else noticed his behavior.

"Just curious, it's not hard to miss I think we all kind of know," Jeff said lowering his voice so not to be overheard, "I really don't think she has a clue."

"Chance, I really think you should relax, I agree with Jeff," Ty stated.

"Fine, but you two try and not make matters worse. It's hard enough on me already just watching her feeling what I feel and not able to do anything," Chance spoke as he looked out the shuttle window back to Earth and shrugged, "she told me earlier that she missed me being around, maybe I should take a step up and let her know how I feel and why I've been avoiding her."

"Don't worry about it now, things will work out, she's had plenty of time to move on and who knows maybe in the back of her mind she feels the same way about you," Jeff assured him, "people change, they grow, and they open up. Who knows?"

"Jeff is right Chance, just let it go for now and see how things play out once we get back home either way we'll both be pulling for you," Ty spoke trying to cheer Chance up.

"I see how she looks at you, the way she reacts to you when you are near her is obvious, and the little hints of unspoken words that she gives. I know Susan, I've known her for nearly fifteen years man I can tell you something is there, and you shouldn't give up. If you feel that strongly about Susan, and you love her don't let her go," Jeff said.

"Thank you. I'll keep that in mind. It's going to be hard, maybe you're right, and she is ready. I do know I have no plans of letting her go, not yet."

"I guess we'd best get ready for reentry. You two head off and get your finals done I'll see you back at control and thanks guys again for taking care of me," Jeff said.

* * *

Everyone finished their checklist and reports as they returned to their seats and strapped in with flight suits on and helmets ready.

I still get excited when we head home. I'm in control of the situation and the shuttle which makes me feel at ease. I can't speak for everyone else. Lord knows my flying makes Abe's stomach nauseous enough and Christina tends to close her eyes and keep them shut until she hears the landing gear smack the Earth.

With everyone ready countdown to reentry started as planned.

"Houston, we are go for reentry," I stated firmly.

"Orion, you are good to go in 5, 4, 3, 2, 1," Banks counted us down.

"Then we were off," I replied.

The Earth never looked more beautiful than it did as we slammed through its atmosphere fully understanding her power and danger.

Ty took pictures through the shuttle window on his side making sure to get plenty of the red glow that created all the special effects to his film. Doc sat alert and smiling with contentment. His wife Patti was due any day with child number three.

"Just like always boys and girls," my voice filled the cabin, "home sweet home."

Thud, thud, down went the shuttle landing gear, and she was landing smooth and safely just like I'd planned.

We could hear cheers and the applauding from flight control as the shuttle slowed on the runway at Cape Canaveral.

"We're happy to see you all safely back on planet Earth," Chief Banks said. "Congratulations!"

"Roger that, happy to be home," Abe replied.

We each stepped out and down the stairs to solid ground. I still to this day never tire of the return home, the bright colors of mother Earth, the smell of fresh air, the birds singing in the distance, and the sight of humans.

We made it down the runway towards our ground shuttle transport to media, family, and friends.

Everyone was waving, cheering, and happy to see us again.

I always dreaded this part. Debriefings sucked.

Each member of the crew had to be debriefed; paper work filed out, and post flight protocol followed. For me, more like seven days of repeating myself over and over from one briefing room to another, shuffled around like cattle. I knew things would not go as smoothly as prior mission debriefings because of our medical hiccup with Doc.

For the next two days, Doc and I attended the same meetings giving our reports, statements on what was done, and why we thought it happened. It was one of my least favorite meetings I must say.

Next time, I'll be more careful and more diligent when it comes to the health of my crew.

By the end of day three, I had wished I could just carry a voice recorder and play back my answers over and over again for each meeting because they all asked the same stupid questions, well okay not all questions were stupid, but the repetition was killing me.

If I could just pass out copies of my report to everyone and that would save time, I thought to myself at one point during day four.

After yet another long day in meetings, I was finally off the clock. I headed home to my condo to relax. Ah, how I loved civilization, hot water, Dr. Pepper, and food that was not already dehydrated. I shivered at the thought of all the dehydrated food I've eater over the year. Yuck!

After a nice long hot shower, I slipped into a T-shirt and shorts feeling renewed.

"Okay, time to check e-mail and let everyone know I'm alive and well," I spoke out loud to myself as the laptop stirred to life and the internet was up and running.

"Three hundred e-mails from who? I'm not that important or that popular," I expressed aloud.

So for the next two hours, I cleared my e-mail files and sent greetings to all my nieces, my nephew, and my mom letting them know I was home and about our adventure to space. I attached my favorite photos of Earth I'd downloaded from Ty's camera memory card earlier in the week and sent off a few official letters to my pen pals from elementary schools across America.

"Done!" I said aloud.

The phone rang.

"Great just when I thought I was going to have the evening off to relax," I said as I picked up my cell phone and saw it was Ty.

"Hello Ty," I stated. "What's up?"

"Hi Susan, I just thought I'd check in and see how you are doing. We haven't heard from you in a few days and wanted to know how all the briefings went," Ty replied as he chuckled.

I could hear Chance in the background making noises with pots and pans.

"Are you guys trying to cook, again?" I asked fearing for their kitchen's safety.

"Hang on," Ty paused and turned to threaten Chance if he didn't shut up, "sorry Susan, jungle boy is loose in the kitchen again," he said as he began to laugh.

"Oh no, get him out of there he'll kill the microwave again," I joked along for fun because I knew I was on the speaker phone by the echo.

"I heard that," Chance smarted off.

"Yes, I know," Ty spoke trying to control his laugh. "What are you up to tonight? Do you feel like hanging out with two wild and crazy guys?"

"Hum. Let me think. Why do you know any?" I teased as I started to laugh uncontrollably.

"Funny very funny Ha Ha," Ty replied. "So are you going to save me from his horrible cooking or what?"

"Sure you two come on over. I'll have the spaghetti ready by the time you get here and I think there's a game on the tube," I said.

"YES!" Chance shouted in the background.

"Thank you Susan, you are an angel," Ty commented back. "I owe you big time!"

"Okay we'll discuss payment later. I'll see you two clowns in thirty minutes, bye," I finished and hung up.

So much for a quiet night at home, but I guess I need a little distraction.

I turned the television on, pulled up the menu, and saw the Rangers were on. I knew Chance would be thrilled, so I clicked on the channel to get the TV ready for the baseball fans enjoyment. Returning to the kitchen I finished making my sauce, got some green beans in a bowl warmed up in the microwave, and the garlic toast out of the toaster oven.

The doorbell rang.

"Come on in guys," I shouted from the kitchen already knowing they'd let themselves in regardless if I'd answered the door myself or not.

"Oh Susan, you are the best thanks for not letting me starve," Ty stated.

"Hey I can cook," Chance spoke up in response while making his way into the kitchen.

"Sure you can," I replied then burst into laughter, "Oh it's okay, you know I enjoy cooking. I'm happy to have the company."

"Rangers are on," Ty said. "Awesome!"

"Cool," Chance said. "Who are they playing?"

With the boys distracted by the baseball game I got back to finish cooking.

"Dinner is ready," I announced.

The boys jumped up and raced into the kitchen. I took a few steps back not wanting to get run over during the feeding frenzy. Once plates were full and beers were in hand, they returned to the TV to watch the game as they ate. It was cute to see them act like teenagers.

I sat in the kitchen enjoying my food in private while I listened to the game.

After I finished eating I went and sat down on the couch.

"So, how much did I miss?" I asked.

"Just the first inning, Rangers are up by one right out of the pin," Ty updated me as he and Chance exchanged an odd glare at each other.

"Good," I replied as I moved over to one edge to avoid getting a shiner from one of the excited fans, as they high-fived, and bounced like children.

Children I thought, yes that would be the best way to describe these two when they got together with food and baseball. I found myself watching Ty and Chance more than I watched the game.

During a commercial, I got up to go to the bathroom to freshen up and change out of my cooking clothes. I could hear them bicker back and forth at each other keeping it too low for me to hear. I returned my focus on the image in the mirror and found myself primping a little more than usual, maybe it was having two men in my home both very cute, nice bodies, and available. Well at least Chance was as far as I knew.

"Okay, pull yourself together Susan," I quietly spoke to myself as I brushed my hair again. "Nothing to think about they're your friends, right?"

With a deep breath I finished and walked casually back into the living room trying not to look at either of them directly turning my attention to the game as I sat back down on the couch. I looked over and noticed Ty had moved over to the love seat and Chance was sprawled out on the couch next to me, both displaying cheesy grins. I tried to ignore the oddness of their behavior and let myself relax and enjoy the game.

During the next commercial break Chance got up to take his turn in the bathroom then followed by Ty.

Chance came back in and smiled an almost evil grin this time.

"What?" I asked puzzled by his expression.

"Oh nothing just a guy thing," Chance replied with nervousness in his voice as he sat down closer to me.

"Okay, either of you need another beer?" I asked as I got up to get myself one.

"Yea, that would be great," Chance said as he leaped up. "Let me help!"

I opened the fridge, grabbed some beer, and almost dropped it as I felt Chance's hand wrap around my waist.

"Oh sorry, I didn't mean to," Chance paused as he realized what he had done, "I didn't mean to sneak up on you like that."

"No, that's okay," I replied trying to hide my excitement at his touch as I leaned back in and got another beer.

Chance shut the fridge door and followed me over to the counter, I got the feeling something was bothering him, or maybe he wanted to talk to me alone about something. It was probably more girl problems, I thought to myself as he stood next to me his forearm touching mine as I popped the lids on each beer.

I could hear his breathing increase and felt my own body go weak at the feeling of his flesh on mine.

"Thanks," Chance said as he smiled towards me. "You're the best!"

As we returned to the living room Ty was back from his bathroom break happy to see a fresh beer. His eyes locked onto Chance revealed concern as if he'd interrupted something major.

I turned around in case I was walking in on a private conversation. I grabbed some chips and dip from the pantry for the long game knowing these two men could eat anyone out of house and home.

"Awe, thanks babe. I don't know what Chance, or I for that matter, would do without you," Ty said.

"Well I'm not so sure about that you two men look like you are doing just fine without me," I replied as I leaned over and squeezed Chance's bulging arm muscles and gave a wink.

He looked back at me in shock, as if I'd stabbed him so, I slowly removed my hand from his arm and slid back on my couch trying to focus back on the game and clear my head from Chance's odd facial expression and reaction.

Chance turned to Ty and the two exchanged another glance then Chance being a little more courageous slid back on the couch to lay down this time turning the opposite direction having his head on my lap and his feet towards the other end. The smile returned upon his face as he winked at me and turned on his side while nesting his head on my legs.

Ty excused himself during the 7th inning stretch something about Stephanie his girlfriend and how he forgot her birthday.

Chance was very still for a few minutes, maybe he wasn't sure how I'd react or if I'd kick him off my lap. I didn't say a word. Chance continued lying on my lap. He's done this before, but none the less it threw me a little after his reaction to my touch. It was just the two of us with Chance's head still on my lap. He laid there with his hand hanging down cupping my calf as the other arm rested on his side. It felt nice, too nice I thought to myself. It felt natural to have him next to me like this, feeling his hand on my leg as his fingers caressed my skin, significantly nice, and I didn't want him to move.

I found myself running my fingers through his hair at one point and he didn't act like anything was wrong with it so I continued softly enjoying the sensation as long as I could.

The baseball game ended.

At first, I wasn't sure if he'd fallen asleep or was just playing possum. He stretched himself out, turning over on his back to look up into my face. Chance had a look of ease about him as he gazed up to me smiling that simple smile I'd always loved seeing.

"So," Chance said. "Now what?"

"Now, you go home and I go to bed," I replied with a giggle.

He frowned, slowly raised his eye brow, starting to speak then closed his mouth as if he was trying to hold his tongue, and stay out of trouble.

"Will you go jogging with me in the morning?" He asked knowing that wasn't what he was about to say.

"That sounds great. I hate jogging alone besides there are too many nut jobs out there lately," I replied.

He sat up seeming to be happy with my reply, put his shoes on, and then I walked him to the door.

He touched my hand as he moved closer to me, sending my body into shock. I'd never reacted this way before to his touch and I liked it.

"Thanks again for dinner and letting me watch the game with you," he softly spoke as he looked deeply into my eyes as if he was searching for more to say.

"You're welcome any time you know," I replied and put my arms around him for a hug.

He held me there in his arms returning the hug and embraced me a little longer than our normal exchange of hugs between friends. I didn't resist and I allowed his embrace for as long as he wanted to hold me in it. I wanted it.

"Thank you," Chance said as he pulled himself back a little and looked into my eyes.

Then, he leaned down towards my smile. I almost forgot to breath. He was incredible in every way imaginable and I was in his arms. My blood surged through my body as a shot of excitement rocked through me again.

He was different this time, his tone, his body language, and his eyes.

"Thank you," I softly replied while taking my hand from his neck and touching his cheek softly. I looked into his eyes seeing his yearning for the first time, my head began to swirl with the knowledge, my heart sped up like a butterfly, and my breath increased as his arms pulled me closer. I could feel the heat from his lips, I wanted to give into him, I wanted to feel his lips upon mine, and I knew he wanted what I wanted.

His lips almost touched mine as his eyes closed and his breathing increased. I could hear his heart kick into high gear. My body ached in his embrace.

"Ring, Ring" the phone screamed. I jumped, Chance jumped and we both broke out in a soft giggle at the tension.

He paused and kissed my forehead. "Well, okay I'd best get out of here. I'll see you at 5:30 for a jog."

"Yes, 5:30 sounds good I'll see you in the morning," I replied as Chance started to release me.

I stopped, leaned up, and kissed his cheek to let him know everything was okay between us.

He smiled and let out a big sigh as he paused not wanting to give up his embrace.

"I'll see you tomorrow," he whispered as he leaned into me and kissed my cheek in return softly and with definition as he released me.

I slowly moved to answer the phone as he snuck out the door closing it behind him.

"Just my luck," I said aloud as the phone stopped ringing. I picked it up to see who had killed my evening, "Ty! Thanks Ty nice timing!"

I found myself still flustered at Chance's embrace and almost kiss. He was different. Could it be more, I thought to myself as I recalled the look in his eyes, the yearning, and had I miss read it. Was this one of those weird moments we both just got caught up in? Or a hormonal induced desire?

No, don't be silly he's just a sweet guy who is one of your best friends. Right? I asked myself. It was a nice thought. It was understandable how I could be so flushed over it. Chance was gorgeous, what woman wouldn't want those bulging arms wrapped around them, I thought to myself as I drifted off to sleep.

For the next week Chance came over to jog with me every morning, but that was it. No more games on TV or late night dinner for the boys. I was okay with it, maybe I did read way too much into things.

Maybe someday I'll find someone to love again, someone who wants to hold me dangerously close, and doesn't care to hold anything back. I allowed myself to drift off into thought as I lay in bed, thinking how nice it would be to find new love, have hope again, and to know I wouldn't be alone anymore. It had been three years since Mike's death. I was finally ready to move on. Maybe my close encounter last week with Chance was all I needed to help snap me out of it and bring me back to the living again.

Chapter III

Burger and Beer

I allowed work to consume me once again, it was a good distraction for now, and I had a lot to think about this past week. An almost kiss and a daringly bold "hug," what am I doing to myself, it was nothing! I reminded myself over and over, but the other half of me thought maybe it was something. I always tried to stuff the "something" as deep inside as I could when Chance was around. It was weird enough between us. I didn't want to make things worse by acting on hormonal frustrations and flights of fantasy.

"Enough!" I exclaimed to myself.

I need to jump in the shower, clean up, and dress to kill. I decided right then and there, I would sulk no more. I jumped up off the couch, cranked the stereo, and let the music envelope my soul. I needed something rocking to get me going.

"This will do the trick. Nickelback now that is exactly what I need," I said out loud and took off to the bathroom. I got cleaned up, dried, and curled my hair, put my make-up on making sure to focus on my eyes, some sultry lipstick, and that new sexy red dress I picked up last week at the mall.

"Okay missy no mercy now go out there and break a heart or two!" I firmly spoke to the reflection in the living room mirror as I grabbed a CD off the stereo shelf and took it with me as I headed out the door. I felt like a teenager ready to sneak into the local club and it felt great. I had always considered myself as the typical "girl next door," but tonight the girl next door never looked this good, I thought to myself as I checked my lips in the rear view mirror.

Once again, I cranked the stereo letting my favorite CD fill the car and rattle the windows and I was off.

The base military police gave me a wave. I saw it was Airman First Class Carbone and slowed down to say hi, since I hadn't been in the gym to work out in weeks. It was nice to see his youthful smile.

"Nice Commander. I love your new Camaro! I didn't recognize you at first. I'll see you next week in the gym," AFC Carbone said then waved me through the gate.

"See you later. Thanks," I shouted back as I waved.

It felt nice to get a double take after wearing military uniform and white shuttle flight suits all month.

I was glad I chose a red dress for tonight. The color looked good on me, putting me in an even cockier mood.

I headed downtown to more familiar sights and sounds. My nephew was booked to play tonight at Murphy's, I hadn't been there in months, and they did have the best burgers and beer in town.

I found a spot in the parking lot nearest the door. I got a few good looks, some nasty, but mostly naughty. I did feel a little overdressed, maybe a little too much on the sultry side. Tonight I didn't care I was going to enjoy myself, and if I pissed off a few of the local trailer-trash, then so be it.

I walked slowly into the pub and was greeted by George, the bouncer, who gave me a hug while he informed me that I was too hot for this dump.

"Flattery will get you everywhere tonight love," I teased back at him.

I surveyed the place to find a spot more towards the back, some place I could sit and assess the situation for my first victim.

My waiter, Hector, failed miserably at trying to keep his mouth shut as he walked toward my table. I knew if he at least got my drink order right I'd leave him a nice tip for stroking my ego.

I ordered a Smithwicks to start off with and then a nice juicy cheeseburger, Murphy style. The waiter smiled and nodded in reply as I ordered. I really hated it when they didn't write my order down. I'll probably get a nice juicy burger alright, so juicy it would start to MOO with one bite. I shivered at the thought.

I sat quietly drinking my beer and enjoying the noise of civilization while I searched the crowd for my nephew Aaron and his band when I thought I heard my name. I ignored it. There were plenty of females in here and I'm sure more than one Susan.

"Susan," The man's voice got louder and clearer. I perked up. I knew that voice.

"Susan, it is you," he spoke as he walked towards me, "I'll be damned you do come out and mingle with the rest of the living," he continued to speak as he laughed out loud and seemed surprised to see me.

I smiled in return. I recognized that laugh, the voice, and that face. My heart almost leaped out of my chest as he emerged from the crowd.

"Chance?" I asked as I played dumb while trying to hide my over excitement at the mere sight of this substantially handsome man. "Well it is you. How are you?"

"I'm good. Wow Susan, you look incredible," he spoke in a softer tone as he stood before me dead in his tracks.

I wasn't sure at first if it was a complement, or if he was just being nice. Then I looked at his eyes, they never lied.

"Thank you," I said as I shied away, again trying to control myself.

"Hey, you mind if I sit with you?" Chance asked.

"Sure, I'd love the company," I nervously replied as he slid in next to me instead of taking the seat across the table.

Great now I've got no escape if he shows signs of rejections. My thoughts fought again as I tried to contain myself. Nervousness was overcoming me due to his proximity to my body. He smelled so good. I quietly inhaled his scent, trying not to give myself away.

It was so hard to hide my expression and be invisible. Once his eyes locked on me, I was dead meat.

"So what are you drinking?" Chance asked.

"A beer," I joked as I held up the bottle for him to review.

"Nice. Good stuff," he said. "Are you eating dinner here too or did you just come to stalk the local prey?"

My mouth dropped in shock at his comment as it caught me off guard.

"I'm sorry Susan. I shouldn't have said that. It was stupid of me," he said as he tried to make a mends.

Even if it were true I wasn't going to tell him.

"It's okay no harm done," I replied as I looked up from the table with a smile flashed across my face.

"So Chance, how have you been lately? I figured you'd be back in Galveston taking a break to hang out on the beach and chase a few of those hotties you and Ty are always talking about."

"Well to tell you the truth," he lowered his voice almost into a whisper as he leaned toward me, looking up to meet my eyes, "I sort of have a reason to stay."

Before I could follow up with my interrogation of Chance, I saw another familiar love of mine walking towards my table.

"Hey Aaron!" I yelled.

"You know him?" Chance asked.

"No, I just like yelling men's names aloud in a pub," I teased as I began laughing at the expression on his face.

"My baby Aaron, how are you?" I asked.

"Hey, Aunt Sue," Aaron replied as he slid into my booth to sit down, "I'm doing great. Glad to see you made it."

I smiled back at him with joyfulness and pride.

"Aaron, you want a drink before you head back up?"

"Sure. I could use a couple. It's going to be a long night," Aaron said with laughter in his voice.

"How's Laura? Where is she? Did she come too?" I asked.

"Yes, she's over there at the band table. She'll be happy to know you're here. You know how much she loves you," Aaron replied.

"Hey, can you get my nephew a Jack and Coke?" I asked Hector.

"Sure," Hector replied. "You need anything else?"

"Yes, maybe another round for the band table on my tab for me," I said.

"Yea, I think they'd love it," Aaron said.

"Where are my manners? Sorry," I spoke, "Aaron, I'd like you to meet Chance Walker, he's a fellow astronaut, and close friend of mine. Chance, I'd like you to meet my wonderful nephew, Aaron Pashka."

"Hi, glad to meet you," Chance said. "You're playing here tonight?"

"Yea, got the band over there," Aaron pointed towards the stage, "we took a short break and are just about to start up another set. You guys sticking around for a few songs?"

"Absolutely and now will you play my favorite song? Please, for your favorite Aunt in the whole world!" I begged.

"You got it anything for you. So, how's work? How's life? Are you going to the Moon or what?" Aaron began to quiz.

"Thanks doll. Well, work is busy as usual. Life, I'm working on that one," I said with a wink, "I doubt I'll see the Moon in person anytime soon," I continued, "maybe after a few man missions. Chance has a better shot at it than I ever would."

"Well, either way I'm pulling for you," Aaron replied with his contagious smile.

I smiled back and gave a nod as Hector returned with drinks.

"He'll need one more for the road," I requested.

"Thanks I guess this was just my night to play. My wonderful Aunt is here in the audience, nice crowd, and good drinks," Aaron said as he sipped his drink. "Life's good!"

"Aaron, how is your CD coming along? I asked.

"Great, we just finished it last week," Aaron replied.

"Make sure I get a copy of it, or I'll write you out of my Will," I joked.

"Now we wouldn't want that," Aaron teased back.

"Here you go. I'll take the empty glass if you're done," Hector said as he sat down Aaron's second drink.

"Thanks, Aunt Sue. It's good to sit and chat for a few minutes. Not long enough in my opinion. I don't get to see much family these days with all the touring and recording. Well, I'd best get back on stage. It's always good to see you and have you both here tonight," Aaron said. "It really means a lot!"

"Anytime Doll. You just need to email or call me. Let me know when and where you're going to be and I'll be there," I replied as Aaron got up from our table.

"Nice to meet you Chance glad to have you here. Thanks again Aunt Sue for the drinks."

"You're welcome baby. Tell your mom and Laura hi and I love her too," I said as I gave Aaron a hug and kiss.

"Sure thing I'll give you a call later next week when we get our gig nights worked out. See you later. Love you," Aaron spoke as he gave a wink.

"Okay, good Luck and I love you too," I shouted as he moved back through the crowd.

As I watched Aaron step onto the stage with his band, I smiled, and a sense of pride came over me.

"Aaron is really a good kid and a great musician," I expressed.

"Nice kid. That's cool, a future rock star in the family," Chance replied.

Aaron's music filled the air just as the waiter sat our food down.

"Here you both go. I added the round of drinks. They all said to tell you thanks and they loved you. Can I get either of you anything else?" Hector asked.

"No we're good," Chance replied.

We sat quietly eating dinner allowing the music and noise of the pub to filter into our private space.

"You're right Aaron is pretty good. Nice vocals and the band sounds great. I'm impressed."

"That's my boy and that pretty girl in front of the stage is Laura my future niece," I said proudly.

"Wow, she's hot and Aaron's got good taste," Chance replied with a chuckle.

We both ate slowly. I figured he was probably debating the best way to ditch me after dinner so not to hurt my feelings, but the way I felt I didn't care. I was having a good time and happy to see Aaron play live music for once.

"Would either of you like dessert?" Hector asked as he returned to remove plates and offer more drinks.

"Yes I think I will," Chance replied, "I think we'll have that brownie thing."

"Good choice. Can I get you all anything else?" Hector asked.

"No, I think that will do it," Chance responded curtly.

I sat in silence as his friends stopped by our table to say hello as they passed by. Chance was kind and kept the conversations limited.

It felt odd having him introduce me as "my girl Susan." I wasn't sure what that meant, maybe home girl or something like that. I just smiled and greeted each one as any friend should.

"Wow. That's the brownie?" Chance quickly asked as he began to laugh, "Susan, I hope you have room because I can't eat that all by myself."

Hector set down the massive blob of brownie covered with chocolate, sitting next to a scoop of chocolate ice cream.

I allowed my eyes to close as Aaron and his band began to play my favorite song.

"I love this. That has to be the best song ever," I said and sighed allowing the music to fill me. "Wildfire!"

"Yea, it's pretty good. He definitely has talent," Chance replied.

I opened my eyes to see what massive blob Chance had requested.

"You want some?" He asked.

"If I do, I'll have to run an extra mile every day for a month just to burn it off," I joked.

Chance tried to lighten the mood. I felt some relief that he was still speaking to me. That's always a good sign, right?

We looked at one another and the laughter just came out while smiling as we both watched the other attempt to eat the plate of brownie blob.

Out of nowhere Chance leaned over and licked my face.

"What are you doing?" I asked in shock.

"I'm trying to keep you from messing up that sexy dress of yours," he responded, only to send me into further shock as he began a wicked giggle.

I was so off guard I didn't know if I could bounce back. I couldn't say a word.

Chance leaned in again this time further into me, "you", he whispered into my ear.

I gazed back at him puzzled. His eyes lit up and a familiar mischievous grin came across his face.

"What? Me. What?" I forced myself to ask.

"You Susan," Chance softly whispered into my ear as the back of his hand brushed my face, "you are my reason for staying."

Oh My GOD! My brain screamed, my heart erupted in jubilation, and my body shivered with pleasure as he once again touched my face with his hand.

I closed my eyes in response to his soft touch as I was over taken by my desire. I tried to calm myself, but it was no use. He noticed my reaction and that was all it took.

I drank in his scent almost forgetting to exhale. I let out a moan as he touched my arm.

How could this be? Why me? Then like a bus it hit me. I was his reason his only reason to stay. My mind played his voice over and over in my head as I pulled my body away from the table to face the voice which burned into my very soul.

I didn't even get a chance to speak as he pulled himself closer to me until he cupped my face into his hands. Our eyes locked and without another word from his lips I knew he was mine.

He held me firm as his lips found mine as he softly moaned sending my body into a whirlwind and my mind went numb. I met his lips kiss for kiss almost with an urgent need while forgetting everyone and everything around us.

"Hu hum," the voice broke us out of our private moment. I couldn't even look up at Hector.

How long had Chance been hiding his feelings from me? How long had I lied to myself that I didn't have those kinds of feelings for him? I asked myself.

"Sorry, we're done," Chance spoke up as he paid the check.

I tried to catch my breath and better compose myself.

"Are you ready to get out of here?" Chance asked.

"More than ready," I replied.

It was all I could muster up while nodding my head in agreement. As we left I waved bye to Aaron as I passed by the stage and motioned for him to call me. Aaron nodded, gave a wink, and smile in return.

Once we stepped out of the bar Chance paused wrapping his arms around me to kiss me once more.

"You got the keys?" Chance asked.

"Yes," I replied as I handed the keys over and my head began to spin at the sweet taste of his lips.

"I'll drive," he insisted.

I just nodded as he opened the passenger door and paused giving me yet another kiss then allowing me to slide in.

He rushed to get in the driver's side. Once inside he started the engine and then jerked back.

"Oh crap," I shouted as I hit the off button on the radio.

"What? Are you holding out on me?" He asked and a surprised look crossed his face as he let out a soft giggle.

"Sorry, I forgot to turn it down before I turned the car off. It's my favorite CD."

"No, that's fine with me. Barry Manilow is one of my favorite singers. I actually have this on a CD or had I should say had it. I don't know what I did with it," Chance responded.

I pointed to the radio.

"That would be it, you left it over my place a few weeks ago, and I've had it in my player at home ever since," I said with a laugh.

He flashed me a smile and turned the radio back up clicking through the CD and stopped at "Could It Be Magic." This was one of my favorite songs on that CD.

As the song began to play, he leaned over the seat towards me, and took my face into his hands holding me still with his eyes locked on mine as he sang the first few lyrics of his song and followed by the most passionate kiss I'd ever had in my entire life. Holding me tight in his embrace while his song filled the air and his kiss filled my soul not stopping until I had understood what this moment meant to him.

"I'd best get you home," he spoke as he pulled himself away and began to back out of the parking space.

Feeling bold and downright aroused and not wanting to wait until we got home, I loosened my seat belt to maneuver my body to face him.

I wanted to see his face as he reacted to my tease. I pulled myself close to his side slowly running my hands over his shoulder, his throat, and then to his hair letting my fingers caress the softness of his skin. I leaned in for the test.

Yes, I wanted to make sure he had no questions about my feelings or excitement towards his kisses of passion.

"You're incredible!" I whispered playfully as my lips found the softness of his cheek bone.

As my hand traced the outline of his chest I trailed soft wet kisses from his chin to his neck pausing to lick his skin following it back to his neck line just behind his ear taking his lobe with my tongue I continued my playful tease while I softly bit down and then released it as he moaned.

"Woman you'll be the death of me," he spoke as he took a deep breath.

"No I have too many plans for you now," I whispered in his ear as my lips pressed against his flesh.

I don't recall ever seeing Chance drive so wildly in all the years I'd known him, but under control.

A man with a purpose, I was thrilled at the thought of a wild man under control with a purpose.

"Wow, I always wondered how fast it could take me to get from downtown to base," I teased.

"You'd be surprised at what I can do when properly motivated," he replied with a snicker.

"Now that is something I'd like to know more about," I said.

From the gate entrance to home all I could do was think why me. There wasn't anything special about me. He could easily have any woman on this planet.

"Susan, are you okay?" His voice brought me back.

"Yes, I'm perfectly fine," I replied.

We made it to the front door stopping for another uncontrollable kiss.

"Are you coming inside or are you going to stand out here and kiss me all night?" I asked.

I rushed to get the key in the doorknob and open the door. He had his arm wrapped around my waist, with his free hand he started pulling my hair to one side, and kissing the back of my neck sending me into near convulsions.

Lucky for me, he didn't stop after we got inside.

We were both out of control, or maybe it wasn't like that at all, maybe just maybe, for once we were in control. Yes, completely without a question in control.

I found the light switch and flipped it on. I excused myself to the bathroom to pee and freshen up.

"What was I doing? Is this a dream? Please GOD if this is a dream, "DO NOT" wake me up," I said to myself in silence as I composed myself best I could after the massive adrenalin rush he gave me and walked back into the living room to face him. I felt butterflies in my stomach.

There he sat on the couch, a beer in hand, the TV on, and talking on his cell phone. I didn't say a word. I watched him in amazement by how at home he looked. It was just like any other night he came to "hang out" with me and watch a ball game or when Ty ran him off so Ty and Stephanie could be alone.

He finished his conversation speaking normal as ever. He laughed a few times and never took his eyes off me as I walked towards him on the couch and he held up a hand to pull me close to him.

"Yea, hey Jeff," Chance spoke as I looked at him in pure shock, "I got to go, my buddy just showed up, and the game is about to start. I'll holler at you later man," he continued, "tell Patti and the boys hello for me and we'll see you later."

Chance hung up his phone and pulled himself up.

"Hello beautiful," his voice called out to me.

"How many beers did you have tonight?" I jokingly asked.

"One, this could be two."

Our eyes froze on one another as neither of us was willing to give up the trance. I took his face into my hands, holding him still as I took in his own beauty. I slowly pulled myself closer to him trying to mesh my body to his.

"I've waited for this day to come for five years," he spoke as his voice cracked and his hands began to tremble.

I could hear his heart beat faster as I lowered myself towards him.

"Why me?" I asked as his hands caressed my arms pulling my body down onto his.

His lips found mine and his kisses became intoxicating as they overwhelmed me.

"It's always been you," calmly he whispered as his lips seared themselves into my skin, "from the first moment that I saw you."

His hands electrified my skin as they moved across my neck and body.

Until three hours ago the man before me was just a friend, my buddy, a fellow prankster in crime, and now he was the very being my entire body longed for. I returned his kiss with fierce passion. As much as the analytical part of my brain tried to rationalize the events of this evening, my body and the rest of me didn't care. Luckily, my body and urge to feel his flesh against mine won.

"You're all I've ever wanted, all I've ever been able to think about, and this moment right now is all I could dream of," Chance declared.

With every kiss and every touch of his hand he owned me.

"My heart, my body, and my soul belong to you," his words trailed his lips across my skin sending me further into a higher stage of need.

"So this is what heaven is like?" I asked.

"I sure hope so and I could get use to this," Chance replied with optimism.

"I'm counting on it," I paused for a moment to see the expression on his face after he'd confessed himself to me. The worry was gone, the months of holding back his desire gone, the self-torture gone, and the selflessness finished.

My hand found the softness of his face as I traced the outline of his chiseled chin and then moving to his lips feeling them quiver at my touch. His eyes filled with desire as his breath increased. With every movement of my hand across his face I recorded every sensual square inch.

His arms wrapped tightly around my body pulling me closer to him with no intention of letting go. I had never felt lips filled with such fury as his lips returned the kisses from mine. It was a rhythm of breathing that allowed me the knowledge and fed my passion.

Without a word, he slowly sat up our bodies in unison pulling me up into his arms as he stood, and carried me off to the bedroom then laying me down softly on the bed. He shed his shirt with one pull and I had my dress off with one movement.

His body was more incredible than I could've ever imagined. I'd never really seen him completely undressed, he was breathtaking. My body shivered at his sight and my eyes quickly recorded the firmness of his muscle tone furthering my arousal.

He made his way slowly across the bed like a lion going in for the kill. I was trying to control my hand quivering as I touched his chest and felt what my eyes had already memorized. I watched his eyes close as a moan escaped his lips. He was slow and methodical in his movement as he passed his hands over my flesh.

My own hands began grasping his arms, pulling himself to me as I felt his body heat radiate over my stomach. I wanted this moment to last as long as possible. I wanted him to take me as slow as he wanted allowing him to marvel in this moment of victory he'd accomplished after years of containment, his desire, passion, and lust was mine to resolve. Nothing was hidden anymore. My lips returned to his flesh with great fever. His kisses moved up my chest and then to my neck only pausing for a moment to smile and sigh as he listened to my own heart beat burst with ravenous joy.

I gripped him tightly as he moved over my body crushing it into his own. I was in total bliss. Every ounce of my being was on fire. I had never known such level of delight, deep want, or the increasing yearning that now filled me. I allowed him to take me over and over without speaking, without compromise, and without hesitation. Everything felt so right like it was meant to be. I was more than willing to accommodate his hearts every desire without yielding another second.

"You are everything I could have ever dreamed of," he whispered softly kissing my lips, "you have no idea how deep my feelings for you run or what I would do for you."

"Thank you for not waiting another moment. I don't know how long I could have waited for you to make the first move," I replied as tears of exuberance welled up in my eyes and I struggled to compose myself feeling his pain and years of yearning, but never being able to share it.

"You are my reason to exist and the reason I am alive," his words comforted me and I felt my heart fill.

The most incredible man in the universe loved me. He didn't have to say it; his kiss, his touch, his smile, and the glimmer in his eyes as he watched me lay in bed were more than enough.

With his strong arms around me to protect me and his lips softly kissing my skin to sooth me I fell asleep.

I woke as a ray of sunlight peeked in between the blinds. Tired, but ever so content I laid in bed watching him as he slept. I allowed my memory to wonder and replay our first night as lovers. My skin covered with goose bumps at the mere thought of the fervor this man had created.

I knew in that moment everything between us had changed. There would be no more avoidance from either of us, no more lying to ourselves, no more hiding our true emotions or our passion for the other, and never again would I allow this gorgeous man to sit by and be forced to contain himself. I knew I wouldn't have to contain myself either.

My thoughts of his internal struggle and how he managed to control himself all those times we laid on the couch after a ball game. The thought of me asleep in his lap or the extended hugs he had to control astonished me. Had I ever had a clue of his feelings, or maybe I did and just didn't react in fear of being rejected. None of that mattered now. He was here now and in my bed. He had expressed himself in every way he could, leaving no more doubt in my head in regards of how he felt about me and the love he held in his heart for me. I was complete. Everything had fallen into place as it should be.

I watched his chest as his breath was shallow. He was sleeping peacefully. He was everything I had ever wanted in a man and he was there for me this whole time. I gazed at his handsome face and knew this would not be like any other prior relationship.

Another chill shuttered through my body as the alarm clock went off and pulled me back from my current train of thought.

I turned and hit the off button and looked back to see Chance laying there with his eyes wide open and the biggest sexiest smile on his face.

"Good morning beautiful," he whispered as his hands caressed my back sending me into frenzy once again.

"Good morning. I guess we can skip our morning jog to-day," I said as I began to place a trail of kisses up his hand and arm making my way back to his lips.

"I'm glad to hear it. I have something more enjoyable planned for you," he replied as he returned to kiss me again while pulling me back into bed.

"You know I could get use to this kind of morning wake up," I whispered into his ear as the intensity of our night returned in full force.

Chapter IV

Chance

It was wonderful to finally wake-up with Susan in my arms two mornings in a row. I wonder how shocked Ty's going to be when I fill him in.

I basked in the moment and the knowledge that I didn't have to hide my feels for her anymore. I felt even more excitement knowing that she did have feelings for me after all. Sure we'd been good buddies and close friends all these years. It killed me when her husband died. I had to stand by and watch her suffer so much. I'd never been married before nor had someone I loved die on me either. I knew back then it wasn't the right time for her to become involved with me, or anyone else. I can't even begin to know the pain she went through. I just wanted to be there for her regardless. I pushed back my overwhelming feelings, the need to wrap my arms around her, the desire to kiss her, and make it all go away, and the longing to feel her flesh burn against mine.

My thoughts paused as I unlocked my apartment door and went inside.

Ty was already awake and sitting in the kitchen eating a bowl of cereal looking at me stunned.

"Chance Walker, where the hell have you been?" Ty asked as he slurped down his milk.

"Sorry Ty," I replied while looking down and trying to hide my expression.

"I haven't heard a word from you since you left here Saturday night to go out," Ty said. "Did you get lucky?"

"Yes, I got lucky, sort of well, real lucky," I said as I nodded in response. I couldn't hold it in anymore I was beaming.

"Dude, that's awesome," he spoke in a happier tone as he walked over and slapped me on the back, "congratulations, I'm happy for you. So who is she?"

"Her name?" I pursed my lips trying to control my gripping smile, "Susan."

"Susan?" Ty asked with a puzzled look. "Is she a local?"

"Yes," I replied letting a giggle slip.

"Susan, hum," Ty paused then his eyes went wide and his face washed over to white, "SUSAN, our Susan," he said as a big grin came across his face and began to laugh.

"Yes, my Susan!"

"Oh my GOD," Ty muttered while allowing it all to sink in.

"It was better than I could have ever dreamed," I replied.

"How? Why? You're joking right?"

"No, no joke. I went to Murphy's to hang out with some of our buddies and she was there."

"What happened?" Ty asked.

"You have no idea," I said.

"Well then, fill me in," he insisted.

"I saw her sitting there in a booth by herself drinking a beer. I figured it would be rude not to go over and at least say hi to her."

"And then what?" Ty asked as he pulled up a chair.

"Well I just went over to her and said hi. She didn't look like anything I'd ever seen before. She had her hair done up, make-up on, and this little sexy as hell tight red dress on," I said as I took a seat feeling my knees growing weak again just at the thought of that dress.

"Sexy red dress? Oh man and I missed it," Ty said. "Damn!"

"Yes, my words exactly. She was radiant like an angel sitting there calling me to her," I shut my eyes trying to recall every second, "I called her name, she looked up at me a little surprised, but in a good way."

"Then what?" Ty asked.

"I sat down next to her, we started to talk. I met her nephew Aaron whose band was playing at the pub. We had dinner and then dessert. She looked great and smelled like heaven."

"Damn!"

"Yea, that's all my brain could repeat in my head for the first hour I sat with her. I'm telling you Ty she was unbelievable. I was doomed the second I saw her. I knew I wouldn't be able to stop myself."

Ty broke out in a hysterical laugh as he fully understood what I saw and felt.

"What I would've given to have seen that," Ty said.

"It was wonderful and actually everything went better than I could've ever imagined it would."

"Everything," Ty snickered, "dude, I want details."

"We drank a beer and ate a burger, then I ordered dessert, she got some on the side of her face near her lip, and I figured now or never so I licked it off."

"No way!" Ty replied with enthusiasm.

I smiled and promised myself not to divulge too much information, but I couldn't contain myself.

"Well things got a little more interesting and then I drove her home," I said.

"Interesting," Ty sighed then raised his brow as the light bulb when off in his head, "Holy Crap! You did it," he said as his mouth opened wide as he went in shock and sniffled while wiping off a fake tear and smiled. "Dude I'm so proud of you!"

"Thanks. I'm pretty proud of myself too. She was just so incredible, she made me weak, and I knew there was no going back once I walked into her place," I sighed as I drifted back in my chair as flashes of ecstasy slipped forward.

"At first I wasn't sure how she'd react to my playful lick, then she gave me a look like she wanted more, I leaned in and touched her face, and she moaned," I said as I continued.

"No way," Ty responded, "too cool!"

"She turned towards me and I laid a long deep kiss on her. By her response I knew I wasn't just reading something else into the look her eyes gave me. I paid the waiter and we left. I gave her another kiss once we got outside and again she responded. I asked her for the keys, she gave them to me, and I opened her door giving her one more big kiss right there in the parking lot to let her know exactly how I was feeling about her. I went for broke. I tell you my heart was beating so hard I thought it would jump right out of my chest."

"Wow," Ty replied in amazement.

"She smiled at me and got in the car. I nearly sprinted to the other side to get in. I started the car up thinking there would be some odd moment between us until we got back home, but then she leaned over and..." I trailed off as my body shivered at the memory, "she leaned over and kept kissing me."

"She didn't?" Ty asked as his rubbed his eyes as if he was fighting off fake tears.

"Yes she did. I swear I could've died happy right then and there at that moment."

"Man I'm in shock. You've got my brain on information over load," Ty said this as he shook his head, "unbelievable, so all this time she had a thing for you too. Dude, what a waste of time and frustration you could've had her over a year ago. Sorry. I mean this is great."

"Yes," I snorted in response, "I drove like a mad man back to base, we got back to her place, and she let me in."

By the look of Ty's face and the fact that his mouth was wide open I knew he was in more shock than I thought he'd be.

"Hey Ty," I said. "Are you okay man?"

"Yea, I'm great," he replied as he snapped out of it smiling at me. "Then what?"

"Well, everything, that's what. What do you think happened? Seriously dude, I've been waiting for this day for five years."

"Cool," Ty responded. "Wait you said everything?"

"Everything," I said as I nodded with a smile streaking across my face.

"Well that changes things. Wow," Ty replied. "She didn't reject you or slap you upside your head or anything?"

"Nope, she just kissed me back, touched me back, and held me tight," I smugly replied.

"Dude you just made my week. I'm happy for both of you," Ty said as gave me a fist tap, "you're my hero."

We both broke out in laughter.

I got up to get a change of clothing and then looking back with a smile, "I may not be home tonight so don't wait up."

The weekend had ended on a high note, it was Monday, and time to work.

I had left her place this morning to come home to shower and dress after we'd opted out of our morning ritual jog for another hour of bliss.

It was nice waking up with her in my arms. Seeing her beautiful face first thing in the morning was better than anything I could've ever dreamt. I had done it. I actually kissed her, touched her, felt her flesh against mine, and I had made love to her. I knew my feelings for her were real, not just something I thought I felt for her. It was all real just like every kiss from her lips to mine. The love I felt for her was overpowering, I wondered how long I would be able to last before I confessed my devotion to her, and spoke those words my soul yearned to say, "I love you Susan," I said a loud to myself.

Now she'd done it, she owned my soul, not just my thoughts like before.

I found myself rushing to get ready. I was eager to feel her body in my arms and wanting to make love to her again with more passion. I didn't have to dream anymore. I loved her and no one else. I would make sure from today on that she knew exactly how I felt about her and how I yearned for her every second of every day.

She owned me.

Chapter V

Mission Training

The weekend had ended and I was feeling fantastic. Chance had gone back to his place to shower and dress for work.

It was nice waking up with his arms around me again this morning. I was still trying to wrap my mind around everything that had happened and fully understand it all. I didn't want to dwell on things too long. I knew things would be different between us from today on and I was thrilled at the idea.

I prepared myself for work and out the door I went, ready for whatever came my way. I wasn't really sure how I would make it this first day back to work knowing things had changed. I knew I would make him suffer no more. I just hoped I could focus on work and hurry to get through this day, so I could see him tonight my pulse raced at the thought. His heavenly face and that rocking body sent a bold rush of energy right to my core.

I didn't linger in the parking lot and didn't want any awkwardness, so I went straight into my office.

Not much was going on for a Monday. We didn't have any training and no meetings to attend until later in the day, so I turned my laptop on and figured I'd check email to see if Mom wrote me back and if Aaron sent an email or one of my nieces. It would help me stay focused and clear my head.

I sat quietly in my office allowing my door to stay open in order to keep me grounded.

Mom sent me a nice letter updating me on my sisters, the grand kids, her health, and sent pictures to me of her most recent cruise she had taken with Aunt Susie and Aunt Sarah. I was named after them and ever since I was a small child both of my aunts had played an important role in my life. I tried hard to be as good of an aunt to my own nephew and nieces as both Aunt Susie and Aunt Sarah had been to me.

I printed off the group picture of mom with her sisters and taped it to my desk lamp, so I could see it any time I started to miss them, and then I returned to my email trying to answer each of them with the thoughtfulness and gratitude that I have for so many people in my life who loved me. I chuckled as I realized I had one more person in my life now who I was sure loved me. Yes I'm pretty sure if he'd been there all this time waiting for me and having feelings for me then this was truly a man who loved me.

"Hello beautiful," I heard his voice speak.

"Hi," I replied as I took a deep breath and looked up to see my current fantasy standing before me with cheerfulness just radiating from him, "I wasn't sure I'd see you so soon today."

"I know I hope it is okay I just couldn't keep away. I'm sorry. Do you want me to leave?" Chance asked.

I sprang up from my chair and shut the door behind him.

"Like hell you will. No, you're staying right here," I declared as he pulled me into his arms. I couldn't speak another word his kisses took my breath away and I wasn't about to refuse him.

"Yes Ma'am," he whispered as his kisses moved along my neck then back up to my chin making my head swirl.

"Thank you," was all that escaped my lips as his lips found mine and my body began to ache.

"I've missed you. You're all I can think about. I can't control myself. You're like a drug and I need my medicine," he expressed while caressing my throat with his hand pulling me closer to his body.

"Well then, I wouldn't want to be accused of denying you your medicine," I replied.

I began to moan as his lips burned desire into my skin.

"I had to see you and feel you close to me to remind me I wasn't just dreaming."

He traced my face with his finger tip as he pulled my body against his setting it ablaze.

"Lock the door," I said.

He complied without speaking and turned his attention back to me. My body ached for him. This level of eagerness was dangerous and I wanted nothing else.

He took me right there just as passionately and completely as he had done so many times now, but every time was as if it were our first. We couldn't get enough of each other. I was lost in the moment. I didn't care who called or who knocked. I wanted him now and I was not going to allow anyone or anything to sidetrack him from his current mission.

As if he read my mind, he pulled the plug on the phone as he laid me back against the desk. Chance proceeded with his insatiable desire of my body. With every kiss and every touch, I surrender to his complexity of need and libido, happily and willingly.

After we sat on the couch in my office recovering from the sense of fulfillment my thoughts of him were incredible.

All these years he was right there just waiting for a sign, a hint, or anything from me to show I was interested in him. I was happy knowing I'd finally woke-up and saw him for the man he was and to see that he was head over heels in love with me and always had been.

"Thank you," I softly spoke as I touched his beautiful face with the palm of my hand taking in just how special this man really was, "you have no idea how happy I am to see you, to feel you, and to be able to kiss you."

"I'd love nothing more than to make you happy every day of every week of every month."

"I'm glad I could be your medicine. I didn't realize until you kissed me just how much I'd already missed you today," I replied with a chuckle.

"Well then I'm glad I stopped by," Chance said.

"Yes," I replied.

"So you feel like grabbing some lunch with me?"

"Yes after that I'm famished," I replied.

After lunch, he walked back with me to my office closing the door and locking it this time behind him. He's a quick learner.

"Oh crap. I forgot to plug the phone back in before we left."

"Yea, sorry about that I just remembered back when we," he paused, "the night Ty and I came over to watch the game and had dinner and Ty left and then I went to leave and we kind of started to have a moment and the phone killed it."

"Not today I wouldn't have answered it even if it had been the President himself calling me," I declared.

"Good to know," he replied as his evil grin returned.

"Well love," I said as I reluctantly pulled my lips away from his, "I have a meeting with Chief Banks and some others from higher up in about fifteen minutes."

"Well I guess I can let you go," Chance replied as he continued to kiss me, "but only if you promise to call me the minute you get home from work today."

"I think I can manage that," I teased as I returned his playful kisses, "the second I get home."

"I'll see you tonight," Chance stated.

"I'm counting on it," I replied.

Chance didn't leave until I was breathless and dazed from another one of his deep celestial kisses.

I cleared my head the best I could and tried to compose myself as I walked into the meeting room. Chief Banks and five other men all in suits had already been seated. I recognized Commander Bower and Commander McKinley both fellow shuttle commanders.

"Good afternoon lady and gentlemen," Chief Banks spoke, "I'm happy to see you all could make it here today for this meeting on such short notice. I do apologize for any conflict in your current schedules this may have caused, but your attendance was required."

We all nodded our heads and understood.

"Doctor Turner will take the floor from here," Banks spoke curtly.

"Hello, I'm Doctor Steve Turner current director of the lunar division here at NASA. We've asked each of you here today because our President has asked us to return to the Moon for further exploration and to start work on a possible lunar base on the Moon."

"Well that sounds incredible," Commander McKinley spoke up first.

Chatter broke out among us as we shared our thoughts of the importance of such a mission.

"Beginning Monday, we will be doing joint training with your fellow astronauts and the robotics division will be hosting your training for the next two weeks in order to familiarize all of you with the workings of the future lunar robots as well as other more advanced technical systems that we will be using during the next five Moon lunar landings. Yes we're going back to the Moon," Doctor Turner said.

"We will have training for the next six weeks, everything from the robotics Doctor Turner has stated to the new lunar Launch Control Team," Chief Banks said as he passed out our work orders for the next six weeks.

"Well so much for a family vacation," Commander Bower responded.

"Gentlemen and lady, this concludes our meeting for today. We'll see you all back here for training on Monday," Chief Banks instructed.

I finished up setting my work schedule for the next six weeks and then headed home.

My brain hurt from the buzzing noise and irritation I got during that meeting. I needed my migraine medication and soon.

It was 5:30 when I got home and just as I promised I called Chance, so he could come over.

I picked up my cell phone and clicked my speed dial for Chance.

"Hi, I'm home sorry it too so long," I informed him.

"Hi, that's okay I had laundry that needed washed," he replied.

"We had a ton of paper work from the meeting. Now my head is splitting," I said.

"I'll be over in thirty minute," Chance said. "Do you need me to bring anything?"

"No, I'll be okay," I replied. "Do you still have a key to my place?"

"Yes," Chance replied.

"Good, I'm going to hop in the shower. You can let yourself in," I said.

"Sure sounds good. I'll see you soon," Chance replied.

"Okay I..," I paused almost letting my mouth slip up and utter words of love, "I'll see you very soon. I'll be waiting. Bye."

"Bye love," Chance finished and hung up.

I got myself showered and ready for my evening with Chance. I wrapped myself in a towel and made it to the bedroom.

"AH," I shouted. "Crap, don't do that you're going to give me a heart attack!"

He was lying on my bed with nothing but his gym shorts on.

"Sorry I did yell hello. I guess you didn't hear me from all the loud music and you singing in the shower," Chance replied.

I walked past him and headed to my closet.

"Not so fast," he said as he jumped up and grabbed my waist laughing as he caught me.

"Hey I need to get dressed," I insisted.

"Um, no you don't," he replied as he raised his brow and that wicked evil grin came screaming across his face as he proceeded to tug the towel off my body and lowered me towards the bed.

"Chance Walker, is that all you think about?"

"No, okay maybe a little," Chance replied.

"I guess I can't argue with a man who's waited nearly five years," I said.

"And suffered too," Chance teased childishly as he frowned with a fake pout.

"I'll never forget how strong willed you are and how I wish the hell you'd kissed me years ago."

"Yes, I've had that thought many times over," he whispered as his lips softly caressed my throat, "but we are in the here and now."

"Yes," I moaned as his lips stirred my soul.

"We're in the here and I want you now," Chance softly declared as his kisses intensified against my bare skin.

I did not refuse him.

Night fell and he'd drifted off to sleep. Not any wonder why. Neither of us got much sleep this weekend and neither of us wanted to sleep much either, as if sleep would have been a waste of time when there was so much catching up to do between us. He had five years of passion, longing, and kisses stored up just for me.

I thanked GOD and all the powers that be for that perfect moment when his lips found mine and the knowledge that this is what we both had longed for together.

I lay quietly propping my head upon the extra pillow. It took every fiber of my being to keep from waking him up. His body glowed under the celestial moonlight casting itself on his body from the heaves above.

He was perfect. Every muscle on his body was tone and tanned. I was going mad and my urge was far too strong. I was weak. It was his fault, I argued with myself. Shame on him. O, shame on me for my wicked thoughts.

Unable to refrain, I softly touched him slowly tracing the moonlight as it shadowed the curvature of his abdominal muscles. I was enchanted by his beauty and awe struck by his perfect physic.

As softly as I could I allowed my lips to caress what my hand had already touched giving up the idea of trying hard not to wake my prince charming.

My teasing was apparently done under false pretense.

He snorted at me and began to laugh. "Stop! Stop your killing me! I can't stand it anymore I give up!"

"You were awake this whole time?" I asked. "Now you're in trouble!"

"I sure hope so."

My heart belonged to him and nothing else seemed relevant. I wanted to lay by his body every night and wake to his smile every morning. I knew right then and there my life would never be the same now that Chance was sharing himself like this with me. I couldn't bring myself to even think of how I had ever lived without him before today. It really didn't feel like I had truly lived at all until now.

My life was clearly with Chance, in the here and now. In his arms, I found the place I'd longed for. He gave me safety, fulfillment, hope for a better tomorrow, and unconditional love. Yes love. Eternal love.

Chance and I had a fairly simple routine now. Neither of us wanted to live without the other. It only made sense that he move in with me since three at his place would be a crowd. I enjoyed my privacy far too much and things just worked out better with him moving in with me. I woke up every morning with his arms gently wrapped around me. Most nights I fell asleep with my head on his chest and my body cradled comfortably in his biceps. Every morning we'd get up early and go for our morning jog, have breakfast, and head off to work either taking the Camaro or our motorcycles if the weather was nice enough. Every day after work we'd come home together, have dinner, watch some TV or read, give into desire, and then fall asleep holding each other tightly as if it were our last night on Earth.

Almost two months had passed since our first kiss. All of it was so natural with Chance. I couldn't be happier than I'm right now this very minute.

Our work weeks had been stressful and filled with the training simulations, Moon rovers, new satellite relay system, robotics, and communication gear.

Today would be interesting because it would be the first group training day for my flight crew since our last space shuttle mission.

I sat in the kitchen reading the morning newspaper and as he approached, I could smell his scent, it was intoxicating. He leaned in and kissed the back of my neck then swiped the comic page out of my hand before I could get a word in.

"It's your turn babe. Better get freshened up today we'll be training on the new lunar orbiter simulator."

"I'm right on it," I said as I hopped up from my chair and proceeded to distract him from his morning comics.

I let my lips trace the contour of his throat and then his ear as my teeth softly bit his lobe. It was futile he didn't even budge.

"You're stronger than I thought," I said.

"You have no idea," he replied firmly as looked up at me and smiled wickedly.

I sulked off to the bathroom to get in a quick wash and rinse.

By the time I was done with my shower he was already dressed and ready to go.

"Hurry up babe," he spoke quickly, "stop primping you look beautiful and come on we're going to be late."

I hated to be rushed and today would be busy enough.

We started with simulator training and had finished with it by noon. Our crew moved into a meeting room along with the other crews for some hands on training with the new rovers.

"Pizza delivery just in time," Ty proclaimed, "another minute more and Commander Davis is going to starve to death by the sounds of her stomach."

"Yes, Susan doesn't he ever feed you," Jeff added.

I raised my eye brow, then the shock, and panic set in. He knows? They all know.

Everyone joined in on the laughter making jokes about my loud stomach growl.

I prayed for time to move fast, so we could get over the last training session of the day.

Jeff then made a comment to Chance saying someone had finally "tamed the lion" or as Ty put it "she's turned Chance into a kitten," then Chance chimed in response to Ty's analogy and proclaimed himself a "sex kitten".

I sat up and looked away. I was overwhelmed with nausea I couldn't hold more than one slice of pizza because my stomach was turning. Chance was sitting up eating his pizza as he chuckled. Their voices repeated in my head and felt like torture. I couldn't find the strength to even speak. I sank into my chair in shock as my face became flush with embarrassment. I understood that Ty knew about us, but the others? I was confused and didn't know what to think or say. I just sat still speechless as I looked down at the floor wishing to be invisible as their giggles grew louder.

Chance grew quiet. I knew he was looking at me and reading my face, but I said nothing.

I wanted to reply to his insensitive statement. I bit my lip.

Did they not think before they spoke? Did they not realize that higher command had no clue about my relationship with Chance? I could get transferred to another position or called back to active duty.

My pulse raced and I felt very sick. As soon as I had the opportunity I bolted out of the room before they got another word in.

After I freshened up and got back some self-control, I decided to go back in the training room and just remain calm and block everything else out.

"Focus on work," I told myself.

I opened the bathroom door and Chance was standing in the hallway in front of me. Nausea filled me again.

"You told Jeff?" I asked abruptly.

"No I didn't tell him. I swear," he pushed his body in front of me to block my escape.

"I don't feel like talking right now," I said. "Let me by!"

"Susan, wait, I'm sorry if they upset you, it's the last thing I would ever want to do to you," he spoke in a lower tone. "Please wait, I had no idea Jeff knew."

The sadness in his voice allowed some relief, but I was still feeling overwhelmed. I just kept walking away and forced myself into work mode as I ignored the boys for the rest of the day. I didn't even give them as much as a glance.

Finally, the workday was over. I left out of the meeting before Major Nancy Blackwell even finished her speech on robotics. I was in my car and out of the parking lot before the others ever made it to the exit door. Chance wouldn't be home for another 30 minutes or more due to his meeting and Ty had already offered to give him a ride home.

I was home in record time. I stripped, showered, and half-dressed before the phone ever rang. I didn't bother to answer it. I was in no mood to talk to anyone right now I just needed to be alone and think.

"Yes let everything sink in," I spoke a loud to myself.

On the couch, I sat mulling over the day's events trying to analyze everything and as I sat alone with my hands over my face, I began to cry.

There was a knock on the door. I didn't answer it. I heard the keys in the lock and the door opened. I sat still and didn't look up. I didn't want him to see me like this. I was a mess.

"Susan, baby I'm sorry," his voice broke and filled with anguish. "Please baby, forgive me!"

I lowered my hand to reveal my eyes over flowing with tears of frustration, but I still couldn't look up to his face.

"Oh GOD Susan, I swear I didn't tell Jeff," Chance dropped down to the floor beside me taking my hands into his after he attempted to brush away my tears.

My eyes met his as he tried to understand my emotionally charged reaction. Without a word, I saw his eyes begin to fill with tears. It was all I could take.

"I know you didn't," I responded to his plea, "I'm sorry I got so emotional and overreacted."

"I would never intentionally do anything to hurt you Susan," his voice softly spoke as it broke. "Please forgive me!"

"There's nothing for you to apologize for," I said as I leaned over and kissed his lips cradling his face in my hands, "there's no need for you to be upset. We knew this would happen and well, it just happened a little sooner than I'd prepared for. I overreacted and I was emotionally overwhelmed, but I'm fine now."

He moved up towards me on the couch taking my face into his hands, holding it as he looked deeply into my eyes trying to find the right word to say.

His lips responded for him without words as they found my lips. I surrendered into his arms. His kiss was more aggressive and urgent. I responded back equally to the urge in his kiss as he crushed my body into his saturating me with more desire. He was all I wanted and nothing else mattered. It was more than before, with intensity and an urgency to let him know exactly where he stood. I held nothing back and he did the same in return. I knew in that moment that every word, every kiss, and every touch that he gave me was the truth. The realization that I loved him was the only truth I knew. Yes, I loved him.

I laid there on the couch in his arms allowing myself to meet his intensity of passion with my own. I wanted him now more than ever.

"You're the most intense woman I've ever known," his whisper soothed me as his lips returned to my flesh. "Now you've gone and done it!"

His kisses tapered off and his eyes focused back on mine as a look of seriousness covered his face. I was clueless.

He pulled himself closer and caressed my throat again with his lips setting my skin ablaze. His breath became more resolute as he slowed and his eyes returned to mine.

"Susan," he spoke my name in a low deep voice and paused, "I love you," he said as he exhaled.

It took me a few seconds to catch my breath. I pulled his face to mine kissing him aggressively with desperation and solitude. I wanted to show him how those words branded themselves into my heart.

His sensual eyes glimmered as he stared down at me as I paused pulling myself back.

"I love you," I softly replied as my hand reach up and touched his face and happiness overcame me and I smiled back, "Chance, I love you," I whispered again as he returned my touch and our kiss turned into tranquility as the rhythm of our passion became incorruptible.

Everything we needed to say had been spoken. Our desire, lips, bodies, and souls became one in that instant as it bonded completely with every fiber of our very being and it was pure.

Chapter VI

Break Time

Today was a new day. Chance and I had confessed our love for one another and managed to talk things over for the most part. We just decided to hell with it. As long as we loved one another and wanted nothing else we would be okay and take whatever life throws at us. Our morning jog was more playful and carefree setting the tone for the day. I relaxed and gave up all anxiety of discovery and just went with the flow.

I loved him, that is all that mattered, and I didn't care who knew. I was already pretty sure our entire crew knew. If Chance had been in love with me from the moment he saw me then I knew I'd find the answers in my photo albums.

I'd finished getting ready for work and had some time to spare so I took out my album labeled "NASA". Right there on the very first picture I opened up to, like a brick hitting me in the head, he was right there standing next to me with an evil grin I knew all too well and his arm wrapped around my waist. How could I be so clueless? Yes I was clueless. I could've had those lips kissing me maybe two years ago. I was disgusted with myself. What did he see in me? That poor man, I thought to myself as my heart ached at the emotional struggle Chance had to go through these past few years. Always wanting to tell me or show me how much he truly cared for me and that he was in love with me.

I sighed as I flipped page after page and photo after photo. He's perfect. He was right there in front of me and I was the only person who had no clue.

Chance came out of the bedroom dressed and ready for work. He was sexy in uniform.

"What are looking at?" Chance asked as he sat down next to me.

"Pictures of you, me, you, me, and you and me," I said as I pointed to each photo with us in it.

"Hey that's a nice one I don't have that one, cool," Chance said.

"You would think after the first ten I would've had a clue."

"Well maybe your heart wasn't ready, or you could just be the most clueless person alive," he chuckled.

"Both," I sighed, "look at you, here and here, standing right next to me in most of them with your arm wrapped around my waist," I exhaled as I gloated.

"Oh baby you're not that clueless. I think more than anything else your heart was just not ready for the likes of me," he teased as he pulled me in for another sexy kiss.

"But you are here and I couldn't be happier than I am right now."

"Well enough of this we have work to do," Chance said followed by one quick kiss as he grabbed the car keys off the coffee table and made for the door.

"Yes I'm ready. You're right," I replied and then paused as an uncontrollable smile gripped my lips, "I love you."

"You don't know how long I've waited to hear those three words come out of those lush lips of yours" he declared as his turned to kiss me. "It was definitely worth the wait!"

"Thank you," I whispered as I ran my fingers over his biceps making him shiver.

"We need to go to work before I decide to call in sick for both of us today," he said trying to shake the goose bumps off his arm. "Out!"

We planned it, so we'd get to work about twenty minutes early today so we could have some "us time" before going in.

Jeff, Ty, and Abe stood in the parking lot hanging out near Jeff's jeep.

We figured something was up so Chance pulled into the spot next the jeep.

"Good morning," Jeff spoke first.

"Good morning," I replied as I got out of the car.

"You guys have a minute?" Abe asked.

"Sure what's up?" Chance asked as he got out of the car.

"We wanted to let you both know we are really sorry for the way we acted and the joking yesterday. If we offended you, we are all really sorry we were just joking around and not really thinking before we spoke," Jeff said.

"It's okay. Really, everything is alright," I responded, "don't worry about it. I realize now that everyone, but me, knew how Chance felt towards me and that information was really no big secret. Actually, it's kind of a relief to have nobody surprised by our relationship. It makes things that much easier for both of us," I said as I held Chance's hand.

"Well knowing that doesn't make up for the irresponsible behavior yesterday Susan," Ty said. "We're really sorry!"

"It's okay there's really no need to be sorry I'm just glad we don't have to hide our feelings anymore when any of you are around," Chance replied as he squeezed my hand.

"Yes don't give it another thought. Now we'd best get before they send out a search party to look for us," I said.

One by one each of them shook Chance's hand congratulating him with "about time" and then gave me a congratulations hug.

It was nice to have our friends supporting us like this. It would make everything easier and with that I relaxed.

We walked together as a group of friends. I took Chance's hand in mine and felt overwhelmed with boldness. I even stopped in the hall before we went into our training class and kissed him right there in front of everyone. Chance's chest swelled and his wondrously handsome smile returned to grace his face.

Our first session was with Doctor Amber Johnson our medical director. She decided in light of what happened with Jeff that we all needed to be updated on standard medical aid during shuttle missions. It was good for all of us and having experienced that kind of panic first hand just made me want to learn that much more.

It was tough sometimes being the shuttle commander, being their leader and friend, and having the responsibility of the crews vary lives in my hands brought enough stress to my life on top of all the other typical stresses of a shuttle mission.

Our class with Doc Johnson was extended from one hour to four hours. She wanted to leave nothing to chance and have all of us go over various medical situations that may occur during a shuttle flight. She took us through every scenario she could think of and then a few that Ty and Commander Bower brought to her attention. Overall it was one of the best training sessions I think any of us had in years.

We broke for lunch for a diet of subs and salads on today's menu. My crew sat together out of habit. Chance positioned himself right next to me leaning over at one point for a quick kiss. It was nice I didn't even blush. He kept one hand on my leg or would shift to lean closer to me so he could put his arm around my waist.

We did get a few gawks from the other astronauts. Nice I'm not the only clueless person here, I thought to myself. I held his hand after lunch as we got up to take the rest of our break outside. Chance made no hesitations or shied away from me in any way and neither did I. We took the notebooks and reference material from the first half of the day back to our car. It was so effortless to be with him.

After he shut the trunk of the car he turned to wrap his arms around my waist and pull me close to him.

"Do you have any idea how happy I am right now?" He asked as his kisses returned.

"As happy as I am I hope," I whispered between kisses, "you have no idea how much I love you," I continued as I moaned as his hand pressed against my back forcing my body to mesh with his.

"I'm glad you do. I can't think of anyone else I'd rather hear those words from," Chance said as his lips crushed mine bringing me to an increased degree of excitement.

"I love you Chance Walker," I said as I gasp for air and tried to contain my hormones.

"I love you Susan, more than anyone in this world and I promise to love you for the rest of my life," Chance replied.

As his words rang true to my heart and his lips filled with fever. If he wanted me to, I would love him for the rest of my life in return. He embraced me in his arms letting me know how much he needed me.

"Come on you two. There's time for that later," Ty shouted interrupting my perfect moment.

We walked back hand in hand as Ty stood at the door shaking his head.

"You two are like love sick teens," Ty joked as he opened the door for us then put his arm around Chance, "I love you man," he said and blew a kiss as he giggled.

We broke into laughter as we walked down the hall.

"Ty, the eternal comedian!" I exclaimed.

* * *

Over the next week our training sessions would be going over various payloads and hardware that would be used in the return to the Moon.

I knew I wouldn't be going to the Moon it would be only sane to have three or four men go back first. It would be just as it was in the beginning of the Apollo missions, except the technological advancements made in the past forty years were astonishing. The astronauts back then would not have dreamed of having some of the everyday advances that we know of that are so common now. Communications satellites are more advanced; weather prediction, robotics, and even the rocket launchers themselves are superior to the old ways. I can't help but think how wonderful science has become and all the advancements. It was like comparing night and day just remarkable. With every training session there is a specific section on safety. We'd learned from past trial and error each time paying closer attention to even the littlest detail can save lives.

I didn't see much difference in having the shuttle orbiter strapped to a giant external tank and a huge solid rocket booster. The lunar orbiter would be sitting on the end of its rocket, but the outcome is the same. Both orbiters are propelled out of Earth's gravity and it's nothing new, just a little different. The overall size of the lunar orbiter was smaller.

I figure whoever is chosen to command the lunar orbiter may have to adjust to a new flight control and electronic system making it a good challenge for any one of us. I could tell the past eight weeks of our training everyone was pretty much excited about the return to the Moon. We all knew it was long overdue and looked at it as another great step for NASA as we moved forward.

Regardless of who gets picked I know everyone will support them 100% and work just as hard in aiding with any lunar training.

Our next briefing involved Mr. Mark Thompson, he was Mission Manager for the return to the Moon, and he would be our training officer for the next two weeks.

Booklets and mission statements were handed out over and over for each training class. We dealt with specific payloads that would be making the trip to the Moon.

Shuttle commanders went over the new simulator information. Engineers went over various robotic arms used for each payload. Medical crew members had specific experiments the science panel wanted to have performed on the Moon.

Everyone was made familiar with each other's tasks.

"I think if I read one more report on propulsion systems my brain will turn to mush," Chance expressed.

We went over hundreds of archive video, notes, and mission operations from all previous lunar missions to help us prepare for what might lie ahead.

"I think I need a vacation," Ty said.

"You think you two have it bad, you should have to watch six hours straight flight coverage from the 1970's," Abe replied as he stuck out his tongue.

"I think we all need a vacation," Chance moaned as he held his head down on the table.

"I heard some higher-up discussing giving everyone three weeks off," Abe quietly spoke.

"Really are you sure?" Ty asked.

"Yes that's what I heard coming out of Chief Banks mouth to General Stewart earlier today while I was on the can," Abe informed.

"When? Did they mention anything specific?" Chance asked.

"September 3 was the date the General gave," Abe replied.

"That would be great. I have some pretty big plans and this would give me the opportunity I need to spring it on her," Chance stated.

"Spring what on her?" Abe asked.

"Nothing I was just thinking of popping the big one on her," Chance replied.

"What?" Ty asked.

"Shish. What the hell are you doing? Nobody else knows yet," Chance insisted.

"Sorry, you think she'll say yes?" Abe quizzed.

"I'm sure she'll say yes," Ty remarked.

"I'm praying for it. I just bought her ring yesterday," Chance responded.

"Cool man. That's awesome. I'm really happy for both of you," Abe spoke as he gave a congratulations hand shake.

"Not a word dude," Chance threatened, "you two are the only other soles alive who know yet."

"No problem. I got your back," Abe said.

"Yes not a word here," Ty expressed.

"Now if I knew that the date for our vacation time off was right I could plan our getaway for the big moment," Chance stated.

"Hey what are you guys up to?" I asked.

"Oh hey Susan," Abe spoke half startled.

"Hey babe," Chance whipped his head back around.

"Just talking baseball, you know us guys," Abe said.

"Well then I guess I didn't miss anything," I teased as I walked over to Chance's chair, leaned over his shoulder wrapping my arms around his torso, and softly kissed his cheek.

Chance let out a soft giggle and then leaned back to return the playful kiss.

"Okay you two stop it," Abe humorously stated, "you're going to make me sick."

"I know the feeling, seriously, they've been at it all day," Ty chuckled.

We looked up and began to laugh. I plopped myself down in the chair next to Chance.

"Oh Abe would you like a little love too," I teased as I blew him a childish kiss.

"O thanks Susan, that's just what I needed," Abe said as he giggled and gave a big smile.

"Hey don't be giving my kisses away I need all I can get," Chance joked as he playfully pouted.

"Are you ready to get out of here this weekend?" I asked.

"Yes," Abe joked. "Where are we going?"

"Oh can I come too?" Ty playfully asked.

"We? Ha! More like Chance and I, alone!" I replied as my hand returned to his face.

"Sounds good I think I can clear my busy schedule," Chance teased me as he kissed my hand.

"Good, how about we take a trip to Daytona for the weekend?" I asked.

"Perfect," Chance replied as he ran his hand through my hair.

He walked me out to our car and pressing himself against me as his lips brushed the back of my neck before I could get the car door open.

"Well then it's a date. I'll see you at home," I said trying to contain myself from his playfulness. "What time do you think you'll be done with your robotics simulator with Ty?"

"We should be done and out of here by 6:00 at the latest. I'll have Ty drop me off and if you can arrange it, we can leave as soon as I get home," Chance replied.

"Sounds great I'll get online and book a hotel on the beach and have our stuff packed and ready to roll."

"Deal," he said as he snatched me up in his arms giving me a more passionate kiss.

"Then I'll see you home," I said.

"Susan," he said my name then paused. "I love you!"

I stopped and pulled his arms back around me.

"I love you too," I replied.

"You make my heart feel like it's going to burst right out of my chest every time I hear you speak those three simple words," Chance replied as he squeezed me closer.

"You have the same effect on me," I replied.

"I'll see you later. Be careful and I'll hurry every chance I get," Chance said.

I gave into yet another long lustful kiss drinking up his affection.

"I'd best get out of here before Ty comes looking for you and yelling across the parking lot at us again," I joked.

"Yes, yes I know. Okay bye; 6:00 at the latest," he said as he shut the car door and gave me another quick kiss.

Chapter VII

Daytona

I arrived home at 4:00 p.m. ready for a long hot shower and to relax before packing to drive up to Daytona for the weekend.

I got online and booked a hotel right on the beach with a cabana suite with direct beach access it will be just perfect. I found availability at the same hotel we had all stayed in two years ago when the entire crew drove up for bike week.

"The Hilton Daytona Beach, perfect!" I spoke aloud.

I went ahead and called to confirm our arrival today and set up dinner for tonight as well. I made our reservations at the steakhouse and our cozy cabana. I set up Parasailing mid-day Saturday followed by lunch at the sports bar and then a relaxing afternoon couple's massage; it was just what we both needed.

Time to get away from work and to relax while being pampered sounded incredible. The more I thought about our weekend getaway the more excited I became. I packed my sexiest lingerie and the skimpiest bikini I owned. I wanted our first mini vacation together as a couple to be as perfect as possible. I made a checklist to make sure I had packed everything I needed. I had clothing for Chance set out for him to review and I would pack his overnight bag while he was in the shower.

I decided to pull out that photo album from our group trip to Daytona and I should have known right there again as big as a train. I shook my head as I realized I was such a dope.

Even in the beach photos of him sitting on the blanket with me while he's rubbing sun block on my butt and that evil grin just like he gives me now when he's up to no good and thinking naughty thoughts.

I made a promise to myself that as long as he lived, I would make it up to him. I'd show him in every possible way how much I loved him, how I can't live without him, and how I won't live without him. I pledged myself to him for an eternity come what may. I'll find a way to show him that I was worthy of his patience and love. I began to cry again. I know it is silly, but every time I look at his angelic face in these photos this level of love for him that I feel makes me emotional. Everything seemed almost alien before our first night together. Chance had awakened my very soul and there was no going back. I cleared my eyes and allowed myself to enjoy my happy memories of that Daytona trip.

5:15 p.m., the front door opened and my heart sang. An overwhelming sensation of enchantment enveloped me once more. I jumped up off the couch and before he could even lay the keys down I rushed to get my arms around his neck and my legs up around his waist kissing him over and over. He was caught so off guard he began to laugh nearly dropping me.

"Wow you missed me that much," he said as he continued to laugh.

"Yes! Yes! Yes!" I loudly replied as I smacked his lips, kiss after kiss, between words.

"Now I could get use to this kind of greeting you know."

"Then this kind of greeting you shall have."

"So what brought all of this on?" Chance asked.

"Just the overwhelming need to have my body strapped to yours," I replied as I giggled.

"Okay more photo albums I see," Chance said.

"Yes I got to thinking about when we all rode up to Daytona for bike week and how much fun I had. Being a glutton for punishment, I pulled out that album and again, there you are!"

"I was always there just like now, only happier," he said as his lips found mine bringing a resurgence of excitement.

"I know me too," I said as I returned his lovely kiss.

"So are we packed and ready to go?" Chance asked.

"Yes everything except your overnight bag. I set out your swim trunks and underwear. You just need to pick the other stuff you want to wear."

"That sounds good. Give me fifteen minutes to shower and shave then we're out of here," he said.

I gave him another quick kiss as he released me.

"I'll get this bag packed and then get it loaded on your bike. Mine is already loaded and ready to go. We just need to stop for gas before we leave. I think I'm at less than a quarter tank."

He nodded in response as he stripped and rushed to the shower.

"Damn," I said with a grin.

He was perfect in every sense of the word. I had to shake off the overwhelming urge to delay our exit plan. I can wait, it's a short drive up the coast to Daytona then I'll have him all to myself all weekend. Chills washed through me and with that I practically ran out to the bike to store his bag.

I folded up our confirmation paper and stuffed it into my jacket pocket. I had already donned my leather riding pants and jacket. I made sure to wear my tight red leather ones and grabbed my matching patriotic helmet.

I was bent over buckling my boots and then jumped.

"What the," I paused as I looked up in shock from his smack on my butt.

"Yea baby," he proclaimed grinning ear to ear, "now that is what I call damn sexy. I don't know babe I may have trouble concentrating on the ride with you looking that hot!"

I laughed at his humor and drank in the compliment as gratification beamed from him.

"I love you," he said.

He was definitely good for my ego.

We were out the door by 5:45 p.m. The ride up to Daytona was perfect we had the best weather and traffic wasn't too bad. We both were speed demons, so I knew we'd make

Daytona in record time. At one point, I clocked us at ninety mph during a long straight with little traffic for about ten minutes. Speed excited me and Chance being a similar being had no problem keeping up. He had a tendency to match my enthusiasm.

The sun was still high in the sky as Daytona came into view. We took our exit and managed to control our speed while in local traffic.

Our hotel was right on the beach. We had stayed there before so I felt comfortable with the surroundings and knew it would be perfect for our return.

We got the bikes parked and made our way to check-in. The desk manager smiled as she said my name and then looked to Chance. Once again we opted to be good ambassadors for our profession and allowed a few extra minutes for photos and autographs. Sometimes being famous in your own state can be helpful. The nice hotel manager, Mr. Cornish, walk with us to our cabana to make sure it was up to our standards.

Everyone treated us so kind it just made things that much better.

Our cabana was beautiful and private. We thanked Mr. Cornish for his time as he left us to our own discretion.

"Wow babe you really went all out, nice," Chance spoke.

"I'm glad you approve. Are you ready for dinner?"

"Starving!" Chance declared.

"Good we have a table reserved for us at the steakhouse," I said as I held out my hand for his.

"You really thought of everything didn't you," he replied taking my hand and then pulling in for a kiss.

"Yes I did. I wanted to make this different than before, special like you!"

He followed me out the door stopping to wrap his arms around me and his hand touched my face.

"I love you," he spoke as I gave into his lips as his kiss electrified me. I let out a soft moan, "everything is perfect just like you," he continued.

The cabana phone rang.

"Nice timing," Chance scoffed as he broke away to answer it, he nodded at the voice on the other end speaking softly, and then hung up.

"That was the front desk and our table is ready," he said as he returned to me on the deck turning to lock the door and with my hand in his we strolled toward Hyde Park Prime Steakhouse.

"This should be good. Jeff and Patti highly recommended we try it."

"Well then I'll have to thank them when we get back home," Chance replied.

Our dinner was just as good as we'd been told. The food was perfect and the service made our first night effortless.

After eating, we took a walk along the beach as sunset was drifting into darkness. The stars began to filter through the heavens above and the glow of the city illuminated the night's sky.

I marveled at the fact that this was our first walk on the beach together as boyfriend and girlfriend. We stopped every so often to look out along the ocean horizon and tried to catch a glimpse of cargo ships or sailboats in the distance. We wrap ourselves around each other taking in the moment. Plenty of couples walked along the shore as did we; maybe for the first time, or maybe the hundredth.

There was something magical about a romantic walk along the shore. Holding hands, walking slowly, not in any real hurry, and feeling completely in love. It was the perfect end to a perfect day. This was a break from our usual routine and work that we both needed.

I smiled as we continued to walk. I had one more surprise for him once back to our cabana.

"Look at that," Chance said as he pointed to a large blanket lying on the beach with a bottle of wine, roses, and chocolate covered strawberries. "Somebody's going to get lucky tonight!"

"Yes you are," I said.

"You did this?" Chance asked as his evil grin returned. "You're good!"

"That's my plan," I said as I sat down on the blanket surrounded by candles I held my hand out to his as he sat down beside me.

"I thought I was always the one who liked to go overboard?" Chance asked.

"Well maybe I've learned a few tricks from your book of romance," I whispered as my finger traced his lips offering him dessert.

Without a word, he opened his mouth and took the strawberry in stopping my hand before I moved back. His eyes locked on mine as he took my finger and licked it sending my body wild as I let out a deep moan.

"You keep that up and you'll get lucky sooner than you think," I said.

"Now that's my plan," he replied as his lips found mine, "strawberry um just as delicious as you."

Our tease of seduction continued as we finished off the strawberries and some wine before breaking to head back to our cabana to continue our nice romance in privacy. We made it to the deck; he swept me up in his arms and carried me through the door. His eyes stared deeply into my own as he laid me down on the bed only leaving me briefly to shut the front door locking it behind him and turning off the deck light.

"Now time to get lucky," he said as he rushed back into the room nearly undressed.

* * *

Saturday began with breakfast in bed.

"So what else do you have planned for our weekend?"

"I have us set up for some Parasailing at 10:30 if you're up to it. I wasn't sure if you'd ever experienced it or not. I thought it would be fun," I said.

"No can't say I've done that, but it does sound fun. Let me get my trunks on and we can go check it out," Chance replied.

The boat was waiting to take us out on the ocean for our ride. After about fifteen minutes of instruction and safety checks Chance was the first to ride. I pulled out my Canon and got as many photos of this historical event as possible. Then it was my turn.

Flight has never scared me; it was the lack of controlling my own destiny that I had trouble with. It was weird being tethered to the boat as I floated upwards as the boat sped through the ocean following the shoreline with its music cranked. It was odd the only thought I had was that this might be 1/10th the experience Chance had experienced during a space-walk, it was exhilarating. The boat returned us to the beach. We thanked our crew for the blast we had and decided to take a swim in the outdoor pool before lunch, since we'd missed our morning jog. Even when on vacations we all had to keep up our physical workout.

The pool was practically empty giving us plenty of room for laps.

"That swim felt great, but now I'm famished," Chance said. "How about you?"

"Yes I could go for a burger and a cold beer," I replied.

"That sounds great," Chance said.

We stopped back at our cabana for a quick change into dry clothing and headed over to the sports bar. I'm sure Chance was more excited about getting to see a game during lunch on the big screen.

Once at our table we ordered burgers and beers while we watched a baseball game.

"I guess we got here just in time," Chance said.

"I told you this would be a good trip for us and all you have to do is simply relax and enjoy."

"What's next on your agenda?" Chance asked.

"We'll have more relaxation with a couple's massage at the hotel spa."

"A couple's massage sounds interesting," he said as he raised his brow.

"You deserve it. This will be a first of many good things to come," I said.

"Everything else is just icing on the cake compared to you babe," Chance replied.

"Are you ready to go?"

"What time?" Chance asked.

"Ten minutes from now," I replied.

"Okay let's get out of here. I'm ready to de-stress," Chance said.

We headed to the spa for pampering. The massage room was already set up with candles, soft music, two massage tables, and two very burly men.

"Hello, come in, I'm Bernard, and this is Thomas. We will be giving your massages to you today," Bernard said. "We're pleased to meet you!"

"Hi nice to meet you both, I'm Chance, and this is Susan."

"Is there any specific area you'd like either of us to pay extra attention to today?" Thomas asked.

"My neck and feet for me," I informed him.

"My left shoulder I guess could use some extra attention. It's been giving me trouble the past few weeks," Chance replied.

"Great we can take care of that," Thomas said.

"We'll wait outside until you call us back in. You will need to remove everything except your underwear. When you are done take your place on one of the tables provided, face up. Use the top sheet to cover yourself up then let us know when you're ready and we'll begin," Bernard said.

"Okay thank you," Chance replied.

"This should be interesting," I whispered to Chance.

"Whatever you do, don't fall asleep on me," Chance said giggling as he got upon his table. "Try not to leave me unsupervised with that one he looks scary!"

"Chance, you're terrible, now behave," I said as I giggled back.

"I'm kidding, but he does look scary," he snickered.

For the next forty-five minutes we had total relaxation to-gether and neither of us fell asleep. It would have been pretty easy to sleep considering how relaxed I'd felt with all the stress and stiffness gone. The massage worked wonderfully and for the first time in weeks I could see Chance was physi-cally more relaxed.

We stopped off at the Pelican Bar to grab a Daiquiri before heading back to our cabana. The beach crowd had returned with locals and tourist alike so we opted to stay in our suite and relax allowing ourselves more time to be alone.

Chance sprawled himself out on our bed while I went to shower and by the time I'd finished, he was out cold. Poor baby hadn't had much sleep between our work and his fam-ished libido. It was sweet to see him lying there peacefully. He was perfect from his head to toe, he was just gorgeous, and he's all mine. I finished dressing and did some primp-ing for our night on the town. We'd left things open and had planned just to wing it. I went back into the bedroom to check on him. He was awake.

"How long was I out?" Chance asked.

"Two hours," I replied.

"Why didn't you wake me or come join me?"

"Because you needed your rest and if I'd come and joined you well you definitely wouldn't have got any rest," I teased as I offered a kiss.

"You look nice and smell even better," he spoke as he moved across the bed towards me not stopping until his arms were wrapped around me.

"I figured I'd let you rest and doll myself up for you."

"I don't know why? You're not going to be in that very long if I have a say about it," Chance said.

"Why not?" I asked as I teased back.

He pulled me tighter kissing me more aggressively each times our lips met.

"I have other plans for your body," he whispered as his lips stroked the skin of my shoulder, "plans that only include your skin."

I shook my head in amazement as with one movement he had my dress off and on the floor.

"You are amazing," I expressed.

"I'm just getting started love," Chance said.

His touch sent my pulse through the roof. His lips only increased my desire to give into his craving once more. There was always a deeper yearning an overpowering need to feel his bare skin against mine, to smell his scent, and feel his breath burn against my throat as I gave myself to him. Pure physical greed that's all I could attribute myself to.

Chance met every kiss I gave him in return with an even greater desire as if my touch propelled his responses higher or drove his libido to extremes. His arms held me tightly not wanting to let me go. His hand caressed my arm then traced its way up my shoulder to my neck only to pause as he pulled me up crushing my flesh beneath his.

His eyes shimmered with satisfaction as he conquered me again as he kissed me softly.

"I love you," I whispered.

He pulled me off the bed taking my hand leading me to the bathroom stopping to give into a long deep kiss then I trailed behind him into the shower.

"This is a nice treat, you and me in the shower and all the things I could do with you right now," he said.

"Do with me as you wish my heart and my body belong to you," I replied.

"Is that right?" He asked with an evil grin and pulled my flesh closer to him as his lips found my neck trailing up to my ear lobe.

He knew just how to drive me wild. Wild was an understatement. I grasp his arms letting out a moan as I melted into his arms. He didn't stop until he had quenched himself once more.

After a second shower, we dressed and got ready for a night on the town. We decided to walk along Ocean Drive to a few pubs and see what bands were in town and maybe check out a few leather shops.

There was a great pub the captain from the Parasailing ride had recommended to us so we figured we try it out. We found the right pub and had a late dinner as we enjoyed the band perform. We didn't make it back to our suite until 2:00 a.m. I'm not really sure how we managed to find our way back since both of us were two sheets to the wind. By some miracle we'd returned safely and gave into a good night's sleep.

Sunday we got up amazingly early considering the night we had and without either of us having a hangover. We planned to take A 1 A highway back down the coast line to give us a chance to view the ocean on the way home.

I tend to have a need for speed and my bike provided it while I was bound to the Earth.

It was a perfect afternoon and a beautiful day for our trip home.

Our drive home was slow and enjoyable. We planned on a side trip into Orlando to stop in at the Hard Rock Café before we headed back to Cape Canaveral. I think Chance had a T-shirt from every Hard Rock Café and collected them from his travels around the world.

The café wasn't too crowded so we had a good early dinner enjoying a few minutes of quiet time together. One of the waiters recognized Chance then a photo shoot and autograph session began. Most were pretty happy to see one astronaut and when he introduced me as the commander of the shuttle Orion, people seemed in shock except for the school children; they knew who we both were instantly. We took photos with the manager Gene and our server Megan.

Then, Gene went to his office to retrieve a shuttle flight crew photo for us to sign he had bought earlier in the summer from his trip to Kennedy Space Center with his kids. I promised we'd get the rest of the crew to bike back up with us one weekend and have the rest of the crew sign the poster for his kids.

Everyone made us both feel so important even though we never really look at ourselves as some kind of celebrity or anything like that. To us astronaut was just our job title.

I promised a little girl Stacy Mitchell from Edgewater Elementary School that I'd love to come to her school for a visit the first free chance I got and I'd try and bring some of my friends. We'd do just about anything for children in the name of science.

Chapter VIII

Rain

"Hey Chance, is everything set?" Ty asked as Chance walked in.

"Yes, I've got the ring, the butterflies in my gut, and anxiety to boot," I replied. "So Jeff, you got our alibi set up?"

"Yes, I talked to Patti already and if Susan calls, she'll tell her we went to the hardware store or something like that," Jeff said.

"Cool. Thanks guys I really need all the help I can get to plan this trip," I said.

"You know we're here for you dude," Ty stated.

"So what's the plan?" Jeff asked.

"Well I spoke to General Carpenter today and got the go ahead for the time off. He put me in touch with his travel agent and even called in some favors for the trip. It looks like everything will be a go for September 4th," I continued as I informed them of our plans.

"So you are sure she has no clue?" Jeff asked.

"No not a clue. She almost walked in on a conversation Abe and I were having a few weeks ago. Abe was quick and told her we were just talking baseball," I replied.

"How long will you be gone?" Jeff quizzed.

"We leave on the 4th mid-day arriving in New York City. We'll stay two nights then off to merry old London."

"Now that sounds like fun," Ty said with a fake yawn then laughed.

Ty had been to London before and it rained the entire vacation so to him no place could be more boring.

"We'll be in London for three days then take the train to Paris. I figure four days in Paris would be good enough."

"Absolutely you will love it," Jeff spoke with enthusiasm. "Has Susan ever traveled there before?"

"No she hasn't I found out a few weeks ago when we were looking over all of her photo albums. She was showing me how clueless she'd been over the years," I replied with a chuckle.

"Yea, her blonde goes deeper than her hair color," Ty joked.

"Funny Ty! Do you have Stephanie and your tickets yet?" I asked.

"Yea, Stephanie is picking them up as we speak," Ty replied.

"Chance, did you get Daisy and your parent's tickets yet?" Jeff asked.

"Yes, last week. My mom was so excited she couldn't contain herself and so was Susan's mom when I called her to ask for Susan's hand in marriage. Daisy started to cry and tell me she loved me. I think our parents will have just as much fun as we will and they're just as excited."

"That's great I'm glad you have such a large group of support. You know it makes all the difference in a marriage having her family and yours 110% behind you," Jeff said.

I pulled out the tickets for our trip and showed the guys the travel itinerary so they would know what day to expect us home and where Ty would meet up with us.

I gave the ring to Ty to hide at his place for safe keeping because it would be hard to hide it at our place.

"I've got a group tour planned for the day after," I said.

"Wow dude you're going all out. I sure hope she says yes," Ty giggled as he spoke.

"I have all the confidence in the world. Don't you go worrying your pretty little head now Ty," I replied.

"Well it looks like you've got everything under control. I'll see you boys later," Jeff said as he gave me a hug and smacked Ty on the back of the head. "Later dude!"

"Alright man thanks again for all your help, both you and Patti. Give her a hug and my boys a nice frog on the noggin," I said with a grin.

"Will do, take care, and I'll see you tomorrow," Jeff said as he walked out the door.

"Later dude," Ty shouted as he waved bye.

"Hey Ty, thanks for all your help man and tell Stephanie thank you as well."

"You know me; I've always got your back. I'm just so excited for you," Ty stated as he smiled. "This has been a long time coming hasn't it?"

"Yes, a long time, but so worth the wait. I've never felt this way about any other woman in my life. She is everything I could've ever asked for and more."

"You deserve it man," Ty replied as he shook my hand and sniffled.

"It's nice to live the dream instead of just dreaming for it to happen," I paused, "she's always telling me how lucky she is to have me. No, I think I'm the lucky one."

"I'm just glad you two finally figured it out. If I had to listen to you one more week," Ty paused as he let out a deep breath, "I was going to sit you both down together and tell you to just kiss and get on with it."

"Yes," I said as I started to recall his interruption call just as I was homing in on her, "you and your crappy timing. I could've had her the night we both went over to watch the ball game and eat spaghetti. Remember?"

"Oh yea, sorry," Ty said as he frowned.

I sat quietly looking over the hotel reservations and our flight to make sure nothing was left out.

"Just don't forget the ring before you take off," Ty interrupted my train of thought, "it's the most important part of your trip!"

"Absolutely," I replied.

"Well you'd best get back home before she starts calling Patti," Ty said.

"Roger that. See you tomorrow dude," I said as I gave Ty a hug and a wallop on the arm before walking out the door.

"Damn it Chance," Ty shouted, "that's going to leave a bruise. Thanks!"

"Anytime," I said as I started up my bike. "Later bro!"

* * *

My workday was done and I was snuggled upon the couch watching Ghost Hunter's on Sci-Fi. Chance was over at Jeff's house helping him paint.

Jeff and Patti had welcomed a new baby girl, Jada, into the world and Jeff decided that it was time to give up his home office for the newest addition to his family. Everyone was filled with excitement for their ever growing family and we all loved Jared and Johnny. The boys asked for a little sister and that's exactly what they got. She was beautiful and already spoiled rotten. It was so sweet to see Jeff light up as he spoke of his little girl.

I had allowed myself to wonder many times if Chance and I ever got married would we have children.

The rain started to come down pretty hard outside. I started to worry about Chance being out on his motorcycle. We hadn't had much rain these past few weeks and the asphalt would be slick. I turned the channel to the local news to catch the weather update and kill some boredom. There was a report just coming on of a big wreck just off base. I watched in horror as the camera panned out to show the destruction and the reporters own voice sounded nervous with a higher level of anxiety.

Then I saw it and my heart sank.

"Oh no," I said aloud as the camera zoomed in on a blue motorcycle wedged between the pavement and a partially demolished minivan.

The phone rang as my nerves cracked and I jumped.

"Hello Chance," I almost shouted as I answered.

"No miss," a stranger's voice replied.

"Where's Chance and why do you have his cell phone?" I asked.

"Miss this is Officer Macias of the Florida Highway Patrol."

Tears filled my eyes, and my mind felt like it was going to explode.

"What's wrong? Where's Chance? Is he okay?" I continued with my questions.

"He is okay as far as I can tell. He's being taken to Memorial. You're number was listed on his cellular phone as home so it was the first number I figured I'd call," Officer Macias explained.

"I'll be there as soon as possible. Thank you sir," I replied.

"Yes ma'am, be safe and I'll keep you in my prayers," Officer Macias spoke as he hung up.

I rushed to get dressed and out the door. I called Ty on the way to the hospital and told him to call Jeff.

I got to the ER as fast as I could. Once through the doors I sprinted to the admission desk.

"Where's he? Where's Chance Walker?" I asked as I took a deep breath.

"He's been admitted and is back this way," a female sitting at the information desk responded.

A nurse emerged through the ER doors letting me through and took me back to Chance.

"Thank you," I said to her as she turned to walk away.

I couldn't see him. The doctors, nurses, and medics surrounded him.

"Chance," I spoke his name as tears erupted from my eyes.

"Miss wait," a nurse spoke up as I rushed forward and then she yelled at me. "No wait!"

"Chance," I spoke his name again.

The doctor moved unblocking my view and I could see him lay there motionless and bleeding.

"Clear!" I heard the doctor yell.

"GOD NO, PLEASE, GOD NO!" I screamed as I heard the flat line.

My heart broke into a thousand pieces as tears overflowed. Rage ran through my veins and I felt as if someone had stabbed me with a hot poker right into my heart.

"Get her out of here," a nurse yelled.

"CHANCE, NO," I screamed at the top of my lungs. "DON'T YOU DARE DO THIS TO ME! NO! CHANCE DON'T!"

My body began to shake as I fought back.

"No let me go!" I demanded as I broke free only to be pushed back by another nurse.

"CLEAR!" The doctor yelled again.

Nothing.

"Please Chance," I begged.

"CLEAR!" I heard again as my heart stopped beating, I felt numb, my voice left me, and my mind was overwhelmed with sorrow.

"Please God don't let him leave me," I said as I collapsed.

"CLEAR!"

* * *

I slowly woke up to strange voices and noises. It startled me at first, then I remembered, and the pain shot through my soul as I began to cry for my beloved.

"Chance," I said his name as I spoke up. "Where's Chance?"

"Hey girl. How are you?" I hear Jeff's voice asking.

My eyes were still overflowing. My heart felt dead.

"I don't give a shit about me. Where is he? Is he okay? Did he make it?"

"Chance is going to be fine," Ty's voice spoke up as my tears poured out.

"He is okay Susan," Jeff's voice came back, "he's right here."

I sat up and wiped my eyes in disbelief as my heart began to beat once again.

"Hello beautiful," I heard his voice sing to me like a song bird.

I leaped from the chair I had been placed in and moved quickly to his side.

"Don't you ever do that to me again," I insisted as he took my hand holding it to his face and kissing it.

"Sorry babe. I didn't mean to give you a scare."

"Give me a scare," I softly spoke, "you have no idea. I thought..." I started to speak and paused.

"No don't even go there," Chance spoke as he placed a finger over my lips.

"Chance, I don't know how I'd ever live without you," I said as tears ran like a river down my face. "I love you!"

"I love you too babe and I'm not going anywhere heaven isn't ready for the likes of me," he said and began to giggle. "So I guess you're just stuck with me!"

"I'll be more than happy to be stuck with you. No more motorcycle riding in the rain," I scolded him then proceeded to kiss every square inch of his face then his lips.

"You won't get any arguments out of me," Chance replied.

I turned to Ty and Jeff giving them both hugs and thanking them for being there for both of us.

"I don't know what I'd do without either of you," I said.

"You both know we care a great deal for you and we will be here as long as you need us," Jeff quietly spoke with words of comfort.

"Susan, you and Chance are my family and I love you both," Ty expressed as he placed his hand on my shoulder comforting me.

"Thank you," Chance spoke as his machines went haywire.

I turned to face him in shock. It was just the blood pressure machine losing battery power. I sighed and pressed the call button.

Chance spent the next three days in the hospital to recover from his wreck as doctors ran tests to try and determine why he flat lined in the ER.

The phone rang in his room and I answered it. It was Robert, Chance's dad, asking how his son was doing.

"His cardiologist thinks it may just have been from the accident itself, overwhelming his system making his heart unstable, but so far everything has checked out fine and all his tests have come back normal," I informed him.

"That is wonderful Susan. We are so glad you are there and he has you in his life. We are so blessed. Thank you. Tell Chance we called and to have him call us when he gets back home. You two take care and we love you both," Robert said.

"Thank you. Tell everyone hello and we love you too. I'll have him call you," I replied.

"That's great. Okay. Take care. Bye," Robert spoke.

"Bye," I replied as I hung up.

Chance returned from his chest X-ray and I told him about his parents calling. He was doing better and finally getting over the soreness from all the bruising.

I skipped work to stay with him. I had no desire to leave his side regardless of his improved condition. I was not budging.

My mind kept repeating that horrible vision in the ER like a broken record. I wasn't about to give up on him not after everything he has been through and knowing he never gave up on me.

For the first time in my life I had a man who loved me unconditionally and without even a glimmer of doubt. I knew I had never been loved so much. He completed my soul. Chance was everything I could've ever dreamed the perfect man to be and more.

I sat quietly watching him sleep. He was beautiful and angelic. My heart sang as love filled it and overflowed into my veins.

Slowly his eyes opened and the smile I'd come to love made its way through.

"Hello baby," I softly spoke.

"Hello beautiful," Chance spoke softly.

"How are you feeling today?" I asked as my hand caressed his face.

"Good just tired from all the laziness," Chance replied.

"You've been through a rough time," I said.

"I'm tough," Chance replied as he let out a soft giggle.

"Yes I'll give you that one, but I can't say the same for your motorcycle. I believe that bikes high speed thrill seeking days are over."

"Damn and I loved that bike too," he said as he frowned.

"Doc says you can go home today once your labs come back."

"Wonderful, I think they tried to poison me with their nasty food," he chuckled as he stuck out his tongue in protest. "I'm starving!"

"Well then we'll stop off at Murphy's if you feel up to it and grab a burger. I'll ask Doc if it's okay."

"Okay? I don't need some quack job telling me if I can or can't have a burger and beer," Chance snapped.

"Fine burger and beer it is," I said.

"Now that sounds about right. He'd better hurry before I spring myself from this joint."

"We have time. I'll buzz the nurse so she can cut these lines loose," I said.

Before I could press the call button Dr. Hodges and a nurse came in.

"How's my patient doing today?" Dr. Hodges asked.

"I'm going great. I can't complain about anything except the food," Chance joked.

"Betty's going to remove that IV and I'll finish your discharge papers if you'd like to go ahead and get dressed. I'll be back in about ten minutes."

The nurse proceeded to remove all the wires and tubes. Chance got up and went to the bathroom to change.

"Okay that should do it. I just need you to sign here stating that you'll be driving him home and that someone will be with him for the next twenty-four hours. Dr. Hodges office will give him a call in a few days and follow up with him," Betty said.

"Sounds good I'll keep a close eye on him," I replied.

"Alright am I ready to go?" Chance asked as he returned.

"Yes I was just going over your paper work," Betty paused, "with your wife and making sure she understands what to do post discharge."

Dr. Hodges returned as she finished going over things with us.

"Great thanks," Chance replied as he let out a quick giggle then looked at me and winked.

I knew he was enjoying the sound of wife. He didn't bother to correct her either, maybe, that was a good sign. His wife Susan Walker, I thought in private. Yes it does sound nice I like the sound of that. There might be hope after all.

"Here you go. Just keep an eye on the cut on your arm. Keep it clean and apply this gel twice a day. You can stop by my office to have these stitches removed in ten days," Dr. Hodges spoke as he handed me the discharge papers.

"I'm free?" Chance asked.

"Yes have a safe trip home. I hope I don't see you in here anytime soon, unless it is as a visitor," Dr. Hodges said as he turned to shake Chance's hand and left.

"Are you ready to blow this joint?" I asked.

"More than ready I'm starving!"

We had dinner and I sat quietly watching Chance eat like a starved child. He was handsome and my heart beat again. Calm filled my senses and I relaxed. Chance would be okay. The near death experience would change us both. I wanted to wrap my arms around him and never let him go.

The days that followed were slow at first. He was still pretty sore from all the bumps and bruises. I kept my own libido in check knowing how passionate he can become on a moment's notice which wouldn't help him heal any faster.

A few weeks had passed by and Ty came over today to take Chance to the gym for their work out on Saturday, which gave me time to call in a few favors with three hours to work my magic. Within that short window of time, I had a new blue shiny Suzuki motorcycle sitting in the garage waiting for its reveal with a new helmet and a new set of leathers to match. Just like the ones that didn't survive his wreck.

At 5:30 Ty and Chance returned. I had dinner ready for the boys and the TV on with a ball game. It was a ritual now, every other weekend they would go workout in the gym for about three hours then return for dinner and a ball game, except today I had other plans after dinner.

Ty had come over on his motorcycle. I had him store it in our garage as part of my bigger plan. Ty was already in on it. After dinner Ty asked Chance if he'd look at his bike complaining of an odd noise that had been bugging him for about a week and wanted his opinion before he took it to the shop. I tagged along playing my part. Chance opened the garage door, clicked the light on, and gasps.

"No way," Chance said as his eyes opened wider, his mouth dropped open, and he began to giggle like a child opening a big gift on Christmas morning.

"Hey look at that somebody left their bike in your garage Susan," Ty said as he let out a giggle.

"Yes I see that," I chuckled.

"You both are sneaky. It's perfect a new helmet and new leather. Wow, this is great babe, thanks," Chance said as he turned to wrap me in his arms for a bear hug and excited kiss.

"Okay you two you've got time for that later," Ty teased. "Dude let's take her out!"

"Thank you. I love you," Chance softly spoke as he kissed me once more.

"Go have some fun, be careful, and Chance, I love you," I replied as I watched him put on his helmet.

"Let's roll!" Chance said to Ty.

They slapped knuckles, started their bikes, and took off for a ride.

Chapter IX

Sunshine

Work consumed us once again with meetings, training, and personal appearances at local schools. Chance and I had resumed our daily routine of morning jogs and driving to work together. I was able to get a yes for my entire crew, Commander McKinley's entire crew, and half of Commander Bower's crew to head over to Edgewater Elementary to keep a promise I made to a very special promising little girl.

I cleared our workday with General Stewart since he was all for any public appearances that involved us visiting school children in the name of science and to see if he wanted to join us.

Those of us who had motorcycles thought it would make a great entrance to have a group of astronaut speed junkies all roll up at the same time to the school with the engines revving and creating a stir.

I called ahead the day before and spoke with Principle Chaffin so we'd have clearance for our noisy arrival.

A loud rumbled filled the air as we drove into the Edgewater Elementary School parking lot.

Lunchtime was winding down and the children came running out cheering. It sounded like the roar of the crowd as chariots entered a coliseum ready for battle. We were filled with delight at the excited welcome from our adoring youth.

Principle Chaffin came out to join in on the applauding and welcomed us to his school.

After getting parked the school bell rang and Principle Chaffin yelled for the children to return to class. Boo's and negative words from the students raised a few eye brows as we broke out in laughter.

"What a real kill joy!" Ty chuckled.

"Hello Principle Chaffin," I spoke up first and extended my hand for a greeting.

"That was just incredible. You guys really know how to make an entrance and get these kids worked up. I haven't seen this level of excitement in years," Principle Chaffin replied as he shook everyone's hand and led us through the halls.

The excitement in the air had over flowed from the classroom as we walked by.

"I'd like to make a stop in Stacy Mitchell's class first if that's okay with you?" I asked.

"Oh that would be wonderful. She'll be thrilled as will the other students in her class. You'll make her day," Principle Chaffin replied.

The entire team followed as he took us into 5th grade math.

"Mrs. Debra Black's class," Principle Chaffin said as he pointed to the classroom door.

"Hello class," I said. "Hello Stacy Mitchell!"

"OH you came," Stacy shouted in excitement. "You really came!"

Stacy jumped from her desk and rushed towards us, or I should say, Chance.

"You came and you brought them with you," Stacy said embracing Chance with a hug. "You're the best!"

The others got tickled by her level of enthusiasm.

"Rock Star!" Ty spoke in a muffled voice as if he were coughing.

"You beat. A promise is a promise," Chance replied to Stacy.

"Welcome to our class. I'm Mrs. Debra Black," the teacher said as she turned back towards her students, "everyone this is Commander Davis and her crew from the space shuttle Orion."

I took a step forward as I glanced with a smile at Chance, who was more than happy to keep his new little friend next to him with his arm around her enjoying the current celebrity status.

"Hello and thank you Mrs. Black for your warm welcome and thank you Stacy for asking us to come visit you here today," I spoke, "I am Commander Susan Davis and this is my crew from the space shuttle Orion: Chance Walker, Ty Lowery, Christina Miller, Abraham McGuire, and Dr. Jeff Brady and along with us today we have fellow astronauts: Commander Frank McKinley of the space shuttle Endeavor with his crew Tiffany Adams, Shaun Mathis, Tara Yarbrough, Alex Griffin, and Dr. Carl Copeland," I continued, "we also have Astronauts Stephen Reynolds and Martha Lopez from Commander Roger Bower's space shuttle Liberty joining us today to tour your school and speak with you all in a few minutes."

It was great to see the children express themselves as a few claimed they wanted to be astronauts like us. Maybe if we can influence one child today to take that step forward and believe in themselves or turn a troubled child onto science with all its possibilities the trip would be well worth it for all of us.

As we finished out our meet and greet with Stacy's class we were taken to the auditorium for a big assembly of the entire elementary school.

Commander McKinley and I would start things off and introduce our crew and then allow each crew member to say hello and give a brief bio on what they did as a member of a space shuttle crew. Things went really smoothly and we each received plenty of questions about why we chose to become astronauts.

As expected Chance, Ty, Abe, Tara, and Martha got most of the questions about their love life and if they were single. It all made for some pretty good jokes later on. Overall it was a great day.

"Thanks everyone for taking time to come out with us to visit the kids," I said.

"Anytime Susan, we're glad we could be here and to do our part," Dr. Copeland replied.

"Yes Susan, it was great, and we even got some new dirt on Chance," Alex also replied.

"Chance sure does have a way with the ladies," Commander McKinley added as everyone broke out in laughter as the teasing about Chance's new admirer continued.

"Now guys you know she's way too young, besides, I like blondes," Chance said as he gave me a wink and smile.

"Next time you need to introduce Abe first and let him woo them with his Aussie accent and charm," Ty joked.

"Yea that's all I need a bunch of little girls running around and screaming my name," Abe replied as he laughed.

"Maybe next time I'll just let you men go and save myself the trip," I teased, "I think overall it went pretty good."

It was a nice day off to visit Stacy's elementary school and it left each of us feeling good about who we are and our personal accomplishments in life.

We finished our workweek back at the training center. Chance got teased for the rest of the week about his new little friend from Ty and Abe.

Training resumed on schedule and for the next two days we went over anatomy, the immune system, and other medical procedures related to Lunar One. I figured after the medical scare I had with Jeff, I'd best learn everything all over again.

Doc Johnson along with General Stewart walked in and interrupted our first aid training.

"At ease," General Stewart spoke, "you kids have been working and training non-stop these past months and I can see some of you are getting burnt out."

We all shook our heads in agreement as he continued.

"So we've decided to give you all a much needed break," General Steward stated.

General Stewart's assistant began handing out letters to each of us stating his approval of time off.

"Three weeks that's awesome," Ty said.

"Enjoy your time off astronauts you've earned it. See you all back here in three weeks," General Stewart spoke as he walked towards the exit door.

"Dismissed!"

Nobody had to tell us twice. A burst of excitement filled with chatter moved across the room as we rejoiced at the good news.

As we walked out to the parking lot Jeff broke the silence.

"This is exactly what the doctor needs. I can go home and finish Jada's baby room and spend some much needed time with my family," Jeff said.

"That sounds great Doc, tell Patti and the kids hi and have a great break," Ty replied.

"Do you think it would be okay if I drove the car and you took my bike home?" Chance asked as we walked hand in hand back to our car.

"Sure just let me get my spare helmet out of the trunk," I replied.

"I really need a haircut and I have to pick up our dry cleaning," Chance said.

"Okay then I'll see you at home," I said as I handed him the keys as he embraced me for a quick kiss.

"I love you," he whispered as he held me tightly in his arms. "I'll be home quickly!"

I swiped another kiss before putting on my helmet.

"Chance Walker, I love you," I replied as cheerfulness filled my heart and I started the bike engine.

I got home quickly and showered, shaved, and dressed for our Friday night on the town. I curled my hair and spritzed myself with some French perfume Chance bought me last week because he claimed it drove him wild. I had plenty of time to perfect myself for him. I was in no rush. It was nice to be alone while I mulled over the changes in my life, his wreck, and the love that flourished between us. Our bond was stronger than ever. I would've never guessed things could be this way, me in love with him. I got goose bumps just thinking about the softness of his lips, how the warmth of his breath felt on my skin, and his sensational kiss. I closed my eyes as I envisioned his arms wrapped around me.

I finished up and sat on the couch putting away our photo albums and stopped to open the album marked "Flight Crew" once again. He was incredibly handsome he even made a space suit look good. I continued my search and came across one of Chance and Ty together. Ty had known all along how Chance felt about me. This would explain a lot of Ty's odd jokes he made to Chance and the teasing. The bonds between those two were more like one between twin brothers. They even finished each other's sentences and thought alike in their warped sense of humor.

Monday night football and pizza the words had been written on the back. Yep, right there Chance's evil grin and all. Chance was always there in the waiting, sitting in the background wanting me and in love with me. I could see clearly everything now. All those heart to heart talks we had after Mike's death. Wow it must have killed him to see me go through that and wanting to hold me to make the pain go away or kiss me to help me forget. I understood why he thought I needed to move on at my own pace. He didn't want to be my rebound guy. If I were to feel the same way about him as he felt about me then I did need time.

We had developed a good friendship and then romance followed. Everything worked out well and he filled my life now with so much joyfulness and love. Yes I was the lucky one.

I laid back to rest with my hand on our new album from our trip to Daytona clutched to my heart. I drifting off asleep allowing myself to be filled with the thoughts of happiness Chance brought into my life.

"Susan," I heard his voice, "Susan, I'm home babe," he said as he sat down next to me and kissed my forehead.

"Sorry I must have drifted off," I said with a yawn," I giggled as I ran my fingers through what was left of his light brown hair. "Nice tan line!"

"Yes I guess I really need to work on evening that out," Chance chuckled.

I sat up to reposition myself as he ran his arm around my waist and brushed his lips against mine as I moaned as his kiss jolted me alive. He released me, went off to shower, and dress. I used the spare time to straighten up the living room and finish putting away the albums.

He was taking longer than normal, so I went to investigate. To my surprise he had our suitcases open on the bed with his already packed and was closing it up when I walked in.

"What are you doing? Going somewhere?" I asked confused and surprised.

"I'm getting ready," Chance replied.

"Getting ready for what?" I asked.

"Our vacation it's about time we blow this joint. We have three weeks of down time and I have no desire to sit here idol and waste one day of it," Chance said.

"Okay so where are we going and when?" I asked.

I started packing my clothing not sure what to expect. He helped me packing his favorite lingerie he wanted me to wear. I just smiled and went along with him. I knew regardless of where we went we'd have fun and more importantly we'd be together.

Chance sat on the side of the bed saying yes or no as I held each outfit up before packing it. He didn't give me any solid hints. He had me pack everything from light apparel to semiformal wear.

"Are you packed and ready to go?" Chance asked.

"Yes my bags are packed," I replied as I zipped it up and walked into the living room.

"Good first dinner then the airport," Chance said.

"We're leaving tonight?" I asked.

"No time to waste!" Chance said.

"Good, then I'm ready to go," I replied.

Chance took our bags and placed them in the trunk as I got in. He gave a quick call to Ty to let him know we were leaving and have him check on the place while we were gone.

Still no clues came from his lips even as he spoke with Ty. Nothing, I was sure whatever his plan was for kidnapping me for the next few weeks would be worth it.

We arrived at the Orlando International with time to spare. Still no word on where he was taking us. I guess that was part of the heightened excitement.

Spontaneous Chance! Always ready to jet off whenever the mood strikes him. I stood back letting him check us in at the ticket counter and allow him his moment of glory.

"New York," I spoke in soft voice as he turned and handed me my ticket. "Nice!"

"Part one," he whispered back.

I was bewildered and curious. Part one of what? I wondered quietly to myself.

"Part one of our vacation is New York City? Wow love you really got my attention now," I said as I smiled.

"Yes babe part one of four," Chance said with an evil grin.

Our plane was starting to board by the time we arrived at the gate. We boarded and found our seats. I let Chance have the window seat making it easier for me to snuggle up as he wrapped his arm around me.

Take off went well. I was so worked up I couldn't rest. Half way through our flight I could hear his breathing slow and his heart beat steady. Chance had fallen asleep. I asked the attendant for a pillow and blanket then placed the pillow between his head and the planes shell. He moved a little to adjust himself then he sighed letting out, "Susan, I love you," barely audible with a childlike smile, his eyes still closed, and his head resting. Even at 37,000 feet he was still confessing his love for me.

I sat quietly watching his angelic face as he slumbered. My thoughts keep drifting to a picture of us I kept in my wallet. He was in his flight suit standing alongside of me with his arm wrapped around my waist. I pulled the picture out of my purse it showed signs of being a little worn out. It was my favorite picture. I had it in my wallet all this time. It was in there mostly for proof since most people didn't believe me when they asked my occupation and I told them astronaut. It usually got a laugh until I pulled this out. I had hundreds of photos of my crew and of all of them my subconscious mind picked this one for me to cherish most. Maybe I wasn't as clueless as I'd thought.

"Oh I thought I recognized you both," the attendant said as she looked over my shoulder. "He's dreamy isn't he?"

"Yes he is heavenly," I agreed.

"Is this you and him?" She asked. "You both look amazing!"

"Thank you. I get a lot of that with this photo," I replied.

"Well I think both of you look really good as a couple. How long have you two been together?" She asked.

"Thank you. We've been together almost six months now, but we've known each other for five years."

"How old is that photo?"

"I think it's around two years old," I replied.

"Glad to see you two together. Nice couple. I guess it's better late than never," she replied.

"Yes I agree. Thank you I must have been the only clueless one in the crowd. He's like this in every photo I have," I replied.

"Congratulations on stealing his heart and you two finding each other. I think it's beautiful," she continued, "well I'd best get back to the others. We'll be landing in fifteen minutes. Let me know if either of you love birds need anything," she spoke with a smile and then walked away.

My eyes drifted back to Chance. He was wide awake staring at me.

"How long have you been awake and how much did you hear?" I asked.

"Long enough," he whispered in my ear followed by a kiss on my cheek as his smiled beamed across his face.

"How long have you had this photo?" Chance asked as he snatched the photo out of my hand.

"I don't remember a year or two," I replied.

He chuckled, "try three years this was the first flight crew picture together. I could barely contain myself. Your very essence drove me wild," he whispered as he kissed my lips softly.

I could barely speak as his kiss left me breathless, "I love you," were the only words I could utter out of my lips.

His hand caressed my face as he stared deep into my eyes, "I've loved you since that very day and now more than ever," his voice was firm as he kissed me delicately again sending my body into melt down.

The pilot came on announcing our decent to JFK and thanking us for flying with the airline.

The flight, for the most part, was uneventful and that made me very happy. We took our time getting out of our seats. We let most of the plane empty before we ever got up. The Captain and the entire crew wanted to say hello, take pictures of us, and get a few autographs.

It was always weird to be treated like some celebrity. Chance was use to the entire fan fair. However, I wasn't use to it. Like the professional that I am, I stuck it out and smiled for everyone until they all had their fill of us.

Making our way to baggage claim I noticed a man in a tuxedo holding up a sign with "WALKER PARTY" on it.

Our bags were the first ones out of the shoot. The limo driver helped us out to the car. Chance couldn't contain himself any longer. Once inside the limo he wrapped himself around me and began kissing me as he pulled our bodies pointedly closer. He was ready to show me how much he wanted me and I didn't deny him his trophy.

Friday night in New York City was off to a great start and my mood couldn't have been any higher.

We checked quickly into the hotel and then off to pub hop a little and catch a few bands. The city was better than either of us had imagined. There was so much to do and see.

We spent Saturday playing tourist as the bright sunshine filled the day and we found the best pizza parlor in the entire city and a Broadway show finished our night.

Sunday morning I had breakfast delivered to our room letting Chance to sleep in. New York City had been a great start for our vacation and I was enthusiastic about the upcoming part two.

The knock at the door woke Chance up and I got up to let room service in.

After breakfast, we packed our bags, checked out, and headed back to JFK for our midday flight.

Again I stood back allowing Chance to check us in not wanting to spoil his big reveal.

Airport security wasn't as easy to pass through on this leg. Chance had to nearly strip down to his boxers before he passed security. He was a good sport about it. Even before he redressed he allowed a few female security guards to take pictures of themselves with his buff body. Yes he was Chance Walker, astronaut extraordinaire.

"Rock Star," I joked.

"You know my fans. They just can't get enough of me," he replied as he laughed.

Making our way to the international terminals Chance stopped and handed me my ticket and passport.

"London," I shrieked out loud, "London really? You're taking me to London?"

I was so excited I stepped up and gave him a big long wet kiss to let him know just how excited this made me.

"Yes London," Chance replied, "only the best for my girl."

He took my hand as we walked toward the gate for check-in.

"Part two?" I asked.

"Yes, that's right," Chance said.

I leaned in for another quick kiss.

"Wow I'm going to have to do this more often," Chance said.

"So how long will we be there?" I asked.

"Three or four days," he replied.

He's killing me. Torturing me emotionally as he only gave me a few hints at a time all the while enjoying his sneakiness.

Chapter X

London Paris

"Welcome to Virgin Atlantic we are now pre-boarding flight 9261 to London," a female voice spoke, "pre-boarding families with small children and those needing assistance with boarding."

The announcement sent a giggle straight through me as I looked up to Chance shaking my head in amazement.

The seats on this flight were larger and more comfortable. I was wide awake the entire seven hour flight to London. Chance meanwhile once again had no trouble falling asleep. He could sleep on a freight train, at the end of a runway, or if a tornado hit. That would be him sound asleep.

What I would give to see a glimpse of his dreams I thought to myself.

I glanced out the window trying to make sense of where over the Atlantic we were. The oceans reflected a deep blue glow beneath us from 35,000 feet.

Sometimes it looked more like the black abyss of space. My anxiety level dropped as I recalled the celestial twinkles of the distant stars off in the galaxy and the planets that surrounded our own Earth.

We'd already been introduced to the entire flight crew before takeoff and I was able to get a few photos of the cockpit and its crew. The pilot incredibly enough was Thomas Anderson an old friend of mine from years ago. He specialized in Hawk 100's for the Royal Air Force and had been stationed near Savannah, Georgia while I was there during cargo flight training years ago. It was comforting seeing an old friend and trusting his skills to get us safely to London.

I sat back in my seat closing my eyes knowing I was in good hands.

The plane made it to London in one piece. I thanked Tom for the great flight and asked him to come visit us during any future down time.

Heathrow was a large airport and it took us an extra thirty minutes to clear customs. Our bags arrived at baggage claim the same time we did.

Another limo driver was waiting for us and helped us to the car. Once again Chance had gone overboard. Our drive to the hotel was wonderful. We saw a few historical buildings in the distance, that sent our excitement soaring.

This was the first time for either of us in London. The hotel was grand, it wasn't as busy as I had expected it to be, the service was quick, and friendly. I got a kick out of British people's English.

We stayed in our room and ordered dinner from room service because both of had jet lag from the seven hour flight along with the loss of time from going eastward with the time zones as we crossed the pond.

Last thing I remember I was laying in Chance's arms, my head on his chest, and his hand softly stroking my arm as he kissed my forehead confessing his love for me once more.

"I love you Chance," I mumbled quietly feeling his arms tightening around me as I drifted asleep.

The next morning we woke feeling sluggish, but excited nonetheless.

It was interesting to see the array of people as we took a walk through town. London was noisy and crowded with punk and gothic dressed locals in a mix of normal everyday looking people. This was nothing either of us had grown up seeing, not too many punk rockers in South Texas or Oklahoma. Regardless of the surroundings, we enjoyed ourselves and it was nice to relax our first day out on the town. Most locals loved Chance's Texas drawl getting a few good laughs and requests for him to repeat "Ya'll and thank you Ma'am." He was adorable.

We caught a taxi to the palace so we could watch the changing of the guard. A nice local couple told us of a great pub with England's finest brew and food for lunch. We took everything in and felt a thrill seeing London so full of life.

Chance insisted we take a double deck bus tour of the city and play tourist. The bus was about ¾ full and we decided to go to the top for a better view. Hand in hand we walked forward and took a seat. A few cameras snapped at us and I felt odd knowing people were taking pictures of us instead of this beautiful city. Most tourists kept their distance except for our fellow Americans. The children waved and told their families who we were as other tourist listened in. "Astronauts," the youngest boy spoke up, "Captain Walker and that is Commander Davis from the space shuttle Orion," he smiled as he continued, "they were on the web I saw a clip of them on YouTube along with shuttle pictures of their last mission it was so cool."

I waved back and Chance nodded while motioning the children to come join us for a group photo. It was great even in Europe children got excited over NASA. They were from Vermont and the other family was from California.

Things settled down and the tour ended up being more educational and fascinating than I'd expected it to be, but after three hours on a bus we were ready for a long walk back to the hotel.

We found a quiet pub, stopped in for dinner, and were lucky enough to show up on a night they had an incredible local band in the house. I took photos on my phone and sent them to Aaron to share our experience since he would be the only one in my family who would fully appreciate it.

The following day was just as eventful with tours of the historic district, museums, art studios, and a few famous pubs where rockers like to hang out. Our last evening we opted to stay in and order room service already having our fill of pub food and crowds.

"So are you ready for part three of four?" Chance asked.

"Sure I'm ready when you are," I replied.

He pulled two tickets out of his bag and began to hand them to me.

"Ah, not so fast," he said as he yanked them back away from me teasing.

"FINE!"

"After we eat dinner then you can peek," he stated.

"I half expected you not to share anything about our trip with me," I said while I frowned and began my fake sulk.

He emptied his hands and moved over to be next to me taking my face into his hands holding it firmly as he glared into my eyes. I tried hard to hide my grin.

"You know how I love you and I can't stand it when you get all grumpy on me," he snickered.

I attempted to shift away from him, but his hold was firm as he began kissing me.

"So is it early to bed so to be early to rise?" I asked.

"Maybe, maybe not," he replied with an evil grin and began to pull me down to the floor.

He pressed his body against mine, wrapping his arms around me, and kissing my lips with furry as I gave in. I longed for his kisses, to have his hands touch me, to feel his flesh against mine, and for his lustful passion. I melted under his kiss as his body moved over me while his hands brought me to a heightened sensual desire. His desire filled my veins driving my need to have him take me right there on the floor.

As if he was reading my thoughts or my soul was speaking to his, he pulled me closer crushing my body beneath his until we were one.

"I love you," Chance softly spoke as he trailed his lips and began kissing my throat.

His touch was slower and more meaningful as his eyes entranced mine as an echelon of pleasure rocked through me. Communication was effortless as my soul screamed out for his body as it was responding to his touch as it ached from deep within. Our bodies lay entangled in silence as he brushed his hand across my face. Then he raised me up in his arms and carried me off to our bed to continue his desire.

"I've always loved you," Chance moaned as my lips returned to his lips with a feverish need, "I could never express the depth of love I feel for you, not even in two life times," he whispered in my ear.

Cradled in his perfect embrace my fingers dug into his flesh as I moaned his name and confessed my love for him once more. His desire for me was insatiable.

"I love you and knowing how much you love me in return makes my life worth living. If it takes me another life time to show you how much I need you, then so be it," I spoke as my lips returned his kiss softly as a filling of completeness and unequivocally love consumed my soul.

* * *

I woke up still in his arms. He'd refused to let me go from his embrace the entire night.

"Good morning beautiful," he said as he stroked my bare skin with this hand as I looked up to see his brilliant smile.

"Morning," I replied as I curled up close to his body.

"We'd best get dressed or we'll be late for our train."

"Train?" I asked.

"Yes I wouldn't want you to miss our train," Chance said.

Still unaware of his plans I complied as I jumped out of bed without another word spoken and rushed to shower. Our bags were packed and down to the front desk in less than thirty minutes.

"You never seize to amaze me," I proclaimed as I stole a quick kiss before ducking into the limo.

"That's my plan," Chance said.

As we approached the train station it hit me.

"A train ride, as in the Euro Star train ride?" I asked.

"Yes," Chance replied.

"As in the English Channel train tunnel, underground, beneath the sea train ride?" I asked as my stomach turned and I frowned.

"What? It'll be fun it's something we've never done before and it just seemed logical," Chance said.

"LOGICAL? You can't be serious? I fly seven hours across the pond just to be drowned beneath it!" I smarted off then my mouth dropped open at the moment my brain finally processed where exactly we were going.

"We're going to Paris? Paris? Really?" I asked with excitement.

"Yes Paris and babe you'll be fine. We'll be okay. People travel this train everyday thousands of them each week. Don't worry it's all good," Chance said.

We arrived on time to board the Euro Star which will take us from London to Paris in just over two hours.

Chance was far more optimistic than I was. I knew I had to dig deep to control myself and I would try not to freak out as the train entered the tunnel of darkness. I felt doomed.

Yes I was a control freak to some extent. My need to control the situation was greatly affected by whether or not I was the one flying a plane, driving a car, or a space shuttle. This was no different. However, I'd never driven a train and didn't like riding in one either. My stomach churned from the anxiety.

It was much nicer to see the countryside between London and Dover and even better once the train came out of the tunnel of doom and darkness. The train made a quick stop at Calais, France.

It just so was beautiful outside. Sunlight, green grass, and the knowledge that I would never subject myself to that insanity ever again brought me great pleasure.

"Next time we're flying," I promised.

It was a nice experience except for the tunnel part. I shuttered at the thought.

The beautiful French country side and perfect weather calmed me.

Chance didn't skimp on the train either. He booked us with premier tickets which were the equivalent of first class with large seats that reclined. Regardless, I decided I wouldn't do it again, even if he paid me.

Our train arrived in Paris around 4:00 p.m. Another limo driver waited on us as we departed the train.

Sounds of a more interesting tongue filled the air. The French language was always arousing. They could curse me out and I'd probably just smile and say thanks. I loved it!

As we drove through Paris historical sights came into view I started to feel excited as I stared with amazement at our hotel. It was incredible.

"Welcome to the Hotel Ritz Paris," the door man spoke as he greeted us pertly.

His smile was contagious.

Chance and I hadn't stopped smiling from the first minute we got off the train. We were like two school kids heading for the playground, only our playground for the next four days would be Paris.

Our room was absolutely breathtaking. Even Chance let out a gasp as the bell hop opened the door and welcomed us in. It was like something out of a 1940's romance movie and was fit for the Queen.

The view from our room was just as incredible. We could see various monuments in the distance. It was perfect and to top things off the hotel indoor pool put any rival in America to shame. The walls had paintings dressed on them with such beauty making the pool look divine.

"So this is how the other half lives," Chance said as a giant smile came across his face as he enjoyed the same experience of visual bliss I was having.

"Honey you really know how to romance a girl and steal her heart!"

"You and I will need to change into something a little more formal for dinner," he replied as he took my hand in his while we finished our hotel tour and walked back to our room.

"Did you see that dining room?" I asked.

"Yes it was just as insane as everything else in this place," Chance said.

"You know we could stay in and just order room service," I replied.

"Not tonight, I want to see you in that sexy new dress you bought back in London it's perfect for tonight."

"Sure and I'm looking forward to seeing you in a tie and then removing it," I teased as I wiggled my brows and smiled.

I went off to dress in our bedroom and freshen up my hair and makeup.

"Oh my!" It was all I could get out as I viewed this perfect man who immediately took my breath away.

"Yea I know I look stupid," he proclaimed as he pointed to the reflection in the full length mirror.

"No you're better than any dream of you I could've ever had," I said.

"You're just saying that because you're so blinded by love," Chance joked.

"Maybe, but if this is blindness then let me be," I replied.

He turned from the mirror to face me and smiled his evil grin.

"You look stunning!"

"I'm glad you approve or are you just saying that because you're so blinded by love," I teased back.

I glanced in the mirror at the image reflecting back at me. The blue dress was stunning and it clung to my body like a glove.

"The way you look and the way you smell," Chance paused as he took a deep breath in, "dinner better be quick tonight because this is going to be pure hell for me with you in that dress."

"I'll try and keep that in mind at dinner," I replied as I moved towards him and touched my hand to his soft face.

"I love you," he whispered as his lips caressed my hand and his arms pulled me into his embrace.

He sent chills through my entire body as he kissed me zealously.

"I love you too," I spoke between breaths, "we'd best get to dinner before I forget why we got all dressed up and start removing that tie," I said as I pulled myself away and took his hand leading him to the door.

He smiled in reply and stopped only to give me another quick kiss, "you have no idea how badly I want you right now," he firmly spoke as he opened the door and we walked out.

The dining lounge was as romantic as anything I'd ever seen. The room was filled with fragrance from the complex arrangement of beautiful Wisteria plants that adorned the entire room, and our table was equally as elegant. We ordered simple foods not really in the mood to experiment this late in the day and kept our choices to familiar foods.

As we returned to our room Chance opened the door and I thanked him for a wonderful end to a perfect day.

"Tomorrow will be burger and beer," I promised with a kiss as I pulled off his tie.

"Anything you want babe," he replied between kisses.

The next two days were filled with sightseeing adventures to the Eiffel Tower in all its glory and the Louvre was the highlight of our trip. Paris was truly a city of love and romance. The food was interesting. We forced ourselves to be opened minded and try as much odd food as we could. Some food was better than others and some was downright nasty.

We took an afternoon to take in some shopping for gifts to send back home. I stocked up on fine perfume and Chance stocked up on T-shirts from every pub we visited. Apparently, the French have a healthy interest and knowledge of NASA and the astronaut program. Many pub patrons bought our beer and one even bought our lunch. We made friends with everyone we met and found the French people to be very complex and wonderful.

Our final night we went pub hopping and had the best time. Chance had plenty of new jokes to share with Ty and

Abe as well as naughty words. His new found French friends had taught him how to cuss and smile. They knew too well how we loved their language and the old joke about thanking them for cursing you. It was great to make so many friends and we invited a few to come out to visit so we could return the hospitality. One pub owner went to his office and printed off our crew photo of the internet, had us autograph it, and then posted it upon his wall with all the movie celebrities and rock stars photos in his possession. He claimed we were his first astronauts.

The next morning we left out of Paris on a rainy day for our last leg of our journey.

Arriving at the Paris International Airport we made our way to the Air France counter. Again, I allowed my prince charming full control over check-in.

Once we got through security and headed towards our flight Chance appeared to become so nervous and began fidgeting his hand as he held mine. It was weird because I was usually the one who was a nervous wreck prior to a commercial flight. I began to worry as he actually started to look like he was getting sick.

"Chance, are you okay? You don't look so good. Let's go sit down at the bar for a few minutes, if we have time."

He just nodded okay.

We sat at the bar trying to relax I was truly concerned about his condition this wasn't like him at all.

"Maybe it's all the mixed food and the time change is finally catching up with me," Chance said.

"We can stay here as long as you need us to okay," I replied.

An announcement came over the speakers for pre-boarding to Rome, Athens, and Brussels.

"Okay that's us," Chance spoke as he stood up.

I just shook my head and tagged along holding his hand waiting for our next over the top destination to come into view.

He didn't disappoint as he walked up to the check-in counter for Rome.

"Italy? You're taking us to Italy," I spoke nearly dumb-founded.

"First class all the way babe," Chance replied.

"So we're going to Rome?" I asked.

"Nope it's just another stop over to part four," he replied with a grin.

"Air France flight 4720 to Rome is now boarding all passengers at this time," a man's voice came over the loud speaker.

Chance squeezed my hand as he held up our tickets to be checked in.

"Thank you. Once you arrive in Rome you'll be connect-ing at gate seven to Venice," the attendant said.

"We're going to Venice?" I asked while trying to contain my excitement and not yell,

"Venice," I kept repeating as I giggled with glee.

Once we found our seats and the time was right I made a strong attempt to let Chance know exactly how thrilled I was. We sat down and I turned to him and before he could speak a word I laid one of the longest, deepest, and sexiest kiss I could conjure up only to be interrupted by our flight attendant.

"Buckle up," she requested.

Embarrassed at my own over enthusiastic display of pub-lic affection, I slowly backed off Chance and buckled up.

"Wow," Chance replied to my affection as he shook his head. "I take it you like part four?"

"Absolutely," I replied as I dove in for another long smooch.

I didn't even bother to look outside our window. I pulled in as close as I could to snuggle up to him once the plane was airborne and lost myself into deep thought.

Chance had to have been planning this trip for weeks if not months. I was impressed he was good, even better at keeping this little secret away from me, and I wanted noth-ing more than to be pressed into his chest and have his arms tight around my waist.

Chapter XI

Part Four

The flight from Paris to Rome went fairly quick, less than two hours. We exited our flight and made our way to gate seven with little time to spare only to stop off for a quick bathroom break and then we made our way to part four.

Arriving in Venice about mid-day was interesting. It was humid. A salty smell filled the air and the sounds of yet another interesting language.

All of this really didn't matter. I was in utter bliss knowing that this gorgeous man who loved me went to extremes and elaborate lengths to give me, us, a vacation of a lifetime. He was truly amazing and I've never felt so blessed.

The hotel escort met us at baggage claim making sure everything was in order for the transport from the airport to the hotel.

Chance had been stationed in Italy years ago before he joined the space program so he was very comfortable with the goings on and knew what to do and who to speak to.

We made it to our hotel water taxi which was an experience all to itself.

When I thought nothing could top Paris, he gave me Venice.

"The Excelsior, Venice Lido Resort is a five star luxury hotel for a most beautiful couple. Enjoy your stay and God Bless you both," our water taxi driver spoke with broken English as he jumped out of the taxi onto the hotel marina slip and helped us out of the boat as the bell hop greeted us with a smile and joyful voice.

Chance thanked the water taxi driver as he turned to me smiling, gave me a wink, and proceeded to take my hand in his as we walked ever so slowly from the dock to the hotel entrance. The hotel was gorgeous and the gardens that surrounded it were splendid, evoking romance, and really set our mood in a positive direction. It was much quieter than it was back in town. My senses were thrilled with the vibrant flowers and the sweet smells whipping up by the afternoon breeze, and we could hear the water lapping on the nearby beach.

I walked around the lobby taking in all the beauty while Chance checked us in and ordered room service for our first night.

Our room was more extravagant than anything we'd ever seen before. The bell hop told us it was an Iberian-Moresque style of décor very favored in this region, he gave us a tour of our suite telling us how things worked, and showed Chance the room service menu he'd requested down at the front desk then proceeded to show us how to place an order. It was a relief to have the hotel staff so considerate and helpful.

We sent in a quick order while it was pretty early hoping to beat the dinner rush. We stuck with the basic menu items Spaghetti, salad, bread, and wine.

"Now this I could get use to," I said as I raised a glass of wine to toast, "to happiness and good food."

After dinner, we decided to take an evening stroll through the property so we could talk over our plans for tomorrow. We made our way to the white sand beach taking our time holding hands. The smell of food grilling in the distance and the odor of the sea mixed as it filled the air as a mild breeze picked up and sent goose bumps across my exposed skin. Chance paused to pull me close rubbing my arms to help fend off the chill. It was nice how he was always one step ahead and knew what I needed without ever asking.

"Thank you," I expressed my gladness of the moment as I touched his face running my fingers along his cheek line feeling his soft skin as his eyes glimmered. He turned his head downward to kiss my hand as it brushed his lips.

"You're welcome. I'm happy I could give this to you and share all the adventures of this past week. This time with you has meant everything to me. I wouldn't trade it for a million moons," he replied as he stopped and pulled me into his arms and his lips found mine.

It was better than any dream I could have ever hand. This experience was real and I knew he was the one for me. He was the man I had always dreamt of and I would love him for all eternity.

Slowing our pace along the beach while holding hands and taking in every second as we talked about our families and our childhood. I was a Navy brat and he was an Air Force brat. We had more in common that I'd ever realized before. Our up brining in military families was similar with a stern father and a mother who showed us what true strength, love of family, and devotion to her husband was all about. Chance had two brothers and two sisters and I had four sisters. We were both the youngest child and thus spoiled. We decided to explore the rest of our hotel on our own. It was incredible every space we explored was equally impressive. Making our way to the outdoor pool we took a spot near the walls edge for one of the most romantic sunsets of my life.

The sea was just as turquoise as the pool and the shadows cast upon the beach below looked to be from another world. The air had a clean mild smell to it mingling itself with the palms as the movement of the flapping cabanas made for an interesting vision in the almost dark background. Focusing on the view before us, I stood looking out toward the sea as Chance wrapped his arms tightly around my waist standing behind me.

"Nothing on the planet compares to you," he whispered as he pulled my hair from my neck to expose it for his lips to find.

A shiver of ecstasy enveloped my body. He was doing it again; breaking down the remainder of my defensive walls crushing every layer with every kiss he gave turning me into mush. He was good, too good. I struggled to contain myself as a moan escaped my lips and my eyes closed at his playful passion. I wanted to turn myself to face him as his arms clutched my body closer. I wanted to be selfish and allow this to last as his concentration excelled. Every kiss upon my bare skin electrified me and set my body on fire. He paused as he realized I was giving into his erotic appetite and pulled away stepping back allowing me to turn to face him.

"I'm sorry I can't help myself tonight everything is just perfect," he said as he pulled my body around to his allowing his lips to find mine and sent me to yet another celestial sensation of desire.

He forced himself to be more contained as other couples appeared to view the night sky and the majestic beauty of the sunset. With a quick kiss we made our way to more private quarters and lucky for me he picked up right where he left off.

Morning came and I was already up. I allowed Chance to sleep in he seemed to have had a restless night sleep.

There was a loud knock at our door and a voice of a female declaring maid service.

I was already up and headed for the door as I stopped dead in my tracks. As if snapping out of a coma or the room was on fire he'd bolted up from bed and literally ran to the bathroom without even glancing at me.

"Chance, babe hey," I said as I walked to get the door.

I turned the maid away and refocused on Chance. I rushed to the bathroom to see what had happen and to see if he was okay.

"Chance," I spoke his name loudly, but still no reply so I opened the shower door. "Chance, look at me!" I demanded.

He was standing in the shower with his back facing away from me and his head slumped down. I stood too frightened by his behavior to move any closer.

Then I saw his face as his eyes met mine the tears ran down revealing his agony. Without a word or even thinking I walked in and grasped his body clinging to it holding him in my embrace until he stepped back and broke free. He looked down at me as if he were still trapped in the hideous nightmare that haunted him before he woke.

He grabbed me with both hands rushing them to my face pulling me to him kissing me so eagerly like he was starved. My eyes filled with tears as I tried to understand what kind of nightmare he must have had to bring him to this point.

With every crushing kiss I returned with equal need. It was killing my soul to see him like this. In all my years I'd known him I had never seen the man who stood before me like this. A man filled with such fear that he kissed me as if it were his last. My thoughts trailed off on those last words. Kissing me as if it were his last and I had known this horror. Chance must been filled with such grief that could only come from a dream of death.

His hands relaxed and his breath slowed as he returned to a state of calm.

"Don't ever die on me," he spoke as tears rolled out of his emerald eyes, "Susan Davis, I love you and I can't even bear a nightmare," he broke off his statement as I placed my finger across his mouth.

"Chance, I have no intentions of ever leaving you, but I will die someday, we all will. Don't you ever think for one second I'll go quietly," I spoke and my words seemed to calm him as he pulled me back into his arms and I placed my head into his chest.

"I've got to lay off those jalapeños," he joked trying to lighten the mood.

"You need to lay off any horror thoughts that I'm going any place without you, not now, not after me going through my own personal hell to come out the other side and have you here before me filling my life with love again. No, you get death out of your brain," I replied as I handed him a bar of soap, "now cleanup we have a busy day of romantic views ahead of us."

He set the soap down and smiled his evil grin and I knew there was no way he would allow me out of the shower now.

He returned to his kissing with greed. I wanted him desperately and I allowed him to fulfill his thirsty desire.

After our shower, we headed down to the lobby to arrange for a water taxi and a tour from Lido to Pizzale Roma. We wanted to stop for a quick lunch somewhere along the way. Rosa our concierge gave us our options as Chance and I considered the best way to make the most of Venice.

Once we had a plan we found our way to the water taxi dock where our guide was waiting on us.

Donatello Lombardi introduced himself speaking perfectly mastered English. We exchanged greetings and names. Donatello's face lit up as he repeated, "Chance Walker," as he smiled.

"You are American astronaut Walker?" Donatello asked.

"Yes one in the same," Chance replied.

"Wonderful this is my lucky day what an honor. Please come, come I will show the best tour ever," Donatello replied as he held out his hand for me to step in his boat.

I grinned at Chance as he boarded and let out a childish giggle.

"Rock Star," I stated as a soft giggle escaped.

"I have no idea how or why some many people seem to know who I am and of all the astronauts in the program I'm not that important," Chance replied.

"Yes only you can be famous worldwide," I snickered as I thought of his now global rock star status.

Chance was loving every second of it with his chest out, head lifted up, and gut sucked in. All I could do is snicker, "Rock Star," again.

"What?" Chance quizzed as he spotted me in deep thought. I didn't reply I just mouthed the words "Rock Star" and burst into laughter.

"We'd best get you two love birds out of here before the mob converged," Donatello spoke as he pointed to a large group of camera crazy tourist who'd over heard his remark about the astronaut.

We laughed as Donatello shoved off and our boat moved away from the dock.

"Astronaut Walker, marry me?" A female youth yelled.

That was all it took and we broke out in intense laughter.

"Astronaut Walker marry me?" I mocked.

Chance jerked to one side looking at me if I had just cursed openly.

"What?" I asked.

"Yes," he replied as he slid back to my side wrapping an arm around me grinning.

"Yes," I said.

"Yep that's what I said," he replied as he leaned over for a quick kiss.

I thought to myself, he's joking right. I was joking right? My brain went into a frenzy over four words and one reply. No, I won't die any time soon, but go insane that's all.

Feeling my awkwardness Chance pulled me close, "I love you," he whispered softly as he kissed my cheek.

Everything was right as sunshine and balance restored as my thoughts harmonized with my soul.

As we rode along the waterways Venice came alive with sounds of water taxis hurrying about and people cramped on the larger one resembled sardines.

Then my stomach spoke growling in protest to my rudeness for not feeding it today.

Our taxi made our first tourist stop a few blocks from a bistro Donatello had suggest would be perfect for lunch Venetian style everything fresh and made to order. Donatello came along as our translator and helped keep us informed on the goings on and culture of his people.

We sat happily at our table after finishing a wonderful lunch to relax. It was then we were made again. A fellow American tourist and his family spotted us and began to waving hello. Thankfully, this family was more in control of their excitement than our public audience from the hotel.

Chance being the gentleman invited the Jonas family from Cleveland, Ohio to sit with us and enjoy dessert; well actually Chance insisted they join us. The parents seemed to get a bigger kick out of our visit than the two teenage boys. Our visitors stayed with us for about one hour as we started feeling like we'd known them for years. We exchanged email and phone numbers so they could call us when they came down to visit the space shuttle launch later this fall and we'd show them a VIP tour and a meet and greet with the rest of our crew. Doug and Chance sat telling jokes while enjoying a beer like two old college buddies. I thought their boys were great and the dynamics of their little family wonderful. It made me feel hopeful that maybe someday in the future when Chance was ready to take that step with me; we'd marry, and have children.

After our last beer we exchanged good-byes and hugs. Chance has and always could win anyone over with his charm, charisma, and Texas size hospitality. Doug and Cindy Jonas promised to write and I knew we'd see them again.

Back to our foot tour of the city we walked the entire Piazza which took us another hour to see.

"We have got to come back and stay longer next time maybe three or four weeks." Chance spoke to Donatello patting him on the shoulder and smiling at his new friend.

I noted that Venice was not as quick spaced as Paris. People were more relaxed and grounded.

Donatello took us for a short ride up the Grand Canal to an area he knew insisting he wanted to take us. We pulled up at a local dock and started our next walking tour.

As the plaza came into view both of us gasp at the size of the buildings and the grand architecture before us.

"Piazza San Marco," Donatello spoke with pride.

"St. Mark's Square," Chance replied.

"Yes my friend this is the heart of our great city. Napoleon himself stood right here and marveled in its spender. His royal palace is there," Donatello spoke as he pointed to the palace.

All I could do was nod and gasp as we walked closer to the center of the piazza. No photo or book could have done it any real justice it was an incredible landmark. It was on our wish list of places we wanted to see while in Venice. We were still filled with amazement as we took our first tour of the Napoleon's former palace, Dogus Palace, and then we walked to the Clock Tower before stopping for short break at Café Florian. Donatello insisted we see the best coffee house in all of Venice. It was beautifully adorned with art, sculptures, and photographs making us feel very privileged to have Donatello think of us as friends and show us such wonderful places we might have otherwise missed.

"This is the best of Venice!" Donatello proclaimed.

Our tour continued as we spent the remainder of our day visiting Procuraties Nuove and a Renaissance building the National Library of St. Mark. Everything was over the top and just amazing. We'd fallen in love with Venice.

As the day started to wind down, we returned to our hotel with promises from our new friend Donatello that tomorrow would be even more grandiose.

"Yes tomorrow my friend we will see you at 9:00 a.m.," Donatello spoke as he winked at Chance.

"9:00 a.m. sounds perfect. Thank you my friend you have made our visit to this beautiful country incredible," Chance replied as he extended his hand in formal good bye.

After waving good bye to Donatello I looked at Chance and almost immediately he knew my exact thoughts as we spotted a crowd coming at us. "Run!"

Holding hands as we ran back to the safety of the hotel lobby before the cheering fans could catch up.

"That was close," Chance stated as the hotel security guard quickly came to our side to shield us if needed and another guard headed to the front door to keep anyone out who didn't belong in the hotel.

A few chuckles came from our lobby audience as laughter overcame us.

Chance grinned as he spoke, "Rock Star. Wow so that's what it feels like?"

The guard escorted us to insure hotel staff or others would honor hotel policy, "for celebrity guest privacy," he informed us as we walked us back to our room.

"That was too funny," Chance commented on our grand entrance.

Back to our suite everything was straightened up and a card placed on our bed. Chance picked it up and read it.

"Your presence is requested for dinner at 7:00 p.m.," Chance read aloud.

We both glanced at each other and snickered at the request.

"It must be one of your adoring fans," I joked.

"Well now we wouldn't want to be rude. We'd best get fancied up," Chance replied as he held the card up to his nose and sniffed. "My favorite perfume!"

I ignored his gloating and got in a quick shower first since it took me twice as long to get ready as he did. I wanted to look extra special tonight to let whatever fan know I was Chance's biggest fan and he was mine.

"6:45 babe let's go we're going to be late. You don't want to keep my fans waiting do you?" He jokingly asked.

"So what do you think?" I asked as I stepped out of the bathroom walking toward him as he sat in the parlor room of our suite.

His mouth opened wide as he exhaled and his face started to slightly blush never saying a word.

"I gather by your expression you approve?" I asked as he held out his hand to take mine.

Chance stood up, more like jumped up, to his feet as his eyes glazed over my body bewildered.

I stood in silence looking at the reflection in the mirror running my hands down my side and then across my stomach as I waited for his response. I turned myself back around to face him, do to his lack of verbal reply, only to find him at my side pulling his arms around my waist, breathing rather heavy, and I swear I saw a drop of sweat come from his brow.

"So what do you think?" I asked again as he tightened his grip and let out a soft moan.

I looked up to see his expression and before speaking another word he crushed his lips to mine allowing the blaze from his lips to tell me of his approval.

"You've been holding out on me," he spoke briefly as he caught his breath and resumed his kiss.

"I take that as a yes you approve," I replied.

"You look incredible," he whispered back.

His watch began beeping startling both us. It was reminding us of dinner as it took us from our tender moment of bliss.

"Dinner it is," Chance said as he held out his arm for me to take.

I tried to compose myself the best I could. My head was still spinning with adrenaline from his lustful kiss.

We walked quietly down the hall to the elevator. Once inside his eyes never left me. He looked incredibly refined in a suit as naughty thoughts pushed their way forward, of me wearing only his silk tie, played over and over precariously through my mind.

"You look stunningly beautiful tonight," Chance whispered softly in my ear as he kissed my cheek and tightened his arm around my waist.

"I have to admit the suit is turning me on it's going to be hard for me to concentrate on dinner," I said as I stroked his tie and winked.

The elevator door opened up to the main lobby and we were met with hushed voices as we passed through on our way to dinner. I heard several gasps and a comment about "American astronauts" and "stunning" coming from the staff at the front desk. I was wondering if they were commenting on him or me.

The matrix of guest already seated in the dining hall lowered their chatter to inaudible whispers.

I thought "Rock Star" to myself as a quiet giggle escaped my lips and caught Chance's attention as a soft shy grin graced his face. The man was even more amazing when he smiled, his eyes glistened, and his stride became somewhat cocky, but still sexy.

The maître looked up and greeted us with a gasp of air, maybe it was shock or the rock star astronaut thing, either way he didn't speak. He took my hand from Chance and escorted us to our table then pulled out my seat while holding his other hand out to balance me as I sat down then proceeded to scoot my seat into a comfortable position as he smiled and then winked at me. He then turned his attention to Chance and pulled out his chair allowing him to sit and continued with his courteousness. He motioned to our waiter then laid the napkin in my lap. "Enjoy!" The maître said and walked away.

"I'm beginning to think this guy takes his job way too serious," Chance joked as he moved his hand to take mine.

"Amazing," I snickered at all the attention Chance gave me keeping his eyes locked on mine like a mountain lion ready to pounce on anyone who touched me.

"We must be early," I said as I looked around the room.

The waiter brought a bottle of wine showing it to Chance and nodding. Chance could hardly contain his smile. What was he up to? He's trying too hard.

"So what would my lady like for dinner?"

"I don't know? You order something for me, something you know I'll enjoy," I said.

"You sure you trust me to do that?" Chance asked.

"Yes I do," I replied.

"Well then this is going to be an interesting evening," Chance responded.

Chance exchanged words with our waiter in a low voice as he kept his menu up to cover his expression as he ordered.

"Good choice," the waiter replied and walked away.

Within minutes the appetizer arrived, calamari my favorite.

"Nice choice," I commented as I realized tonight was a set up.

Chance set the whole thing up just to spoil me even more. He was amazing.

The food flowed across the table like a well-planned movement of professionalism and never taking too long between courses. It was nice feeling so pampered.

Chance suggested that we skip dessert and take a stroll out to the pool and catch the sunset. I was more than happy to agree.

From the dining hall we made our way out to the outdoor pool to watch the sunset from the terrace. It was different tonight the pool had flowers and large candles floating on its surface, the terrace was covered with candles, and flowers wrapped around the railing. The smells of roses were everywhere. I stopped to take it all in as Chance wrapped himself around me to enjoy this moment. We were the only couple out tonight and I felt romantically charged knowing of our current privacy as we stood in our embrace Chance kissing the back of my neck and he began to hum. It was the melody to my nephew's song. I turned my head toward his face to allow him to see my smile and kiss him for his efforts. He was so sweet trying to make our evening so perfect.

"I love you. Thank you for a wonderful evening. This day and this night have been so incredible, I feel so blessed," I softly spoke between kisses. "Thank you!"

He pulled me close to his body as his kiss surged with greed feeding my hunger for him. As he continued his affection the music filled the outdoor space. I slowed my response and moved my head as the music grew louder.

"I know this song," I said as the acoustic guitar played my favorite song.

"Yea it does sound familiar," Chance replied.

I gasp as I heard the voice.

"No way did you get a recording of Aaron and have the hotel play it?" I asked in shock.

"Something like that," Chance replied with a wink.

Pulling from his embrace I turned to see where the music was coming from.

"What are you doing? Oh my GOD," I said stunned. "You flew Aaron here to sing for me?"

"Surprise!" Chance replied.

I shook my head in amazement at the lengths this man went to give me a vacation of a life time. As my eyes drifted across the pool area other people emerged.

"What? Who?" I asked as my eyes grew bigger.

"Only the best for you babe," Chance said.

"Ty, Stephanie," I paused becoming overwhelmed with joy, "Mom."

"Yes and my parents are here too," Chance replied and pointed.

"Oh my, what is this? Chance, you really out did yourself and you went way over the top!"

I started to walk towards our family and stopped when I realized Chance wasn't walking with me. I turned back to see what happened. My mouth fell open. He was bent down on one knee holding out his hand for mine. I slowly walked back and took his hand as tears filled my eyes in disbelief my brain was on overload.

"Susan Hall Davis, I've loved you from the very moment I laid eyes on you and I have never stopped loving you. You are my lover, my best friend, and my life," Chance spoke with firmness and an absolute tone as a calmness came across his face and devotion in his eyes beamed, "I will love you until the day Earth no longer exists. I love you with every fiber of my very being," then he held up a box in his other hand and opened it before me.

"Susan, will you marry me?" Chance asked as his hands began to tremble taking the ring out of the box and offering it to me.

Tears ran from my eyes as my entire body shivered with excitement and I placed my hand on my forehead trying to compose myself as my brain and heart began to scream.

Then from my lips I spoke, "Yes! Yes Chance Walker I will!"

He put the ring on my finger and stood up cupping my face as his lips found mine. Tears began to flow from his eyes.

"I love you," Chance proclaimed.

"I love you Chance Walker, God as my witness I love you," I said as I surrendered myself completely and totally to him as my heart sang.

We both broke our kiss at the sounds of the loud praise and clapping that now filled the night air. It came from everywhere, the hallway, the lobby, and even the beach.

I was so overwhelmed at the intense jubilation I just wanted to hold him close and never let go.

Chance wiped away my tears and kissed my lips once more. Taking my hand in his we turned ourselves to greet the crowd of onlookers who just witnessed the best day of our lives.

"Mom and Aaron you two are in so much trouble," I said as I hugged them both.

"I'm happy we could be here for you honey. We love you both," Daisy replied.

"It was his idea," Aaron stated as he pointed to Chance and began to laugh.

"Thank you for the serenade and for being here. Your song was perfect and I'm sure Chance will owe you big time after this," I replied.

We continued our hugging and hand shaking with everyone we knew as well as few new friends who showed up to share in our engagement.

"You have some serious planning skills," I said to Chance as we finished our greetings.

"Yes I know and I'm good," he replied as he began proclaiming his victory with a soft kiss.

Chance stepped over to a table near by picking up a glass of wine as he took his free hand in mine.

"Thank you all for being here tonight. I would like to formally introduce you to my beautiful fiancé," he said as he held up my left hand.

Chance then asked everyone to join us for drinks and dessert.

I looked up to see his expression and he was just radiant as he smiled.

"Chance Walker, you never seize to amaze me I don't know how I got so lucky."

"I'm the lucky one," he replied as he stole a quick kiss and his hand softly caressed my cheek, "thank you for making this the best day of my life and for every day from this moment on. I love you more than words can describe. You have made me the happiest man on Earth," he paused, "and in space."

Chapter XII

Venice

I lay in bed as minutes pass by. I could hear the shower running. I was alone in my thoughts to reflect on last night's events.

"Engaged," I softly spoke as I took a deep breath pulling my left hand up to view. "Yes! Yes! Yes!" I declared to myself as my eyes focused and complete delight wrapped itself around my body like a warm blanket. The ring was beautiful a brilliant solitaire perfectly centered with three more diamonds trailing down on each side. They were smaller yet equally as brilliant the ring was over the top just like everything else. I was so emotional last night I didn't even really look at the ring. It was impressive, big, and perfect just like the man who gave it to me. I started to feel guilty as I held my ring up into the sunlight as it gave off a brilliant shimmer. Everything was perfect, my ring, this vacation, and Chance.

"The most romantic man on this planet, who is caring, loveable, dreamy eyed, with an angelic face and that rocking perfect body, is all mine," I softly spoke while my eyes closed to envision his splendor, "my Chance," I said as my mind repeated our incredible evening.

My thoughts stopped as I realized the water had stopped and the suite was oddly quiet. Slowly, I opened my eyes only to see him kneeling down by my side. My eyes were fixed on his expression of amusement as his smile was soft and divine.

"How long have you been there?" I asked as I began to blush.

"Long enough," he exclaimed as he took my hand lifting back up to the suns reflection. Then he softly kissed my hand and held it to his heart.

"I love you!" I smiled as his words brought my soul to the infinity of euphoria.

"I love you. Thank you for everything you've done and given to me. I never knew I could be as happy as I am right now," I replied as my lips returned to his.

"We have a 9:00 a.m. tour," Chance said as he released me and held up his watch tapping the surface.

"You've got one hour to get ready, make that forty-five minutes and Susan," he paused trying to make a straight face as he clutched my arm then broke into laughter. "Hurry up!"

"I love you," Chance shouted as I sprinted to the bathroom.

Room service delivered breakfast and we rushed to eat as I finished dressing. We had twenty minutes left before our tour and we still had to meet everyone down stairs in the lobby.

"Are you ready?" I asked.

"I was born ready," he smarted off. "Let's go!"

We headed out the door and to the lobby where our family awaited to join us for a tour of Venice. Our guide Donatello and one other water taxi were waiting for us at the docks. Aaron, Mom, and Chance's parents rode together in the first taxi with Donatello. Ty and Stephanie rode with us in the other taxi.

"Today will be extra special," Donatello spoke aloud as he pushed off from the dock. "Congratulations Chance and Susan," Donatello continued as he introduced himself to our family and we made our way through the canal towards the heart of the city.

Chance sat quietly with his arm tightly wrapped around me smiling from ear to ear. I snuggled happily into his arms as it seemed to be the most natural place for me to be. I glanced up to his face to steal a kiss to let him know how happy I was. It was more obvious than ever he was truly head over heels in love with me. Every now and then, I could feel his arms tighten his hold while he leaned into kiss my cheek and smile. I could've spent the entire day wrapped up in his arms tour or no tour. His arms are where I belong, this is where I felt complete, and I was unequivocally in love with him.

We stopped at every possible square of historical importance making sure we took the family to St. Mark's square and to Rialto Bridge.

The tour of the Rialto Bridge was exciting over four hundred plus year market had lined the steps. We made our way to as many shops as we could absorbing it all in.

"The history this bridge could tell us if it could speak," I said.

"Oh Yes, many wonderful stories I am sure," Donatello responded.

It was nice to stop at the market. The men seemed more interested in the musical instrument shops and sweet shops as we ladies took to the spice venders and textile shops with great enthusiasm.

Donatello reminded us that it was nearly noon and most shops closed up for lunch so we'd best make our way through the shops we wanted to see and then head off for lunch.

We all decided that lunch sounded good and set off to a nearby "Ostaria" a pub like Italian restaurant. "Antico Dolo" was our pub for the day. We made it in before the crowds and managed to get a large table towards the back. Everyone enjoyed the atmosphere as we recapped the events of last night for Donatello and our other guide Tony. The food was the best we'd had thus far and the service didn't disappoint either.

"Amazing we travel half way around the world and still we can enjoy something from home," Chance spoke as he held up his beer for a toast with Ty.

They had a strong bond stronger than most siblings. Ty and Chance were roommates in college and now astronauts together. Ty stood up and cleared his throat as he held up his beer to make a toast.

"Here is to two of the best people I know. Chance, it's about time and Susan, congratulations on the engagement," Ty's words were sincere and welcoming.

"Thank you man," Chance replied as he turned to face his best friend, "thank you Ty for all your help, encouragement, and for never letting me get side tracked."

Both men hugged and the rest of us clapped as tears began to swell in my eyes at the thought of how long Chance had waited for this day and for us to be together and how his best friend never allowed him gave up on his dream.

I got up and hugged Ty as tears flowed freely, "Ty, thank you for being such an incredible friend."

I turned to face our family.

"Thank you all for being here with us today and last night. I'm sorry I'm so emotional right now. I just feel so much love and so blessed to have every one of you in our lives," I said as I wiped my tears trying to get a grip.

Chance turned to embrace me bring calm back to my emotions.

"I love you," I whispered into his ear as he held me tight. "I will love you forever!"

"I love you too and thank you for making today and every day hereafter the best days of my life," he replied and kissed me tenderly.

Everyone started applauding and we broke off in a giggle having almost forgotten our audience.

"You two were destined for each other. I don't know what took you so long any fool could tell by the way he stared at you he was in love with you," Daisy spoke up as she giggled.

"I know I know. I keep hearing that a lot," I replied as I looked back, "better late than never."

After our incredible lunch Donatello arranged for everyone to take a Gondola ride through the great canal and he'd meet us further down at our next tourist stop.

We broke up into four Gondola's, Ty and Stephanie in one, Aaron and Mom, Robert and Linda, and then Chance and I.

As we floated through the canal enjoying our moment of privacy, I didn't pay much attention to our surroundings Chance and his lips were all I was interested in. During our silence, our captain broke out in Italian song and we snuggled closer as we took in this romantic moment.

"I wonder how long it's going to take them to come around," I said as I pointed back to Ty and Stephanie.

"Any day now," Chance replied with a chuckle as he waved back to our friends.

Our next stop was the Dorodeo Sestiere District of Venice to start our museum tour.

Donatello met us at the dock as promised and held his hand out to take my mom's first. I looked at Chance and we both giggled.

"I think he's taken a liking to Daisy," Chance whispered as we sat in awe.

As we went along with our walking tour Donatello offered his arm to my mom as her personal escort through the plaza and museum. Aaron slowed and tagged along with Chance and I not wanting to crowd in on his grandma's new admirer.

"Aren't they just the cutest? I haven't seen grandma light up this much in years," Aaron spoke as he gave me a half hug.

I entered the museum arm in arm with my two favorite men in the whole world.

Most people thought Aaron was my son, by the way we speak to one another, and he'd smart off or joke around with me. I think when you only have one nephew and six nieces it'll do that to you. I hoped that one day I could give him a little male cousin one for Aaron to spoil and be the big brother type to. I could only hope for such wonderful things to come.

I took great exhilaration in knowing my mom had lived long enough to see me love again and be happy once more.

She absolutely adored Chance. Seeing her today so happy and enjoying her time with Donatello seemed to come full circle. My dad had spoken of his naval stopover in Italy during a submarine cruise in the Mediterranean and had always wanted to take mom here for vacation. In part he was here with us. I couldn't help but think how much Aaron favored dad and had the same quirks and gestures.

The museum tour was by far our favorite. It had been an art school in a previous life and it was fascinating. The museum had twenty-four rooms displaying all works of art from a variety of periods and everything from Paolo Veneziano's work from the late thirteen hundreds to 17th century art adorning the walls including a most famous DaVinci. The tour finished and everyone agreed we needed a break to stop for coffee before seeing more of the sights.

For the next four hours we took short tours of each sestiere or district of Venice. Donatello wanted us to be exposed to the best of Venice.

Upon returning to our hotel we all parted to shower and get ready for our family dinner at Ristorante Parco dello Rose located in the community of Lido along with tourist shops and sweet shops.

We sat outdoors in the garden area. The restaurant canopy seating was beautifully draped with flowering bushes and a mix of local trees making for yet another romantic meal.

Sitting around our big table we discussed all the priceless art, culture, and fairy tale type architecture we'd all experienced. Each of took turns describing our favorite part of the tour. To me this entire day was my favorite, everything in it and about it. I was able to share Venice with our family and the most wonderful man that has ever existed and said yes to him. My life could not have been more perfect than it was today. Seeing the smiles and excitement on everyone's faces, I had all but forgotten home.

After another round of drinks had finished each guest excused themselves to enjoy the night life on their own or go back and rest after the long day of excitement. Ty and

Stephanie took Aaron club hopping while our parents went back to the hotel to rest. We told Ty we'd meet up with them later on we had an evening stroll along the beach to take care of first.

"Thank you for bringing my mom and Aaron all the way here for this. It meant the world to me and them," I shared with Chance as I wrapped my hands around his adorable face and proceeded to kiss him eagerly.

"You're welcome. I'm glad we could share last night and today with our family. They have always been so supportive of us and it wouldn't have felt right not having them here to share that perfect moment," Chance said as his arms gave me a squeeze.

We went back to our suite after a short stroll along the sandy beach. We opted to skip out on club hopping and save it for tomorrow night before everyone flew back to the states.

Our hotel room was once again a place of refuge and silence.

Chance stopped once inside as I closed the door behind us. He took me into his embrace and I gave into one of his deep kisses of greed.

"I love you," he said to me as he paused to caress my face.

His eyes swelled up and tears began to trickle down as his expression changed.

I touched his face catching his tear feeling confused and concerned something was bothering him.

"I love you," I replied as I kissed the trail the tear left behind, "I love you."

"You have no idea how incredible those three words are to me and how they make me feel," he whispered as he pulled me closer to his body, "I love you Susan," his voice cracked, "I love you," he continued as he kissed my hands, "you are the love of my life and when you said yes, you completed me."

"I've loved you from the first kiss. I belonged to you from the first touch, and I knew I'd marry you before you ever kneeled," I softly replied as I kissed his lips not giving him time to reply. I wanted the full range of emotions I felt to fill my lips and share them with him and never let go.

His touch, his lips, and his pulse all increased as it spiked an erotic yearning. A deep yearning that only stirred our very souls.

"Incredible," he moaned as he returned my kisses with equal urgency.

Every movement that followed was even greater than our first night together. I couldn't get enough of him as if I were possessed.

I wanted to be taken so much that the experience we shared was almost sacred.

* * *

I woke up at 6:00 a.m. remaining in his full embrace even in sleep. He had refused to let go declaring his devotion to me as we slept. Slowly, I managed to release myself from his clutch he moved slightly too deep in his slumber to notice. I took time to shower, dress, and then call for breakfast in bed. I had the door partially open hoping to get the door before the knock. It was Rose our regular morning breakfast host. She quietly pushed the cart into our room as I pointed back to the bedroom and put my finger over my lips to signal silence then I mouthed. "He is sleeping, thank you."

I quietly shut the door and then proceeded to wake my beloved. It only took a few kisses on his chest to create a rush of energy to his heart and bring him around. I had a tray waiting by our bed side.

"Good morning love," I said as I traced his face with kisses.

"Hi. Good morning," Chance replied as he took a deep breath in and opened his eyes, "wow breakfast in bed, you'd best be careful babe I could get use to this kind of pampering."

"I'll keep that in mind," I said playfully as he returned kisses to my lips, "you'd best get to eating our parents will be down in the lobby in less than an hour to say goodbye before going back home. I'm not sure if Aaron's is going back with mom or not."

"I don't know. He seemed to be having a great time last night and I'm sure he had a blast with Ty club hopping," Chance replied as he finished his breakfast.

"Yes I'm sure he had the time of his life with Ty the party animal!" I joked.

"He was wilder back in his youth," he chuckled.

"I can't imagine Ty being any wilder than he is right now," I said as I laughed. "Well we'd best get!"

"Okay just let me get dressed, grab my wallet, and I'm ready," Chance said.

Making our way down to the lobby holding hands I felt some level of sadness because our parents had only been able to stay the weekend to share in our vacation.

"I love you," I said before we entered the lobby.

"I love you too babe. What brought that on?" He asked looking puzzled.

"You're what brought everything on. You were determined to give me the best vacation, romance, and engagement day I could have ever dreamed of and more."

"I wanted it to be right. Perfect just like you," he said and smiled as he stole a quick kiss.

Everyone was waiting in the lobby for our water taxi ride back to Venice.

"Aaron, are you going back or staying a few more days?" I asked.

"I spoke with grandma this morning she said she was fine if I stayed. Her flight back is the same as the Walkers all the way to Atlanta and I think they had some wedding plans to discuss," Aaron replied as he wrinkled his nose at the idea of wedding planning.

"Already, they'll talk the entire flight and your poor dad won't be able to get any rest," I said with a giggle.

"I figured that much my mom and Daisy seemed pretty excited when I shared my plans with them last month," Chance replied.

We all made our way to the water taxi and headed out for the airport. I was relieved that mom would be with Robert and Linda all the way back to the states and excited that I would be getting to actually spend some quality time with my nephew. Everything had turned out better than planned. With our parents safely on their way back home the rest of us went off to explore more of Venice. Chance had a cathedral tour set up where we'd tour various important historical churches of Venice and a few other historical landmarks.

I enjoyed having Stephanie there to hang out with during lunch at a local bistro. A major football game was on and being the sports nuts they are Chance, Ty, and Aaron ended up staying to watch the last half of the soccer game while we girls went off to check out the boutiques for some sultry outfits for us to wear tonight to one of the night clubs Ty had discovered last night that played top forty American style music and as Aaron put it, "they have a wicked sound system."

Stephanie and I figured what the heck we'd find something a little on the skimpy side to insure our men kept their attention on us and not on any hot Italian babes that might be there stocking the clubs for rich American tourist.

Shopping turned out to be more fun than work. Italy had always been on the cutting edge of top design and elegance. It took us two hours in one shop to buy one outfit each. There was such a variety of choice and everything we tried on fit like a glove and would be perfect for making a statement.

"You know Stephanie, I could see myself living here someday," I said.

"I know it's just so dreamy and relaxing. I just wish Ty could learn to relax and maybe he'd enjoy this trip that much more," Stephanie responded.

"What he's not enjoying himself?"

"Yes he is, but he just seems to be preoccupied these last few days like he has a lot on his mind. He won't tell me what it is or what's going on."

My brain reminded me of what Chance told me yesterday "any day now".

"You shouldn't worry too much about it. He was probably concerned for Chance you know how those two are, glued at the hip and brain," I assured her.

"Yea you're right he did tell me he was pretty excited for Chance and you and how everything finally worked out like it should be. He was really sweet about it."

"Thank you again for being here with us and sharing last night with us too. I know it meant everything to Chance to have his best friend right there to witness his crowning moment," I replied with a giggle as I recalled our engagement.

"Susan, we are both so happy for you and Chance. I can't think of two people who deserve so much happiness," Stephanie said as she hugged me and began to tear up.

"Oh don't start you'll get me crying too. I love you and thank you. Your friendship is so important to me and I'm really blessed to have so many wonderful people in my life right now."

"Well we'd best get back to the boys before they find more excuses to sit and drink beer all day," Stephanie said.

The game was just minutes from finishing when we arrived back at the bistro. The men didn't look like they'd missed us much. Chance, Ty, and Aaron sat with some locals at a table close to the TV yelling and hooting like they'd belonged right there. It was so cute.

"Hey beautiful, over here," Chance yelled to get our attention as his concentration broke from the game to see us standing at the bar watching them from a distance.

I waved as we walked toward them and found Chance's arms waiting to embrace me.

"You girls shop until you drop already?" Chance asked as he leaned in for a kiss.

"Yes we found the perfect sexy little dress just for tonight," I replied.

"Do I get a preview later?" Chance asked as he wiggled his eye brow.

"Absolutely," I replied as I gave into another lustful kiss from his lips.

"Dude, don't you two ever stop?" Ty asked as he rolled his eyes.

"NO!" Chance chuckled as he returned to my lips.

"Come on I think I'm gonna be sick," Aaron chimed in. "Are they always like this?"

"Yes they are. You'd think they'd be tired of one another by now," Ty replied as he began to laugh then muttered. "Sex kitten!"

That was all it took and we all broke out in hysterical laughter.

"Meow!" Chance replied as he continued with the joke.

"My hero," Ty responded as they smacked fists in unison laughing louder yet.

"We'd better get out of here before someone starts to complain," Aaron spoke up.

"Yes there's so much to see. Let's go," I replied.

We finished up our tour of the Piazza and headed back to the hotel, so we could spend some time on the beach while the weather was still good and the sun high in the sky.

The men played on jet skis the hotel provided as Stephanie and I laid upon the beach working on our tans.

"Look at those speed junkies," I pointed to Chance and Ty as they sped past the beach weaving back and forth between each other's wake.

"It never surprises me when those two get together and there's speed involved they practically revert to children. And look at Aaron, he's no different."

"I know Aaron," I chuckled as I watched my nephew keep up playing his part in the speed junky game, "I'm surprised, he didn't turn out to be a fighter pilot or some adrenaline junky bike racer. He definitely has a wild side that can only come from my side of our family."

"Are any of the nieces like that?" Stephanie asked as she pointed toward the jet skis.

"Yes, actually my niece Tammy, she's in the U.S. Coast Guard stationed in Alaska."

"I beat that would be just as exciting as a fighter jet."

"I'm sure sometimes it is. They go out on the chopper and jump into that freezing water to save a fishing boat crew all time. I don't think I'd have the nerve to jump from a perfectly good helicopter," I said as I had a vision of Tammy jumping in.

"I don't see the difference? You strap your butt to the end of a massive rocket and fling yourself into outer space!"

We both got so tickled at the analogy she was right I was just as crazy.

"Speaking of crazy," I said as I pointed to the men returning from their fun.

"That was awesome," Ty spoke first smiling like a kid who just won the big race.

"Awesome doesn't cover it," Aaron replied.

"Yes you two should have come out with us," Chance said.

"We had just as much fun watching you three men drive like speed demons," Stephanie replied.

"Aaron, you are just as bad as they are," I joked.

"It's in my blood. I can't help it," Aaron chuckled.

"Yea he was pretty good out there at one point he had us both beat coming down the line," Ty replied.

"Well if you boys are done playing with your toys, we'd like a nice dinner, and then a fun night on the town," I stated.

"Sounds good I'm starving," Aaron replied.

"I am too. I could go for some surf and turf," Chance said.

"Well what are we doing standing here," Stephanie replied. "Let's go!"

Once back to our room I headed for the shower first only to find Chance had already jumped in.

"What? I thought we'd share," he said as his evil grin flashed up.

"Yes that does sound like a perfect plan," I replied as I took his hand.

"I've been waiting all day for this," Chance quietly spoke as he rubbed soap over my body sending me into complete excitement.

"I'm glad we both share the same desire for showers," I said as I kissed his neck and moaned as his hands electrified my body.

"You're all I can think about. I can't seem to get enough of you. You're all I want."

"Then take me right here right now!" I demanded and he complied.

After a long passionate shower we dried off and I began to primp and get prepped for our evening out. I wanted to look as irresistible as he made me feel. Naughty thoughts charged my mood as I thought about the night of fun in store.

"Holy crap!" Chance said as I walked out of the bedroom and his mouth dropped.

"I take it you like what you see?" I asked as I smoothed out the fabric.

"You could say that," he said as he got up from the reading chair and quickly made his way to me.

"I'm glad you like it. Stephanie said I was sure to get a double take or two," I said.

"Look is all they'd better do," Chance said as he looked at me and frowned.

"Oh honey you're too sweet," I replied as I gave into his kiss.

"We'd better stop before I call in sick and stay in for the night," he chuckled.

I smiled and took his handsome face in my hands offering a kiss of delight to let him know I have only room in my heart for him and I belonged to him.

"Now this will be an interesting night," he said as he opened the door for us to leave.

Ty, Stephanie, and Aaron sat in the bar waiting on us to accompany them to dinner.

The bartender recommended we try a local steak house with the freshest seafood and finest steak in all of Venice. The choice was made to go check it out and off we went.

Dinner was the best meal any of us had had in years and the service was just as wonderful. After a big meal like that we figured we take a walk around the Piazza before going out to the night club scene and do some bar hopping.

"Thanks Aaron for staying an extra day to go hang out and party a little with us," I said.

"You're welcome. I'm just glad I had enough down time with between gigs to make it," Aaron replied, "thanks Chance for everything man you're alright."

"Sure I'm just glad you could be here I know it meant everything to Susan," Chance spoke.

"Yea Chance, thank for picking the greatest city on planet Earth to invite us to," Ty remarked as he slapped Chance on the back.

"It wouldn't have been the same with you dude," Chance replied.

Our one hour stroll around the piazza was perfect. The weather was mild, the air felt fresh, and the breeze just enough to keep that sticky feeling from emerging.

The club was incredible. Ty didn't disappoint with his choice of party venue.

There were plenty of local scantily dressed young beauties for Aaron to have his pick and enjoy another night of fun.

"He's going to break someone's heart one day," Ty said as he pointed to Aaron surrounded by four girls all clinging to him.

We laughed at the sight.

"If I'd only brought my camera the trouble he'd be in," I chuckled.

"Camera? Use your cell phone," Ty replied.

"Yes thanks, now I can black mail Aaron for the rest of his life," I teased as laughter broke out again.

Our night ended early in the a.m. hours as we made our way back to the hotel.

"I guess Aaron is playing the good boy because lord knows he could have had any one of those girls tonight," Ty chuckled.

"Yes he is a good boy and he knows Laura would kill him," I said with a giggle.

"Ty, wait until you meet Laura and you'll understand why. He'd have to be insane to mess that one up," Chance commented.

"That good," Ty replied.

"You could say that," Chance said as he tried to cover his mouth to muffle his voice from my ears. "She's seriously hot!"

Then they started to giggle like school boys again getting a naughty peek under the bleachers.

"You two are seriously too much like twins," I replied. "Are you sure you weren't separated at birth?"

"Maybe," Ty said as he broke out into another loud laugh.

Once back to our room we laughed over the day's events and found ourselves happily in each other's arms again.

"You know there's no place I'd rather be than right here with you in your arms," I confessed.

"In my arms is exactly where you belong," Chance replied as he began kissing my neck and unzipping my dress, "you know I've been dying all night to do just this."

"Really, well then let me help you with that," I said as I pulled his shirt off and threw it across the room. "Now that's more like it my hands on your flesh!"

"My flesh is all yours!"

"Yes and I am so glad," I replied as I pulled him to bed to feed my greed once more.

Chapter XIII

Home

The journey home was far less stressful for both of us and everything worked out the way it should be. Chance lay back holding my hand to his chest as he slept peacefully. Our trip back to Rome was short compared to what lay ahead on the flight back to JFK.

Ty, Stephanie, and Aaron had left earlier in the day to fly to Atlanta before heading home.

Everything had changed now I would never be alone again. I had found the man who would love me for an eternity. I marveled in the thought of introducing him as my husband and the pride of that knowledge sent my heart singing.

"Susan Walker," I thought to myself, it does sound as right as anything in my life has ever been.

I leaned up to take a look at his face while he slept. Chance was wonderful and he loved me. I recalled what I thought of him the first time I met him during his first shuttle simulator training. He was good looking, better than the boy next door. My first impression of Chance was that he was cocky, self-centered, and a prankster. He was still the hunk, the cockiness was just a front to impede any suspicion of how he really felt about me, the furthest from self-centered any man could ever be, he was sensitive, caring, loveable, and the most considerate person I'd ever known.

Chance had become the man I could not nor would not live without.

As I sat looking out the cabin window he came alive once more.

"I love you," he said as he pulled me back into his waiting arms. "Can't you get any rest?"

"No it feels weird going back through the time zones now gaining the hours we lost on the way here. It's going to take the rest of our time off just to readjust our sleeping habits back to Eastern Time."

"My nights and days will take at least that long to get back to normal," Chance said.

"I don't mind staying awake. It gives me time to think and watch you sleep," I said.

"So you've been watching me sleep and thinking of what?" Chance asked.

"Thinking about you, me, work," I replied.

"No thinking about work," he teased. "We my dear are still officially on vacation!"

"I know. I'm just thinking how nice it will be not to hide our relationship from anyone now," I said.

"Yes that's right. I'm happy about it too. You know being engaged is the next best thing and it clears up a lot," Chance said.

"So what would be the best thing?" I asked.

"You and I married," Chance replied as he gloated.

"Chance, you always know what to say. Yes, married would be the best," I said as I gave into a soft romantic kiss.

"You sure you don't want to hop on a plane to Vegas next weekend?"

"Don't tempt me," I declared.

The flight back to JFK was long and uneventful. Chance snuggled up to me once again and began caressing my arm as my eye lids lost the battle, my brain gave in, and my body felt protected by the one person I'd give my own life to protect in return.

* * *

Finally home back in our condo. It was strange walking in knowing that Chance would now become a permanent fixture. Five months had passed bringing us to this point. It felt like we'd been together for years rather than months.

Chance went off to the gym to work out with Ty and I stayed home doing tons of laundry. I was glad we had the extra days off just so I could get caught up on everything. My mood was jovial, so I checked e-mail and stopped cleaning house.

I had dinner ready by the time Chance and Ty got home. Ty even got in a shower; he'd left extra clothing in the guest room for his ritual dinner night.

"Doesn't he ever help you out Susan," Ty teased as he poked Chance in the ribs.

"Well you see he does try and he's thoughtful," I replied trying to keep my laugh in.

"So basically he sucks at laundry," Ty replied as he broke out into laughter.

"You see I'm kind of a control freak and I've got a method already down on how I like things done around the house," I said as I joined in on the laugh.

"Great this isn't funny you two tag teaming me," Chance pouted turning to give me a wink then back to Ty for a frog on the arm.

"Maybe she'll have better luck training you than I did," Ty continued to joke.

"Yes maybe, either way she's a much better looking trainer," Chance leaped from the couch to snag me into his arms, "besides I rather enjoy her rewards for good behavior," he chuckled as he began kissing me.

"Don't you two ever take a break? I think I'll pass on the ball game tonight," Ty replied as he got up and headed for the door.

"Night Ty, see you tomorrow," Chance spoke as he turned his attention back to me. "Now where was I?"

He raised a brow and took my arm pulling me back into his arms never skipping a beat.

"I guess I'm done for today. I think it's time for bed Mr. Walker," I teased as I slipped out of his arms shutting off the kitchen lights.

He wasn't far behind cooing at me as he followed me into bed.

"Reward time," I offered in a low volume.

"More training?" He asked between kisses.

* * *

5:00 a.m. the alarm went off it was time to get up and start back to our workweek routine. We started with our morning jog feeling the energy that the new day brought and ran at a comfortable pace allowing ourselves to readjust to the climate and sea level changes. Neither of us tired since we'd done so much walking on our vacation and tried to swim at least every other day to help keep up our fitness routine.

This week would be our pre-mission fitness test and physicals before the next space shuttle launch a month from now. I felt pretty confident that we'd both do well and might end up on another mission together before NASA breaks for the winter.

The weeks that followed would be stressful enough with extensive hours in the orbiter simulator. Chance would be immersed back into robotics and working with any payload that would be going up as well.

By mid-week my day planner thinned out and I found myself in my office pre-occupied with the pending marriage. We still haven't set a date and I knew our parents would want something nailed down before the holidays.

I got to thinking about our living arrangement and even though it was nice having a place on base it would be better to have a bigger home off base if we'd ever planned on entertaining the thought of having little Chance's running around. I smiled with enthusiasm at the thought of one, two, or maybe three little boys running around the house playing tackled with dear old dad. The more I allowed my visions to expand the more tickled I got at the idea of Chance being a dad. He loved children and he was wonderful with Jeff and Patti's kids.

I don't plan on flying shuttles for the rest of my life and I need a backup plan.

"Hello beautiful!" He spoke as he walked into my office holding a rose.

"Hello. Wow. This is nice," I replied as I greeted him with a kiss.

"I was just in the neighborhood and was thinking of you, again. We finished up early today. I'm taking the rest of the day off to spend with the sexiest woman alive."

"You are? Does she know this?" I asked as I chuckled.

"She will soon enough," Chance said as he playfully teased pulling me into his arms.

"I'm happy to see you. I can't concentrate on anything today except for you," I said.

"Lucky me," Chance replied.

"I was actually thinking about going house hunting later, but since you're here now," I said smiling as I waved a print out of area new home listings.

"You work fast. My thoughts of you and I, spending quality time together was as far away from this as it gets," he said as he wrinkled his nose up in protest.

"And I'm guessing you have other plans?" I asked as he kissed his way up my neck line.

"Oh yes love I have plans for us," Chance replied.

"Chance Walker, what I am I going to do with you?" I asked as I shook my head.

"I can think of one, two, three, maybe four things right off the bat," he snickered as he continued his erotic tease of my flesh against his lips.

"If that is your plan and you're sticking to it then we'd best get out of here," I replied.

"I'll drive," Chance said as he released me.

"We can always look for a new house tomorrow," I concluded.

"Deal," Chance replied.

I made sure to clear my schedule on Thursday, so we could take the afternoon to drive around various subdivisions near, base looking to see what was on the market and in the size of home we both felt comfortable with.

"We'll need a fenced yard, a shade tree or two and four bedrooms minimum."

"How did you come up with that?" Chance asked.

"I want us to have our bedroom, a guest bedroom, home office, and a future ideas room."

"Future idea room," he said as he raised his eye brow as he cocked his head.

"You know future idea," I said as I rubbed my tummy.

A look of shock came across his face and he gasp.

"No dear not a "now idea" room, but a "future idea" room," I clarified.

"Okay, you caught me off guard on that one, not that I wouldn't mind a "now idea" room," Chance said as he grinned big and wiggled his eye brows.

"Yes way in the future idea room," I insisted.

"Then I like your plan. A house like that would fit us perfectly. As long as it has a big yard and garage I'm good with it," Chance said as he smiled.

"Well then where to first?" I asked.

"The west side of base is probably going to be more protected from weather. So maybe we should start our search in one of those subdivisions first."

"That sounds great," I replied as I snuck a quick kiss.

"Maybe we can get one with a swimming pool and I'm not a big fan of two-story houses especially if we have kids because I've heard too many horror stories of toddlers falling out of windows," Chance said.

As we drove around each subdivision, I started to feel the excitement building as the love of my life spoke of our children and future. For the next three hours we drove from house to house getting out looking around the property and seeing if it met our want list.

We found six possibilities and took pictures of each making sure we got a good photo of the front of the house and the back yard.

The next week we called Charlotte Lowery, who is Ty's cousin, and a local realtor.

Charlotte set up viewing at the first three homes on our list.

"I've got time today if either of you would like to see the house over on Dalewood?" Charlotte asked as we exchanged information over the phone.

"I'd love to. Let me call you back in a few minutes I'll call and see if Chance is available to go as well."

"Sounds great just give me a call when you're ready to go and I'll meet you over at the house." Charlotte said as we ended our call.

I pulled up my house hunting file on the laptop. "Dalewood, which one was Dalewood?" I asked myself aloud.

"Dalewood got it. That's our number two pick, nice."

I picked up my cell phone and called Chance.

"Hello beautiful," he spoke as he answered.

"Hi love. I just got off the phone with Charlotte Lowery she wants to know if we'd like to see house number two on our wish list. Are you available?"

"Actually I am. I just finished my physical over at the flight clinic and should be out of here in about ten minutes. Do you want me to come by your office and we can go together or do you want me to just meet you girls there?"

"You can meet me out in the parking lot. We can go together," I said.

"Alright then I'll see you in a few minutes," Chance replied.

"Great I'll call Charlotte back and tell her to meet us at Dalewood," I said.

"Sounds like a plan. I love you," Chance said.

"Love you too. Bye," I replied then hung up.

I quickly called Charlotte back to set up our visit to the house and made my way to the parking lot.

"Hey Susan!" A man's voice spoke loudly from behind me.

I turned to see who was calling my name; it was Major Ryan Harrison from flight command.

"Hi Major nice to see you," I said as I greeted him.

"Congratulations on your engagement to Captain Walker. Jill and I were thrilled when we heard the good news," Ryan said.

"Well thank you Major I appreciate the support. I was just on my way to meet up with Chance in the parking lot. Come on we can talk as we walk," I said.

"That would be great. I haven't seen Chance in months," Ryan said. "How are things going? Have you two set a date yet?"

"Things are wonderful. No, we haven't set a date for the wedding as of yet we have a few different dates picked, but nothing specific," I replied.

"Jill wanted to host a bridal shower for you if you'd allow her the honor," Ryan said.

"That would be wonderful. Tell her thank you and I'll give her a call next week," I said.

"Sure. Hey it was good to see you. I'm really happy for both of you," Ryan replied.

"Hey Ryan," Chance said as he walked towards us. "What's up my man?"

"Hey Chance. Long time no see. I'm doing great. I was just talking with Susan about you and congratulations on the engagement," Ryan spoke as he offered a handshake.

"Thank you," Chance replied as he pulled his arms around my waist.

"I'd best get I've got a staff meeting to attend. It was good to see you. Give me a call sometime buddy and we'll go golf," Ryan said.

"You know I will and it was good seeing you man," Chance replied as he turned to me for a quick kiss.

I smiled and allowed myself to pause in the comfort of his embrace.

"I've missed you today," I informed.

"You have?" Chance asked as his lips offered a more passionate kiss.

"I'm miserable when you're not around," I pouted and returned his kisses.

"We'd best get before you get me all worked up and we miss our appointment with Charlotte," Chance said.

"Alright I'll behave," I said with repose.

Within minutes, we arrived at the house on Dalewood. Charlotte had already arrived and had the front door open. It was a great house. It had most of our wish list criteria except a pool.

"Hello Susan and Chance. Glad you could make it on such short notice. Come in," Charlotte spoke.

"Thank you," Chance replied.

"So let's start the tour. The house is four years old, it's 3,800 square feet, and of typical Floridian design. We have a great room with an open floor plan allowing flow from the living room into the kitchen and then the dining area. It has five bedrooms and four and half bathrooms. The kitchen has all new appliances included."

"This is perfect. I love the idea of being able to cook and still visit with the guys as they watch a ball game," I said.

"Yes that would be nice for a change and the kitchen is nice enough to even encourage me to learn how to cook," Chance replied.

I just looked at him and giggled.

"Let's see the rest of the house," Charlotte said as we walked down the long hallway, "and here is the master suite."

"Wow this is big," Chance said as a smile streaked across his face.

"This is definitely big enough," I responded.

"You have two walk-in closets, linen closet, large master bathroom with double vanity, separate shower enclosure, and a whirlpool tub," Charlotte continued to describe the suite.

"A whirlpool tub is perfect. I love the oversized shower," Chance spoke with an eager tone as he turned and gave me a wink.

"Okay then let's see the other bedrooms and bathrooms," Charlotte replied.

I knew exactly what Chance was thinking. Oversized shower for two I quietly giggled to myself.

"Well Charlotte this is great. This house so far has everything we are looking for," I said.

Chance walked out the back door to inspect the yard as I followed.

"This is nice and level. It shouldn't be too hard to add a swimming pool later on. What do you think Susan?"

"Honey, I think it's great. It looks big enough to have a pool and yard left over."

We returned to Charlotte back inside the house and continued our tour.

"This area here is the laundry area with a walk-in pantry. This door leads to the two car garage," Charlotte spoke as she opened the door and turned on the lights.

"Wow that is a nice garage and it has enough room for our motorcycles and two cars," Chance replied.

"So what do you two think?" Charlotte asked.

"I think we both like it. We'll give it some serious thought," I replied.

"Thank you for showing the house to us. We'll get back to you later after we've had time to talk things over," Chance said.

"Great, I look forward to hearing from you soon," Charlotte said as we walked back to our car. "Take care!"

"How would you like an early dinner tonight?" Chance asked.

"Sounds wonderful I didn't get a break today so I didn't get lunch and I'm starving," I said.

"Well I can't let that happen," he teased as he opened the car door on my side.

I gave him a quick kiss and slid in.

"How about going to Murphy's for dinner?" Chance asked.

"Perfect," I replied.

We continued our conversation about the house on Dalewood as we ate dinner. Murphy's wasn't too busy or loud, and we were able to have a normal conversation, for the most part.

"So what do you think about this house?" I asked.

"Well so far I think it is the best one out of all six we've looked at and it has everything we want except the pool," Chance said.

"I think so too and we can always add a pool later on," I said.

"Do you want to make an offer on it?" Chance asked.

"Yes I do," I said.

"I agree," Chance smiled and replied as he held up his beer for a toast.

"Then I'll call Charlotte tomorrow and give her the good news," I said.

"This is amazing. We're buying our first house," Chance said. "Wow!"

I smiled at his reaction and couldn't contain my self-control any more. I pulled myself as close as I could get to his body and wrapped my arms around his shoulders.

"I love you," I sighed as I spoke, "you have made me so happy. Yes, our first house."

"I have a feeling this will be the first of many new things for us," he replied as he offered a kiss.

He was radiant as ever. I could see and feel his energy as it pulled me in.

"Maybe we should call Charlotte tonight," Chance insisted.

"Okay I'll call when we get home or should I call her after we finish up here?"

"Sure you can call her after dinner that would be great the sooner the better," he said.

I gave Charlotte a quick call to tell her we wanted the house on Dalewood and set up to make a formal offer on the house at 9:00 a.m. tomorrow.

"We're set, she can stop by my office at 9:00 a.m. tomorrow," I informed Chance of our conversation and how Charlotte would've done it tonight, but she was in the middle of a house tour with another client.

"Tomorrow it is. I want to close on this puppy before the next shuttle launch," Chance said.

"It will be good to have buying a house out of the way and maybe moved in before the launch too," I replied.

"Yes I agree and the sooner the better. I'm more than ready to start our lives together."

"You are? Then I guess we'd best work on setting that date for the wedding," I said.

"Is tomorrow too soon?" Chance asked as he snickered.

"Yes, I think that is too soon. You know both our moms would kill us both," I stated.

"I almost forgot. You're right she would kill me. She called me today matter of fact asking me for the wedding date," Chance said.

"Well then, we'd better get something worked out. I'll get out my appointment book once we get home, and we can work on a specific month and day."

"Yes the sooner the better," he insisted as I gave into yet another intense kiss.

Chapter XIV

Holidays

∞

Moving day started off smoothly as planned. We had some of our friends over to help out. Our condo didn't have a large amount of items to move. We'd already furnished the new house with a new couch, dining room set, beds, and had most of the old furniture was donated to charity. We made the move in one truck load and the weather had cooperated bringing us a mild sunny day for late October.

While the men unloaded the truck Stephanie, Patti, and I went to work in the kitchen cooking up a feast for our hard working boys.

I had bought Chance a big new barbeque grill and outdoor furniture for the patio. Jeff helped out by offering his grilling skills for our big lunch.

Stephanie and I had already been back and forth to the new house all week prior to the move getting the pantry sorted, the bedrooms decorated, and the living room furniture moved into place.

"Alright that does it. The truck is empty and we are officially moved," Chance proclaimed.

"Good timing lunch is ready," Jeff replied.

"You guys go wash up and meet us outside on the patio," I said.

We carried the food out to the oversized patio table and enjoyed our first meal in our new home with the people who had supported us and shown so much love to us over the past years.

"Jeff, this chicken is the best yet," I said.

"Well it wouldn't be much without all the food you ladies provided," Jeff replied.

"I agree. These ranger potatoes are killer," Ty added.

"Thank you, we're glad we could contribute," Patti responded as she passed out some of her famous cherry cobbler.

"Now this is what I've been waiting for. Patti, you're an angel," Chance said as he licked his lip and proceeded to place a large helping of cobbler on his plate.

"Yes Patti, you have to share your secret with me," I insisted.

After lunch the men went off to hook up the big screen TV so they could catch the last half of the Cowboys game while the ladies cleaned up after the big meal.

"So Susan, how are things going?" Patti asked.

"Everything is good it seems like things just worked out for the best," I replied as I smiled.

"Now that you have the man and the house, when is the big date?" Stephanie quizzed as she popped grapes into her mouth and grinned.

"New Year's Eve," I said proudly.

"That's wonderful a New Year's wedding. That is so romantic," Stephanie replied.

"Are you getting married at midnight or what?" Patti asked.

"Chance has already set everything up with Chaplin Moore for the service at the base chapel and the reception will be at the Ballroom House just off base."

"Susan, that is going to be incredible my friend Elizabeth had her reception there and it was perfect," Stephanie expressed.

"My mom and Linda are thrilled to the have a wedding this soon. Chance and I figured why drag it out another year, so the sooner the better."

"I think it's a great idea," Patti said as she offered a hug.

Shouting came from the living room. Chance and Ty got the TV working and just in time to watch the second half of the game.

"Babe, are you girls going to get in there and watch the game or stand in here all night?" Chance asked as he entered the kitchen.

"Be right there," I replied as he gave me a quick kiss and returned to the living room.

"They're having far too much fun," Stephanie insisted.

We finished putting the dishes in the dishwasher and took some beer from the fridge before joining the men.

"So who's winning?" I asked as Chance rose off the couch to greet me.

"Cowboys," Chance replied as he put his arms around me, "I love you."

It was all I needed to hear and with three simple words my life was complete. I smiled with excitement as he pulled me closer. I looked over to the couch and everyone had taken their seats to watch the game. I stepped back and took his hand pulling him back into the kitchen with me.

"I love you," I replied as my body found its way back into his arms and my lips found his.

"Thank you I needed that," Chance quietly replied as his lips offered more zeal.

"And you are exactly what I need," I whispered as his lips caressed my neck.

"So what were you girls discussing?" He asked.

"New Year's Eve and New Year's Day," I said.

"Ah wedding talk. I'm glad I missed it," he chuckled, "I had enough of that with mom earlier today."

"How is she?" I asked.

"Ecstatic! She told me to tell you she loved you and can't wait to see you for Christmas."

"My mom is the same way. I'm surprised they both didn't already have everything planned out for us and all we'd have to do was show up," I said.

"Well I can have that arranged," Chance teased.

"No this is for us and I want New Year's," I said as I returned kiss playful kisses.

"We'd best get back to the game before Ty comes hunting for me."

"Yes, by the way, next time you talk to your mom tell her I'll have all the invitations mailed out by this next Friday," I said.

"Sounds great do you have enough invitations?" Chance asked.

"I sure hope so. I'm mailing out four hundred," I chuckled.

"Four hundred? I didn't know we knew that many people," Chance responded as he shook his head in disbelief.

"Yes we do know that many people, added with the people on your mom's invite list and my mom's invite list, we end up with four hundred," I said.

"I think we need a bigger cake," Chance joked.

"I'll keep that in mind. Patti offered to take me cake shopping next weekend," I said as I snarled my nose up at the thought of sampling cake after cake until my tongue shriveled up from too many sweets.

Taking my hand in his we rejoined our waiting friends who seemed focused on the game and didn't seem to miss our presence.

* * *

Before we knew it the Christmas holiday was bearing down on us. I had so many people to shop for. This year our crew opted for drawing names for our annual Christmas party at Jeff and Patti's house. I drew Ty and Chance drew Abe this made for easy shopping since we both knew exactly what they wanted. I gave Chance the task of picking out the gifts for them.

I had bigger things to worry about. I had no clue what to buy a guy that claims to already have everything in the world he'd ever need. My mind was blank. Then I remembered a story his mom told me of their dog Roscoe and how Chance loved that dog. Maybe I'll get him a puppy? If I did get him a puppy it would have to be a breed I knew he loved. An Irish-setter would be perfect and the more I thought about it the better I felt about a puppy.

I didn't have much time so on my light workday I called several breeders and pet stores in the area to see if they would have an Irish-setter available for Christmas.

I worked out my plan with Ty since he and Stephanie would be over for Christmas brunch they could keep the puppy and bring it when they came over.

Things between Ty and Stephanie had progressed forward and Stephanie moved in with him. Ty finally committed to asking Stephanie to marry him on Christmas Day at our house. He figured he owed Chance the opportunity to witness the big event and he knew Chance would kill him otherwise.

We'd traveled back to my parent's lake house for Thanksgiving in Oklahoma. It was good to spend time with mom and my sisters with all their kids. Everyone seemed excited about attending a New Year's Eve wedding and New Year's Day reception party in Florida. My sister Brenda had already starting to fake bake a good tan on her skin so she wouldn't be to pasty if they went to the beach. Peggy and Aaron wouldn't miss the wedding for anything. I had already roped Aaron into walking me down the aisle since dad had passed away and he was the only nephew. It was only fitting that Aaron be the one to stand in for dad. The other sisters would bring the entire clan promising a wild bachelorette party.

The weekend before Christmas we flew out to Galveston to see the Walker family.

It was nice to get in another short trip before the wedding and it gave Chance time to visit some old friends.

The first night in town he took me to a local pub his friend Brad Owens ran and we ended up visiting until sunrise. Brad and his wife Sandra had been high school sweethearts. Brad and Chance played football together and had stayed close through all these years. Brad had an entire wall in the pub dedicated to Chance. I called it, "Chance's Shrine."

Sandra made sure to add a print out of the Orion flight crew and had it dead center among all of the newspaper articles and other photos of Chance Walker, the astronaut. I took a photo of the wall to take back home to show the others, none of them would believe this otherwise.

"Rock Star," I teased as we walked from one end of the wall reading articles to the other end.

It was then I spotted the reason so many knew who Chance was. It was a People magazine article claiming astronaut Chance Walker as one of the top twenty sexiest men in the world for 2007. I had never seen the article before only heard about it through the office gossip, since those types of magazine aren't my typical reading material, and from the occasional joke Ty and Jeff would tell about Chance. It was impressive and I finally understood his star status.

"See I told you I'm famous," Chance chuckled.

"Yea, he was famous alright. He was famous for breaking hearts," Sandra responded.

"No not Chance," I said as I giggled.

"It's true as soon as that boy heard I love you, he was gone," Brad informed me as he agreed with Sandra.

"So what does that make me?" I asked.

"A first," Sandra replied and laughed.

"The only one," Chance proclaimed, "one is all it takes. I just knew she would be out there somewhere and I was right."

"I can't argue with him on that one. He knew he wanted me and that was it," I replied as I stroked Chance's soft face as he nodded in agreement.

"Well honey I don't know what you did, but I'm glad you are here. I couldn't be happier for the both of you," Brad said.

"We knew any woman that could hold his heart had to be the one he'd marry," Sandra said.

"Thank you, but I feel like I'm the lucky one," I quietly said as I felt my heart flicker with joy.

"How about you and I going for a stroll on the beach and let these two close up?" Chance asked.

"That sounds wonderful," I replied.

"Thanks for the great time and we'll see you two later on," Chance spoke to Brad as we left the pub.

"Sure see you New Year's Eve!" Sandra shouted back.

It felt good to have the cool sand beneath our feet as the warm southern breeze picked up and flowed over the gulf waters.

"Another sunrise on the beach, I could get use to this," I said walking hand in hand.

"It is beautiful isn't it," Chance said.

"Yes it's beautiful and romantic," I replied.

We paused to watch the Seagulls fly overhead and as I looked back down I felt overwhelmed with dizziness and nausea.

"Babe are you okay?" Chance asked as he grabbed my waist to hold me up.

"I don't know my equilibrium must be off this morning probably from lack of sleep. I'll be fine after we get back to your parents and I get some rest," I replied.

"Maybe we should go eat some breakfast first then to bed with you," he stated as his arms found their way around my waist as he pulled me in.

His kisses seemed to electrify me even to this day. He sent a burst of energy right through me. I didn't need caffeine I had Chance as my own personal adrenaline rush.

Once back to the Walker home I went off to bed and was already asleep before Chance ever had an opportunity to wrap himself around me.

Three hours later I woke up and rushed out of bed to the bathroom feeling the overwhelming urge to vomit.

It must have been something we ate the day before. I don't recall ever being this sick. Lucky for me Chance's brother David was a doctor and he took a look at me later in the day when he and his family arrived.

David agreed more than likely food poisoning and suggested various over the counter nausea medicine to help with my stomach so I can keep some solids down.

Our fun for the weekend was shot for sure now.

Chance being the bright light in anyone's day was right there by my side every possible minute to make sure I was doing better and to care for me.

I didn't deserve such a man.

"I love you!" I told him as I laid my head in his lap as we sat on the living room floor watching his nephews and nieces open their Christmas presents we'd given them.

It was so wonderful seeing them light up with excitement at the discovery of what fabulous gifts Uncle Chance had given them. He went overboard as usual. The children were still young enough to really enjoy Christmas. My nieces and Aaron were all post teen and opening presents was more of a chore or duty than an adventure.

The day we left Texas I finally started to feel like my old self and knew whatever bug I had was gone and I could go home and start focusing back on the wedding and making sure all the last minute details had been taken care of. I enjoyed our trip, but I was so happy to be home.

Our home was decorated with garland and the smells of pine. In one week we would take that next step in life and stand before all professing our love.

Tuesday evening we all gathered at Jeff and Patti's house for our group Christmas. They had their house all lit up with lights and holiday décor. Patti cooked enough food to feed an army and everything had gone smoothly until dinner. I had to excuse myself midway through and make a run for the bathroom.

"Not again," I spoke out loud.

"Susan, are you okay?" Jeff asked from the hallway.

"I don't know. I think I had food poisoning last weekend. I thought I was over it, but just now after eating, I just can't keep anything down. I get sick just over the smell of most food," I replied.

"I've got some Pepto-Bismol under the sink. You should try and hold some of that down and see if that helps with the nausea," Jeff said.

"Okay I'll give it a try. Thank you," I replied and gulped some down and went back to join our friends.

After that episode I didn't eat much else I was too worried I wouldn't keep it down long so I ate some bread and drank water to help fend off future nausea.

"Are you feeling any better?" Chance asked as we walked away from the table.

"Yes I feel fine. I must still have some traces of whatever stomach bug left in me," I said with a frown.

"Let's go watch the kids open gifts then we can get out of here and go home so you can rest."

"Alright," I sluggishly spoke.

It was nice to see the boys get excited when they opened Uncle Chance's gift, a new X-box with at least ten games to go with it.

More cooing and snickers came when Ty and Abe both opened their gifts to find they too had a new X-box game station with several new games. We gave a gift card to Toys-R-Us to Jada, since she wasn't really old enough to know what Christmas was yet. Stephanie, Christina, Patti, and I all got a day at the spa while Chance and Jeff got a free round of golf at the country club.

After everyone opened gifts we excused ourselves so we could go home, get some rest, and hopefully fight off any recurrence of my virus.

In Chance's arms was all my body needed to relax. I gave into the comfort of his kiss.

"I love you Susan," Chance quietly spoke, "I think after we get married, we should attempt to start a family. That is if you want one?"

My eyes opened wide as I was filled with shock and amazement.

"You want to start right away?" I asked.

"Yes I'm ready. After seeing Jeff's family tonight and the inner workings I just wanted it all," Chance said.

"Wow I'm stunned, but in a good way. I really didn't know you'd given children too much thought. I figured sure maybe after a few years you'd want to start, but now is good," I replied smiling as I looked up to him.

"I want it. I'm ready I just know it. Now is the right time," Chance said as his lips returned to mine.

* * *

Christmas morning came and we allowed ourselves to sleep in knowing Ty and Stephanie wouldn't be over until at least 3:00 p.m. right before the big football game.

I made a quick phone call to Ty while Chance was in the shower to have him go ahead and bring the puppy over and I'd leave the garage open so he could slip in and out. Ty's apartment was only six blocks from our new house so things timed out well. The puppy would be in the garage safely awaiting Chance's discovery within the hour.

Chance was still in the in the bathroom when Ty pulled up. I went out to the garage to let him in and check on the cute puppy.

"Hi Ty. Merry Christmas," I said as I gave him a hug.

"Hi Merry Christmas," Ty replied. "Where's Chance?"

"He's taking a steam shower so your timing is perfect," I said.

"What's the plan?" Ty asked.

"After he gets done with his shower I think I'll have the puppy in the house sitting under the tree and ask Chance to check the gifts again to make sure I wrapped Stephanie's gift."

"Good plan. I'd best get out of here. I'll see you at 2:30," Ty said.

"Thank you Ty," I said.

"Anytime," Ty replied as he snuck back out of the garage and drove away.

I placed the puppy in red box with a big red bow on top then hurried to set my plan in motion.

As I walked into the bedroom Chance had finished dressing and moved quickly to take me into his arms.

"Merry Christmas," Chance spoke as his kisses greeted me.

"Merry Christmas to you too," I replied.

Not wanting to interrupt my plan I pulled myself slowly back and proceeded.

"Chance, have you seen the gift I bought for Stephanie?" I asked as I pretended to undress for my shower.

"No I can't say I have. Where did you last see it?"

"I'm not sure if I took it into the living room or guest bedroom to wrap it. Can you look for me real quick while I get in a shower?"

"Sure," he replied as he walked down the hallway.

I could barely contain myself as I pulled my shirt back on and followed from a safe distance waiting for his reaction.

"Susan! Hey Susan!" Chance shouted.

"Did you find it?" I asked as I let out a quiet giggle.

"I'm not sure. Is it this big red box?"

I walked into the living room just in time.

Chance jumped as a ruckus came from the box.

"What the heck," Chance said as he walked towards the tree to inspect the gift.

I watched in excitement as he read the tag.

"To: Chance," he read the tag aloud as he turned around.

I was standing there behind him with my hand over my mouth trying to keep the laugh in. The look on his face was curiosity and amusement as he started to understand the gift.

He bent down and yanked the top off.

"RUFF," the puppy barked with excitement.

"What? How?" Chance asked as he picked the puppy up and embraced it. "He's beautiful!"

I could only smile as I observed him kiss it on the head and walk towards me grinning ear to ear.

"You are wonderful and you got me a puppy for Christmas," he spoke as he took me with his free arm and pulled me close, "I love you."

Chance kissed me quickly over and over. I was happy he had reacted so well to the puppy. It was a long shot. I really didn't know how he would react. Overall I'd say he loved his gift.

"So what should we name him?" Chance asked.

"He's your puppy you get that privilege," I replied.

"Let me think about it. He is so cute. I still can't believe you got me a dog. That is so cool! Where was he earlier? I didn't hear any puppy noises from any place."

"Over at Ty's place and I had Ty bring him over while you were in the shower," I said.

"That sneaky little devil," Chance snickered.

"I take it you like your gift?"

"Like it? Susan, this is perfect. You just keep on amazing me every time I turn around you've gone and done it."

"Done what?" I asked.

"Taken my heart and pulled me in," Chance whispered as his kisses became passionate. "I love you!"

"And I love you. There nothing I wouldn't do for you, to see you smile," I replied.

He was all I had ever wanted, every square inch, and my desire for him only grew with every day that passed. He was the amazing one and in a few days I would be his for eternity.

At 2:30 sharp the doorbell rang and Ty walked in with Stephanie.

"Merry Christmas," Ty shouted.

"Hello, come on in," I replied, "Chance is outside with the puppy. Go see him, he's like a little boy with that dog, it's so cute."

"Hi Susan," Stephanie said.

"Hi Stephanie, Merry Christmas," I said. "How are you?"

"I'm doing great. How are the wedding plans? Do you still need help Monday with flowers?"

"Yes I do. Would you like to help out?"

"Absolutely, I'm so excited for you," Stephanie replied as she hugged me.

"The pre-game show is already on. I could use some help getting this food into the living room," I said.

"Sure," Stephanie said. "You need help with anymore cooking?"

"No, I actually have pizza for the big game. I sat it back in the fridge and all I'll need to do is pop it in the oven and we're good."

"Oh look, the puppy is so cute. We had so much fun yesterday playing with him. He's an active one," Stephanie said as she paused to look out the back door watching the guys roll a ball around the yard as the puppy ran back and forth between the two.

"Looks like we have three amigos now," I said as I pointed outside as Chance picked up the puppy and Ty scratched the puppy's head.

"Like little boys all over again," Stephanie commented.

"Exactly," I replied as I opened the back door, "the games about on. Chance, come on in and get ready."

"Be right there," Chance said. "Can you bring out a bowl of water for Bruno?"

"Bruno?" I said as I raised a brow and laughed. "You named your dog Bruno?"

"Ty and I tossed around a few names and when I yelled Bruno his ears perked up and he came running," Chance said.

"Well then Bruno it is. I'll grab some water and you two go wash your hands." I said.

I finished setting up the living room and set a bowl of water out for Bruno. We figured it would be better to keep him outside for the afternoon so he can get use to the fenced back yard and get his energy worked out.

The Cowboys football game was getting ready to start on the TV and the aroma of the two large pizzas baking filled the air.

Abe showed up during half-time after he had finished visiting with his cousin Lucas and his family.

I was in the kitchen when Chance came in looking all excited and smiling.

"What's going on?" I asked.

"It's almost time for the big reveal."

"Really, are you sure Ty's going to go through with it?" I asked jokingly.

"Yea that's what we were talking about outside earlier. He showed me the ring. I think he's ready," Chance replied as he pulled me into his strong arms holding me closer, "I know exactly how he's feeling right now and how great he'll feel in about ten minutes."

"I love you Chance Walker," I said as I gave into his deep kiss, "I know exactly how she will feel."

"It is wonderful, isn't it," Chance uttered, "I think I'd best stop before I end up kidnapping you to our room."

I giggled as I took another kiss and enjoyed thoughts of how our relationship had been forged between us over this past year and the level of tranquility allowed for everything to just flow.

We walked back into the living room to join our friends for the half-time show.

Stephanie had gone to the bathroom and the men stood quietly awaiting her return.

Ty nodded his head and I returned to the kitchen as Stephanie came back to sit on the couch.

"Chance, can you bring Abe in here for a minute and help me with the pizza?" I asked so to allow Ty and Stephanie to have their moment alone.

They both moved quickly as if the house was on fire. I just giggled at the excitement. We all were so excited for this moment.

Chance muted the commercial on the TV so we could listen in as we watched from a distance pretending to be occupied with pizza and beer at the kitchen table.

"Stephanie," Ty spoke as he dropped to one knee next to her, "I love you and for the past two years you've stood by me through thick and thin. I just wanted to tell you how much you mean to me and how wonderful it has been having you in my life," Ty continued as he placed her face in his hands and kissed her softly.

"I love you too Ty. You are so sweet. What brought all this on?" Stephanie asked as she smiled.

"Stephanie, I love you," Ty said as he pulled the box out from under the couch. He took the ring out and held it up in his hand, "Stephanie, will you marry me?"

She gasped as his proposal caught her by surprise.

"YES!" She shouted as she fell off the couch and landed right on top of Ty.

We all broke our silence with laughter at the sight. It was great.

Stephanie just kept kissing Ty over and over until they both joined in the laugh.

"Congratulations!" We shouted in unison.

"About time," Chance remarked as he held a hand out to help Ty off the ground. "The suspense was killing me!"

We all offered hugs as we congratulated the newest couple to take the next step.

Nobody really paid much attention that the football game had resumed. We all went back into the dining room and began to enjoy the pizza as we talked about Ty's proposal and cooed over the pretty ring on Stephanie's left hand. She was beaming with happiness and Ty was like a proud man who'd just won his trophy.

After we ate, we all returned to the game to finish out our evening. Christmas turned out to be a wonderful day for everyone.

* * *

The days that followed were as crazy as expected. Stephanie and Patti helped out as much as they could as we got everything ready for the influx of guest. I had mailed out four hundred invitations and as luck would have it two hundred and eighty-nine replied with RSVP stating they would be there. Panic set in I wasn't even sure the chapel held that many guest. Chance reassured me everyone would fit, they might have to sit like sardines, but they'll fit.

I had a final fitting for my dress on the 30th, so I took Mom and Linda with me since neither one of them had seen the dress yet, and this way I could include them in my joy.

"Okay you two are you ready for the big reveal?" I asked as I peeked out the curtain.

"Yes, we've been ready for nearly thirty minutes," Mom joked.

"Ah Susan, the dress is gorgeous," Linda responded.

"Susan, it is perfect and you look like an angel," Mom said.

"Thank you. I just hope Chance likes it. You don't think it's too plain?"

"No honey I think it is just perfect. It's simple and elegant. There's nothing plain about that," Mom replied.

I smiled at the reflection in the mirror as it looked back at me. The dress was simple, elegant, more traditional, and not so "princess" drama.

"Yes, just like me, simple," I said.

After the fitting, we stopped off for a quiet lunch before heading back to the house. Chance and Robert went to Orlando to pick up his sister, Kimberly, who was flying in for the wedding. Kim was serving in the Army and was stationed in South Korea. This would be the first time in almost a year any of his family had seen Kim. We had a big dinner planned to welcome her home. I'd never met Kim and knew she was closest to Chance. We'd talked every time they'd call each other so it seemed like I already knew Kim. I was equally excited to have her in our home and be able to make it to the wedding.

My mom, Chance's parents, and Kim stayed with us as the other siblings would be flying in today and stay in rooms we had reserved for everyone over at the Hyatt.

I found having a house full to be a lot more fun that I'd ever imagined. Everyone got along so well. Everyone pitched into help me clean, cook, and tending to Bruno.

Chance had already started house training Bruno and yesterday signed them up for puppy obedience classes. He had that dog with him every place he went. Today he took the dog to the office to meet and greet everyone on base. It was comical to see him with Bruno.

"Honey, did you get some more puppy chow for Bruno?" Chance asked.

"Yes, it's in the trunk still. I'll go get it. Here you take Bruno outside to play," I said as I headed back into the garage.

"Chance Walker, what have you done?" I asked and stood in awe of the massive bouquet of roses sitting on the top of the car as my brain became pensive.

Everyone came rushing into the garage to see what happened as I stood still as my eyes filled with tears shaking my head. They were so beautiful I couldn't utter another sound. Then I felt his arms wrap around me from behind. My eyes closed as the tears poured out. He stood behind me pulling my hair from my neck and kissing it.

"I love you," he whispered into my ear as he swayed my body in his arms.

"They are breathtaking. I don't know how I deserved such a man," I replied as I turned to face him. My eyes were still overrunning with tears, "I love you! I love you!" I repeated as I held his face in my hands and kissed him.

"I've never felt more loved than I do right now. I will love you forever," Chance replied as he returned my kiss with ardor.

We once again had forgotten we had an audience. Our entire family stood there speechless as they witnessed our exchange of kisses and confessed our deep love for each other.

I don't think there was a dry eye in the house. I have never felt so much love from our family. It just brought everything full circle.

Mom put her hand on my shoulder, "I love you baby. I'm so happy for you both," she quietly spoke as the tears ran down her warm face.

Then we all had a group hug and returned to the living room to freshen up for our family dinner.

For a brief moment, we were alone in the garage. I stopped and turned back to face Chance. My body found its way back into his waiting arms. My lips found the remnant of enthusiasm it desired.

As our embrace grew tighter and our kisses grew softer a sudden repose filled my senses as I knew everything would be effortless tomorrow.

We rejoined our family shortly after allowing us some private time together in the garage.

"So who's hungry?" Robert asked as he rubbed his stomach.

"I'm famished," Kim spoke up first.

"Yes this emotional roller coaster day has my appetite in chaos today," I remarked.

"Well then we'd best get some food in you before your stomach starts to scare everyone off with its evil growl," Chance joked.

Chance and the boys opted for golf earlier today in lure of a bachelor party. I think Chance didn't want any awkwardness about having a wild bachelor party with our parents staying at our home, golf was the alternative. The girls had already given me a bridal shower a couple of days earlier.

After dinner Ty came over to pick Chance up to sleep over his place in keeping with tradition of the groom not seeing the bride before the big wedding.

It would be our first night apart in months and the thought of his absence in our home made me sad even though tomorrow would be the best day of our lives and we'd never have to spend another night apart again.

We had a few minutes of private time before they'd leave.

"So you and me, tomorrow at 11:45 p.m., the base Chapel," Chance said as he wiggled his eye brow with a big grin on his face.

"I'll be there eagerly waiting for you," I replied as I gently kissed his lips knowing that this time tomorrow I would be kissing him for the first time as my husband. The very thought thrilled me to the core. "I love you!"

"I love you too. Don't let things get to you tonight. Just keep in mind tomorrow night and our big celebration, I know that's what I plan on doing," Chance said.

"Okay, well you'd best get so we can all get to bed. Tomorrow will be a long day," I replied as I gave into to yet another insatiable kiss before letting him leave.

I finally got some food to stay down and starting feeling better.

The house was quiet and it still felt odd not having Chance to snuggle with. I surrounded my body on both sides with pillows hoping to give me some comfort from his absence. My body and mind were more exhausted than I'd realized. I quickly drifted off to sleep feeling content with the knowledge that tomorrow would be the best day of my life.

Chapter XV

New Year's Eve

As midnight approached, our family and friends gathered in the chapel. All dressed for the big celebration. New Year's Eve was upon us. I was minutes away from tranquility. I had waited a lifetime for this moment and for this man. I fidgeted in front of the mirror trying to fix my bridal veil.

"Susan, you look radiant," Peggy spoke as she fixed the pin that held the veil in place.

"Thank you. I can't help it, I'm just so nervous. I hope Chance likes it," I replied.

"I don't think you have to worry about if he likes your dress or not. The man loves you," Peggy chuckled. "He'd love you in a paper sack!"

Her words brought a smile and helped break the tension.

"I just want everything, my dress included, to be perfect for him," I said.

"Honey everything is perfect. Now you just go out there and say yes," Mom responded.

"Yes I got it," I repeated as I shook my head in agreement and exhaled.

There was a knock at the door. Peggy slowly opened it as I stepped back to avoid being seen.

"HI. Can I come in yet?" Aaron asked.

"Yes doll, come on in," I replied.

"Oh my Aunt Sue, you look incredible," Aaron commented as he gave me a gentle hug.

"Thank you baby you look pretty dashing yourself," I said.

"Yea right," Aaron replied with a snort. "I'm not comfortable in this monkey suit!"

"Oh Aaron, behave. You can ditch the jacket before the reception," Peggy rattled off.

"Well thank you Aaron regardless, for being such a good sport," I expressed as I placed my hand on his left arm. "Okay I'm ready!"

"Alright then let me go get Stephanie and Brenda and then make sure Jared is ready too," Peggy said as she went to leave the room.

The main area of the chapel quieted down and a hush came over the crowd as Chaplin Moore, Chance, Ty, and Jeff walked up the aisle to take their place.

"Okay everyone's in place. Susan, you're on," Peggy said as she popped her head in the room to inform us.

John, Chance's brother, performed Usher duties along with William, Ty's cousin.

Each parent walked down the aisle first then the wedding party.

Jared, Jeff's youngest son was our ring bearer and Stacy Mitchell, our little friend from Edgewater Elementary, was given the honor of flower girl. Patti was my matron of honor and Stephanie the bridesmaid.

The music quieted down and then wedding march began. Everyone stood and turned around to view our entrance. My heart sang like a hummingbird when I saw him at the other end of the aisle. He was stunning and his smile radiant.

Aaron took a deep breath as he took the first step and with my hand holding onto his arm, we proceeded forward.

There were gasps, whispers, mouths falling open, tears running down faces, and then there was Chance. He was all I could focus on. I fought the overwhelming urge to burst into tears of fulfillment.

Aaron paused and turned to face me, lifted my veil, and kissed my cheek, "I love you," he quietly whispered and smiled. He then turned to Chance and shook his hand.

Aaron nodded at Chaplin Moore then placed my hand into Chance's, turned, and went to sit next to Mom.

As I slowly looked up to see his eyes an un-measureable nirvana filled my soul. He was breathtaking and he was mine.

Chance softly squeezed my hand as we turned to face the Chaplin.

A prayer was spoken asking for GOD's blessing upon our union then we exchanged our own vows. We wanted something more meaningful to express our love and commitment to each other, so we wrote our own vows.

Chance began his first as he held both my hands in his and smiled with amazement.

"Susan LeAnn Hall, today before GOD and family I proclaim my undying love for you. I promise to be there for you when you need me, to never let you down, honor you, and love you until my time on Earth ceases to exist. You are my world. You have brought a sense of purpose to my very being. Words could never express how I truly feel for you. I loved you from the moment I saw you. I will love you for all eternity."

"Chance Thomas Walker, you are my life, my love, and my reason for living. You are my best friend, my soul's companion, and I promise to love you until my heart beats no more. I promise to be there for you in good and bad times, to honor you, and to spend the rest of my life devoted to you. Without you in my life there would be no reason to breath. I knew I loved you from the first kiss. I will love you for all time."

Chaplin Moore spoke up asking for the rings and then placed them in our hands as we turned to face one another again.

We spoke our sacred vows then paused as the chapel bells signaled midnight.

"I hear by pronounce you husband and wife," Chaplin Moore spoke as the last bell struck, "Chance, you may kiss your bride."

We stepped towards one another and Chance took my face into his hands as his lips kissed mine ever so gentle, and with calmness.

"I love you!" I said as the applauding began and I paused to see his face full of happiness.

"I love you Mrs. Walker!" Chance replied with excitement.

"Ladies and gentleman I am proud to introduce for the first time Mr. and Mrs. Chance Walker," Chaplin Moore spoke aloud, "Happy New Year's everyone!"

Clapping and cheering erupted filling the great hall.

We glanced back at each other and took a few steps forward to offer hugs to our parents before continuing down the aisle hand in hand.

My heart swelled with pride as my soul overflowed with love.

The wedding party stayed as the guests exited the chapel to make their way to the wedding reception.

My niece Amy, a blossoming photographer, was our official wedding photographer and took charge of placing everyone in position for our group photos and family unity photos, as well as all the photography shots for the reception. I knew everything would turn out great Amy did wonderful work. I had complete confidence in her abilities to really shine tonight.

"I love you," I whispered into Chance's ear as we embraced for our couple's photo session.

He held me tightly as he placed a delicate kiss on my forehead.

"You have no idea how much those very words electrify my soul," Chance replied as he moved down my face to kiss my lips.

Yes electrifying my soul that is what he did and to hear him express the same to me gave my devotion to him a more meaningful description. My soul has never felt as loved as it does right now.

"Okay everyone. That wraps it for this part. It's time for us to join the rest of the family at the reception before people think we've gone AWOL," Amy said.

We piled into the waiting limos and made our way to the Ballroom. Once we arrived, the wedding party entered the banquet room first giving us a private moment before our grand entrance.

All I wanted at that instance was to be in his arms right where I belonged.

"You have made me the happiest woman in the entire universe," I decreed as I cupped his face in my hands and kissed him lovingly.

Chance let out a soft moan as his lips returned my affection.

"The first day as husband and wife this is going to be best day of my life," Chance quietly spoke as his hand caressed my face, "I love you with every ounce of life left in my body, I love you."

His kisses continued to softly express what his words could not.

"Not again. Don't you two ever stop to breathe?" Ty asked sarcastically.

"Yes we do just not around you," Chance replied back as he slapped Ty on the back.

"Well I love you both and I couldn't be happier to see you two finally tie the knot," Ty commented, "now it's time for your big entrance."

Chance took my hand in his as we proceeded forward following Ty's lead.

Aaron was on stage with mike in hand.

"Ladies and gentlemen give it up for Mr. and Mrs. Chance Walker," Aaron announced.

The noise level rose as the applauding returned. We entered the room waving as a radiant glow came over both of us. I could feel his pride in this moment and his undying love.

Aaron had already set up for his acoustic performance of "Wildfire", his wedding gift to Chance and I.

Chance lead me straight to the dance floor not missing a beat as Aaron began to sing.

Aaron, in his entire splendor, began his acoustic performance of "Wildfire" the first song that evoked the flame and our first kiss.

The song was perfect. I felt at ease as Chance pulled me into his arms as we danced and whispered part of the lyrics softly into my ear as he kissed my cheek making his way to my lips. My heart lifted as my head spun from the intoxicating kiss my husband shared with me. It was always far too easy to forget our audience. My mind could only zone in on Chance and nothing else.

We remained in our embrace even after our song had finished not wanting to let go.

Chance had hired the band South Jordan to perform during the reception. I'd heard their music from the CD's Chance had and I got the opportunity to meet the band two days ago after they had arrived in town. Chance told me how he met Michael, Greg, Mike and Bobby at a club they'd performed at in Bloomington, Indiana last year during a trip he and Ty took up there for their buddy Blake's wedding.

Chance loved their music and insisted they play the reception if he could manage to bribe them to come down to Florida and perform.

As it would be, Aaron tapped my shoulder and asked for the traditional father daughter dance as he stepped into represent dad. I smiled and took his hand as Chance smiled back and went to stand next to his parents.

"Thank you Aaron for everything baby," I said as tears filled my eyes and my emotions broke forth with memories of dad and how much he would've loved Chance and how proud I was of my nephew and the man he'd become.

"You're welcome Aunt Sue. I love you and I can't think of any place I'd rather be," Aaron replied as he embraced me into his arms giving me a good bear hug.

"Thanks I needed that," I sniffled in response.

I looked up and nodded at Chance who then took Linda's, hand leading her onto the dance floor to joins us for the mother son dance.

It was a beautiful sight to watch. One by one our guest entered the dance floor to join us.

After the song had finished Ty took the mike and asked everyone to be seated.

We made our way to the main table as Ty held up his glass of wine to offer the first toast.

"Chance and Susan, two of the most loving people I have ever known. We sit here before you today to witness your union, your love, and your commitment to one another with pride and honor. Chance, you are the greatest friend anyone could ever ask for and thank GOD you never gave up your dreams. Susan, my dear friend you are like the sister I never had and now I do. Thank you for bringing me home safely and for finally shutting Chance up," he laughed as he poked fun at Chance's unwillingness to give up on me, "the two of you have come so far and inspired so many. Here's to life, happiness, and never ending love," Ty finished and held his glass high and gave a nod. "Cheers!"

I was the first up from my seat to offer a hug for his beautiful words and support followed by Chance.

"Thank you Ty, for that wonderful toast and your kind words," Chance responded. "Now let's eat!"

After dinner, we cut the cake and allowed for a lengthy photo-op to take place. Chance was very reserved in his feeding and only took a brief opportunity to place a finger full of icing on the side of my lip so he could lick it off.

"Now that brings back some good memories," I replied to his playful gesture, "yes I recall your lick and then as I remember it was followed by one of the most excited kisses I'd ever had."

"I'm saving that for later," Chance replied as he winked and started to snicker.

Once again, the music returned to a live performance as the band South Jordan took the stage and their music filled the air. Throughout the night Michael and Aaron traded off vocals on various songs keeping the party alive.

"Overall I think Aaron and Chance's band South Jordan worked out perfectly," Stephanie stated.

"So how is Aaron related exactly?" Sandra Owens asked.

"Aaron is Susan's only nephew and an amazing musician," Stephanie replied.

"Well they both sound wonderful," Sandra said.

"Hi ladies are you enjoying yourselves?" I asked as I gave Sandra a hug.

"Yes we are. We're just talking about how much we love Aaron," Stephanie said.

"Yea Aaron gets that a lot. Either it's his music or his good looks," I replied as I looked to Aaron and waved, "he's a great kid."

"Stephanie told me you have a niece in the Coast Guard?" Sandra asked.

"Yes, my oldest niece Tammy, my sister Brenda's daughter. She's stationed in Alaska and she'd the only one of my nieces that couldn't make it today," I replied.

"I'm sorry to hear that. Who else is here from your side of the family?" Sandra asked.

"My niece Amy you met her earlier, she and Tracy, the one over by the band, are also Brenda's girls, my sister Brenda is the one with the fake tan over near the bar," I said as I pointed each of them out, "my sister Peggy is over there, and you met her at the wedding, she's Aaron's mom, my other two sisters Kathy and Christy are the blondes, who helped serve the cake. Christy just got married last year and has a new baby girl Daisy, whom she named after our mom, and Kathy just got divorced," I said as I continued to point out the rest of our family. "The two girls that are coming out of the bathroom are my nieces LeAnn and Lyn, they're Kathy's daughters."

"That is nice you have just about everyone here to see you two married," Sandra replied.

"Yes and Chance has his entire family here so the party just keeps growing," I said.

"I went to school with all of Chance's siblings, except for Mary. She's the oldest and had already graduated high school when their family moved to Galveston. Kim and I were in the same grade. David and John a few grades ahead," Sandra spoke kindly.

"I love his family. Everyone has always treated me like I'd been a part of the family for decades," I replied.

"They are great and Chance I think he's the best one of the entire bunch," Sandra said.

"I can't argue with you there," I chuckled.

"Speaking of the devil," Stephanie spoke up.

"Hello beautiful," Chance softly spoke as he wrapped his arm around me pulling me to his side.

"Hello," I replied as I raised a brow.

"What are you ladies discussing?" Chance asked.

"Susan was bragging on you and the family," Stephanie said.

"She was, well, I thought I felt my ears burning," Chance chuckled, "well if you'll excuse me ladies, I'd like to steal my wife for another dance."

I held my hand out for his as we walked towards the dance floor.

"Are you having fun?" I asked.

"Yes actually I am and I think everyone else is too," Chance replied.

His arms pulled me in closing the gap between us until I could feel his heart beating. His eyes started firmly at me and never broke away.

"I love you," Chance whispered as he leaned into kiss me.

I smiled and returned his kisses,

"You're all I need," I said as my hand caressed his jaw line.

His hand moved to grasp mine holding it still as he kissed the back of my hand then turning it to allow his lips to kiss the other side.

"You're all I have ever wanted," Chance replied as he continued to hold my hand to his chest close to his heart.

"I love you Chance Walker. Today has been the best day of my life, and as long as I breathe, I will love you, and I will make sure every day I let you know how special you are to me and how much I need you."

Chance looked over to the stage and gave a nod. The band played "Under Orion", another one of our favorite songs that Aaron had written and recorded. Chance pulled me in crushing my body close to his and with an eager surge gave me one of the deepest erotic kisses my lips have ever had the pleasure to experience.

He didn't need to tell me another word. His kiss always spoke the truth, his hands always allowed me to feel the truth, and his heartbeat always sang in unison with mine bringing me to a point of spiritual elation. He completed me.

We were still swaying together as the music softly finished and my lips refused to release his.

I didn't want to release him. I wanted to stay right there in his arms and never let go.

Finally, our kiss became more playful as we'd both realized we were now the only people on the dance floor, and we had an audience.

The music stopped and the clapping began louder than before and with a few whistles from Ty and Abe.

Pausing from our embrace Chance turned to wave at Ty and Abe giving them the "thumbs up" for the support of his passionate public display of affection.

"Are you ready to get out of here Mrs. Walker?" Chance asked as he stole a quick kiss.

"Yes I am Mr. Walker," I replied as I giggled.

Walking around the ballroom we gave hugs and said our good-byes to our family and friends. It was 3:00 a.m. and the party was still going on. We had reserved the ballroom until 5:00 a.m. since we knew some of our friends and family would like to celebrate the New Year a little longer.

Our plan was to go back to our home and spend the night then fly off to the Island of Atlantis in the Bahamas later in the day.

Linda, Robert, and my mom had already arrived home and were in bed when we returned.

Trying to be as quiet as we could, and we snuck our way back to our master bedroom for the beginning of our honeymoon.

"I've wanted to do this all evening," I insisted as I slowly pulled off his tie as his lips burned the flesh of my neck, "I love you."

It was all I could say as Chance lifted me up and carried me to our bed. His hands rushed to remove my dress. He only stopped to finish removing his tuxedo and then like a love starved man, he moved his body meticulously towards me, his hands and lips slowly worked their way from my chest towards my face. My breathing was erratic and I snapped. I moved so quickly it caught him off guard as I pulled his body down onto mine and flipped him over on his back. I slowly returned the flesh tease to his own chest as my hands traced every curvature of his well-defined body. Chance moaned and closed his eyes. His flesh was hot and sweet bringing me to higher arousal. His hands moved across my body pulling me on top as I crushed my flesh into his taking him insatiably as if it were our first time, and he gave himself to me eagerly and unrestrained.

His hunger filled my senses and my desire. He was divine.

We woke mid-morning. Chance got up to shower, and I ventured off to see what the rest of our family was up to.

Our plane didn't leave until 5:00 p.m. so we all had plenty of time to rest and recover from our evening.

Mom and Linda had brunch ready for us.

"Where's Kim?" I asked.

"I don't know she didn't come home after the reception," Linda said.

Silence filled the kitchen and I took a sip of orange juice not wanting to add to the odd situation.

Five minutes later Kim walks in from the garage. I looked outside and I saw Ty's bike.

"What the f-," I stopped before I dropped the f bomb in front of my mom and mother-in-law.

Kim looked at me smiling as she wiggled her eye brow.

I excused myself and followed her into her room.

"Kimberly Walker, what they hell have you done?" I asked demanding an answer as I closed the bedroom door.

"Wait just a minute Susan, it isn't what you think," Kim replied.

"Well then inform me on what you are doing on Ty's bike after a night out?"

"I stayed the night at his apartment," Kim said.

"You what?" I asked confused still not sure if she meant as a friend or something else.

"Yes, you two missed the big fight after you left Ty and Stephanie was out in the breeze way yelling, or I should say she was yelling at him. Cursing saying hateful things I couldn't believe my ears. Ty stood there and took it. Then she went to slap him. I stepped in and grabbed her by the hair and threw her sorry little ass out the front door."

"Oh my GOD. What happened? Why?" I quizzed.

"At first I didn't know I just walked in on the whole drama as it was finishing according to Ty. Stephanie had been missing for almost thirty minutes and Ty went looking for her. He found her alright, sucking face with some young airman in his car. Ty said his name, but I can't recall who it was. Apparently, they all knew each other and the guy didn't know she was still with Ty. She had told him they had broken up which they weren't at the time, but they're broke up now!"

"Holy crap! So she's been screwing around on Ty while she was engaged to him? I think I'm going to be sick," I said as I quickly sat down on the bed, "well, don't say anything to Chance right now okay. You tell Ty I'm sorry for all of this.

I'll break the news to Chance later and more than likely he'll call Ty to make sure he is okay."

"Oh Ty will be okay," Kim said as she grinned. "He'll be more than okay!"

"Kim, what did you do? Did you sleep with Ty?" I asked.

"Slept with him hell yes. I rocked his world," Kim replied as she started to laugh, "I've always had a thing for Ty for years. I know it may not have been the right time or whatever, but it just happened. He was crushed by what Stephanie did to him. You know how he loved that stupid white trash."

"Yes I do and I know how it must have killed Ty to see her kissing another guy," I calmly spoke.

"Poor Ty he didn't deserve that not from her or anyone. We sat outside the ballroom for an hour before he asked me if I needed a ride home I said yes. We sat in your driveway for nearly an hour and then he asked me if I'd like to go see the sunrise with him so I did and one thing led to another," Kim explained.

"Just be careful. You don't need to get hurt by his rebound," I replied as I gave her a hug.

"I'm not worried about getting hurt by Ty. This isn't our first rodeo, and as I was saying, we went for a walk then ended up back at his place after that. We started talking, then he leaned in for a kiss, and I didn't want to stop him. One thing led to another and we had one wild night," Kim said with a wink.

"Are you going to see him again this week?" I asked still feeling nauseous.

"Yes he'll be here in about fifteen minutes. He's jogging over," Kim replied.

"Okay, well he's got clothes in the closet I know he'll want a shower. I guess he can use your bathroom when he gets here. Just let him know I know and it's okay with me about you two, nothing weird. I just want him to be happy and you too," I replied as I gave her a hug.

"I will. Thank you for listening and understanding whether you realize it or not I am in love with Ty. I have been for years," Kim said.

"Wow, no I had no clue, funny it seems I'm famous for that," I snickered.

"Would it be too weird if he stayed here with me while you're in the Bahamas? That is if he wanted to stay here with me."

"No, zero weirdness. It might be good for him to hang out with you for a few days," I said as I walked out the door to return to our parents in the kitchen.

Chance had finished showering and Ty let himself in and was already at the kitchen table stuffing his face. I walked over to Chance and placed my arm around him for a kiss on the cheek before sitting down. I patted Ty on the back, smiled, and gave a nod letting him know I knew.

Ty got up from the table and went off to Kim's room. A few minutes later Kim came out. I could hear the shower running. Kim sat down next to me and leaned over to whisper that she'd spoken to Ty and everything was okay.

With balance restored to some odd level, I set into enjoy my brunch with our family.

Robert, Linda and my mom all had flights out of Orlando close to the same time Chance and I needed to be at the airport, so we all took a limo to the airport in style.

Ty and Kim stayed behind. Ty gave me a hug and said thanks before we left.

I wasn't sure the history between Ty and Kim, but they have been down this road before. I relaxed knowing Ty, for the most part, wouldn't have to go through the first few days of his break up with Stephanie alone. He would have an old friend there with him to help comfort him and who knows maybe Kim is Ty's long lost love.

We said our good-byes to our parents and made our way towards our gate to begin our tropical honeymoon.

Our flight to the Bahamas was uneventful and wonderful. As the plane circled the island to land, we could see the turquoise water as it lapped against the white sandy beach below. The weather was warm and the air still sticky as ever.

This wasn't our first time in the Bahamas, our flight crew came here for a group vacation three years ago, so Chance and I both knew we'd have a relaxing honeymoon and be able to spend plenty of quality alone time together.

For the remainder of our first day, we stayed in our room, sleeping, eating, and feeding each other's ravenous desire.

Day two of our honeymoon was a bit more adventurous as we took a scuba class and had the opportunity to scuba dive along the native reef system. The water was crystal clear, warm, and full of life. We'd snorkeled the area last time we were here and scuba diving was high on our list of must do's. Our evening revolved around dancing at a local club.

Day three we shopped the local bazaar for gifts to bring back for Kim and Ty. Chance broke down earlier in the morning and checked in on Ty. I explained what had happened after we left the reception and Chance told me how Ty had confided in him that he suspected something wasn't right with Stephanie, and she was hiding something big. Big was an understatement when it comes to sleeping around on the man you just got engaged to a week prior and all the time she knew she wasn't going to marry him. The thought made me sick at how Stephanie lied to all of us and how it would destroy Ty's ability to ever trust another girlfriend ever again.

"Are you ready for lunch?" Chance asked bringing me back into focus.

"I'm starved," I replied as I took a quick kiss, "I love you!"

"I love you too babe," he softly responded as his hand caressed my cheek.

"Is everything okay with Ty?" I asked.

"Yes, better than expected. Ty and Kim are keeping each other company, so they're staying at our house until we get back tomorrow," Chance replied.

"That's good. I think Kim still has some unresolved feelings for Ty," I said.

"I think they both do. You know he's always been in love with her."

"You don't say. Well then that's nice," I replied as I raised my brow recalling my conversation with Kim.

"So what's for lunch? You feel like having a burger? Or surf and turf?" Chance asked.

"A burger would be good, but steak and seafood seem more logical since we are in the Caribbean enjoying romance and fun on a beautiful tropical island," I said.

"Surf and turf it is!" Chance replied.

We made our way back to the hotel room to change out of our swimsuits and slip into something casual for lunch.

The hotel Atlantis had several dining options everything from the pub, traditional buffet, and then a steak house. We opted for the steak house and a relaxing meal for our last lunch on the island.

"I've noticed you are feeling better these past few days. Is your stomach better?"

"Yes it is I have been feeling pretty good. I haven't had any more sickness in days. I guess my bug just ran its course," I said.

"I'm glad I was beginning to worry there for a while everything made you sick even smelling food," Chance stated.

"I know, but today I feel great," I said. "Weird isn't it?"

"Next time you start feeling that way maybe you should go to the clinic and make sure you didn't end up with E-coli or some other bad stomach virus," Chance said.

"I will don't worry. I don't think I want to go through all that again," I replied.

We continued to have our steak and lobster while enjoying some light hearted conversation. After lunch, we decided to try our luck in the casino. We'd been there for three days and hadn't even stepped foot in the casino.

"I feel lucky," Chance said as he gave a wink. "How about you?"

"I'm born lucky," I replied as I squeezed his hand. "I have you as proof of that!"

Chance stopped, turned to face me as his arms pulled me close, and laid a wild kiss on me.

"I'm the lucky one," Chance firmly spoke as he released me and began walking towards the poker table.

I just smiled and followed behind him hopelessly in love.

"Good afternoon. Place your bets," the man at the poker table spoke.

We sat down next to each other and nodded that we were in. The table was full.

I placed my bet and Chance doubled it. He must be feeling lucky.

I matched his bet and sat back watching the other players match it as well.

"Seventeen," our dealer said.

One by one each player turned their cards face up. I smiled at Chance's hand, twenty-one. He was lucky. With luck on his side, we continued to play for another thirty minutes before calling it quits and heading over to the roulette table for more fun.

"Now watch and learn," I snickered to Chance as I placed my chips.

Finishing our afternoon in the casino on a winning note we decided to go out to the pool, get in some laps, and work on evening out our tans.

The rest of our day was lazy and filled with relaxing around the pool while enjoying some people watching. There was a large family next to us. The parents sat on the lounge chair while watching their children of various ages all playing Marco Polo in the pool. It was so cute seeing the childish play and got me dreaming of little Chance's running around our pool back home in the near future.

As if he read my mind. I felt his hand caress my arm. I turned to look to see his smile.

"How about we work on that "future idea" again?" Chance asked as he wiggled his eye brows and his evil grin streaked across his lips.

"I'm ready," I pertly replied as I quickly stood up and grabbed my towel.

"Future idea it is then," Chance said as he let out a soft giggle.

We walked quickly back to our room. Once inside Chance kicked the door shut behind him and grabbed my waist and lifted me up off the floor into his arms.

His lips worked feverishly over mine as he rushed me to our bed. We gave into a greedy kiss. My hands gripped his flesh with greed as I pulled him down onto mine own flesh feeling the warmth that remained from the suns radiation as it mixed with the smell of coconut oil and the sweet taste of his tongue. His body crushed into mine as his hands ripped my swimsuit off my body and tossing it over his head. His lips never broke stride as they continued to bring my flesh a whirlwind of pleasure. Every moment I shared with Chance seemed to bring forth an overwhelming urge to give myself to him completely and with erogenous passion that could only come from deep within one's very soul as it burst to the edge of spontaneous obsession.

The mission to work on our future idea never looked so good.

Chapter XVI

Surprise

Ty and Kim greeted us once we arrived to baggage claim at Orlando International.

"Hi I'm so glad to see you two," Kim spoke with excitement.

"We're glad to see you two as well," I replied as I gave her a hug.

Kim was glowing and Ty had this crazy grin, like a child who just stole a cookie from the cookie jar or something.

"Hey dude. How was the Bahamas?" Ty asked as he gave Chance a brotherly half hug and a pat on the back.

"Hi. It was wonderful, plenty of sunshine, and the best company ever," Chance replied.

"Well are you two hungry?" Ty asked.

"I am starving to near death. I need a burger," Chance said as he rubbed his stomach.

"How about we have lunch at the Hard Rock Café?" Kim asked.

"That sounds perfect," Chance responded as he offered her a hug.

Our bags and the extra souvenirs we brought back with us barely fit in the Camaro.

Not wanting my honeymoon to end, I hopped into the backseat and pulled Chance in after me.

"Ty knows the way he can drive," I remarked.

"Roger that," Chance replied.

I snuggled into my husband and allowed my body to be enveloped into his strong arms as I pulled my face close to his and to begin my playful kisses. Chance was more than happy to oblige.

I observed Ty holding Kim's hand and caressing it ever so often while glancing over to see her face. Kim had a radiant smile. It was odd at first to see the two of them together, but Chance had filled me in on their history, and it made sense.

Then I saw it. I gasp trying not to give away my vision not knowing if Chance had seen the same glimmer I just spotted. I allowed an internal giggle and a smile. This is going to be good.

We arrive at the Café within minutes.

"I think Ty just set the land speed record for fastest drive from the airport to the Hard Rock Café," Chance chuckled as we exited the car.

Not wanting to give any news away, but still feeling curious I took my arm and put it around Kim's shoulder and pulled her close for a whisper.

"Is that what I think it is?" I quietly asked.

She smiled and nodded without a word then pulled away to take her place in Ty's waiting arms.

I just smiled back feeling a strange level of excitement for them both.

Who am I to deny those feelings of love found again between two people who had similar levels of undying love for one another?

Our new friend Gene, the manager, met us at the reception podium with hugs and congratulations on our wedding and proceeded to sit us at a quiet corner table.

"We brought you another astronaut to sign that group photo Gene," I commented as we took our seats.

"I'll be right back and I'll get you a round on the house," Gene spoke as he turned to the bartender, "Tim will you get a round of Smithwicks for my favorite astronaut's?"

"Will do," Tim replied.

"Hello. Welcome to the Hard Rock Café. I'm Jorge and I'll be your server today. What can I start you all off with?"

"Gene has the beer covered. How about some cheese fries?" Chance replied.

"Sounds great I'll get that order in and give you a chance to look over the menu," Jorge said and walked away.

"This is more like it finally a good burger and good beer," Chance said as he placed his hand on my leg and began to caress it.

I raised an eye brow in response to his playful tease of my flesh and goose bumps invaded my skin. I leaned in for a quick kiss.

"Yes, that's what I'm having too. I'll have a burger and some water," I said as I took my hand and placed over Chance's giving it a squeeze.

He just lowered his head nodding as he smiled and squeezed back.

"So Ty, how are you doing?" I asked.

"I'm great never better," Ty replied as he put his arm around Kim and pulled her closer.

There it was I saw it again. Blazing in the artificial light this time I couldn't hold back my gasp. It wasn't just any ring, it was a wedding ring.

Chance looked at me then looked at his sister. His mouth proceeded to drop open as he sucked in a huge breath of air.

"What the hell?" Chance asked in shock.

"What you like it? It's pretty isn't it," Kim snorted as she held her left hand up to make the diamond glimmer again and then sighed.

"Ty, is there something you'd like to tell us?" Chance curtly asked.

"Where do I start? The ring is pretty isn't it? Let's see, you guys left for the honeymoon, I went over to your house, and stayed with Kim and one thing lead to another, and two days ago we flew off to Vegas and got married," Ty informed us then lifted his chest with pride and turned to kiss Kim.

"You did WHAT?" Chance asked aggressively.

"Now Chance, do you really think I'm going to let him get away again?" Kim asked as she smiled.

"No, but married? Why?" Chance asked with pursed lips.

"Why the hell not," Kim replied quickly back.

Chance sat there in a daze not speaking another word. He was in shock at the sudden news of his favorite sister and his best friend running off to Vegas and getting married.

"Wow you Walker's do work fast," I teased as I tried to ease some of the tension at the table.

Kim laughed in response as she shook her head in agreement as the food arrived.

Chance was reserved and only spoke simple words for the rest of lunch as he slowly ate his burger and then asked for another beer when our server returned to check on us.

I'm not sure what all is going through his brain. I really don't think he expected this from his sister or Ty.

"Kim, I got you the cutest dress. I can't wait for you to see it and see if it fits," I said trying to change the subject and once again lighten the mood.

"That is so sweet thank you. Yes, I'll try the dress on as soon as we get back home," Kim replied as she gave me a wink.

"Would anyone like some dessert?" Jorge asked.

"No I think we're good, just the check please," Chance replied coldly.

I looked up at Ty and I could see his eyes glazed over. He knew Chance wasn't happy, but I felt that maybe Ty didn't expect Chance's cold reaction either. Ty's only human and a wild spontaneous one at that.

We paid for the meal and left without another word being spoken. Chance and I returned to the back seat as Ty took command of driving once again. I took Chance's hand into mine. He responded by looking at me with a soft smile. I took that as a good sign and shifted my body closer to his and placed my hand on his thigh to allow his arm to wrap around my waist. I took the opportunity I was given and reach my hand to his tender face caressing it as I pulled him towards me.

"I love you," I said and smiled.

A grin broke across his face as my lips found his. My hand freed itself from his face and slowly moved down his chest caressing his firm abdominal. He pulled his face to my ear to speak.

"You're getting into risky territory Mrs. Walker," he whispered.

"I know that's my plan. Live dangerously and love hard," I snickered as I kissed his neck moving my lips across his flesh up to his ear lope and stopping to take a soft bit before releasing it as a low moan escaped his lips.

I didn't care who saw what I wanted my husband to know he was all I thought of, and he was all I wanted right now.

His lips returned my erotic tease with his own trail of kisses up my neck as he bit my skin between his playfully.

"You're going to be the death of me woman," Chance quietly moaned into my ear as my hand moved slowly across his skin.

"All I want when we get home is you," I whispered as I inhaled feeling extremely aroused.

"All of me, you shall have," he replied as his kiss got wild and frantic.

"Home," Ty said as we drove into the opened garage.

"Thank God," Chance replied as he tried to compose himself and I did the same.

An evil grin came across his face as he took my hand in his.

"I think we need to freshen up a minute. Ty, just leave everything in the car and we'll get it later," I said as we got out of the car.

Chance let out an evil laugh and grabbed me into his arms lifting me up.

"Welcome home Mrs. Walker," Chance said as he gave me a soft kiss carrying me through the threshold.

I remained in his arms until we entered our bedroom. Softly he rested me onto the bed and ran back to the door to shut and locked it.

"Now where were we?" Chance asked as he shed his clothing.

After an intense lovemaking session we showered, dressed, and decided to have our talk with Ty and Kim.

Kim was resting on the couch curled up in Ty's arms as we walked into the living room.

"Hi," Kim said. "Did you two get some rest?"

"Something like that," I snickered.

"I was thinking of grilling some ribs for dinner if you're up for it later," Ty said.

"That sounds great," Chance replied calmly.

Maybe my talk settled Chance down some. They were both adults and we both know Kim and Ty had a lot of unresolved feelings and issues. Both were extremely spontaneous.

"Kim, can I borrow you for a minute in the kitchen. I need some help peeling potatoes?" I asked.

"Sure I'd love to help," Kim replied as she sprung to life from Ty's lap and made her way into the kitchen. "So what's up?"

"Chance wanted a moment alone with Ty to talk, you know guys stuff," I said.

"Is everything okay?" Kim asked.

"I think so we talked things over and Chance may be ready to let up on the whole marriage issue," I replied.

"Good because I'm staying married to Ty. I love him and I'm not about to let that boy out of my life, not now, not ever again," Kim remarked as she washed potatoes in the sink.

"I'm still in a slight stage of shock. I'm happy for you don't get me wrong. It just took us both by surprise," I said as I began to peel potatoes and place them in a large bowl.

"Susan, I love Ty and I've never been surer about anything in my life than I am right now," Kim expressed.

"Well let's get these potatoes cut up and into the foil then I've got some corn in the crisper that needs shucked, we can grill that too and maybe make a salad," I said as a sudden hunger hit.

"Wow Susan," Kim chuckled, "that sounds like a lot of food."

"I don't know what it is lately. One week I'm sicker than a dog and the next I feel like a starving dog. Go figure," I replied.

"Hey Chance," Ty said first as Chance sat down on the couch. "How are you doing?"

"Things are going great. I really love the married life. How about you?" Chance said as he smiled.

"Well, so far so good. I know it was crazy, but something just clicked. It's hard to describe," Ty said.

"Try me, I'm listening," Chance said.

"I guess seeing Kim again stirred up all those old feelings and then the bull shit with Stephanie. It wasn't strange or anything. I saw myself with Kim and I wanted it, all of it. Can you understand?"

"Yes I can understand. I know all too well. That's why I'm not going to give you any crap about running off and marrying my sister," Chance replied with a snicker and a smile.

"Thanks man that means a lot. You know I would never do anything to hurt her. I love her," Ty responded.

"I know you do and deep down I am happy for you both," Chance said.

"So you're not mad at me or going to kill me?" Ty asked.

"No I was never mad at you. More like shocked and well my feelings were hurt. I figured if you ever did get married I'd at least be there to see it."

"I'm sorry about that. I know we probably should have waited. The good thing is we will have an actual wedding later in the spring. Kim doesn't think it's a good idea to spring the news on your parents just yet," Ty said.

"I agree," Chance chuckled, "Dad would be okay, it's mom you have to worry about."

"Yes that's what Kim said. So we figure we'll have the formal ceremony back in Texas that way Linda can make a big deal out of it," Ty said.

"She'll get a kick out of that. I don't think you should tell either of them you two are already married. It might spoil their fun," Chance commented.

"Kim said the same thing," Ty chuckled.

"Well brother dear," Chance snickered, "that's going to be weird for a while, brother."

"Everyone thinks we're brothers half the time anyway. I guess it was just meant to be that we were brothers," Ty said as he smiled.

"Welcome to the family dude," Chance replied as he offered a hug.

"Thanks Chance, you don't know how happy I am to hear it," Ty replied.

"So let's get that grill going before the girls end up doing all the work," Chance said.

"Sounds great let's do it," Ty replied.

The men got the grill started just as Kim and I finished prepping all the vegetables we wanted to grill and mixed a salad up as well.

Everything seemed fine between Ty and Chance, which helped relieve a great deal of tension. They were outside warming up the grill and playing ball with Bruno just like old times. My heart felt satisfied as the sense of normalcy returned to our home and family. Love would always win the day over in the end.

During dinner Kim and Ty discussed their plans with us concerning Kim's tour in South Korea, which would be ending at the end of this month. Kim would put in for her transfer to an Army base near us in Florida. Ty would take three weeks of leave time off to fly back with Kim to South Korea and help her with the big move.

* * *

The following weeks sped by quickly as we busied ourselves with work and dog training classes for Bruno.

We'd returned to our normal work schedule and resumed shuttle training for the following spring shuttle launch date that was announced for March.

Kim and Ty would be returning today.

Chance had been stopping by the old apartment every other day to check the mail and water the planets while Ty and Kim were away. Kim had already had most of her belongings shipped to our house for storage until they arrived. Our garage was beginning to look more like a storage shed than a place to park the motorcycles and car. I had Molly Maids do a big clean up several days earlier at Ty's apartment, so they could have time to recover from the extremely long flight.

I drove by myself to the Orlando International airport to pick up Ty and Kim. Chance had an extended robotics simulation to finish before meeting us back home. I'd already taken the day off so I could get to the airport before all the Friday afternoon traffic crowed the highway.

The plane was on time and our wait for luggage was brief. Most of their clothing had been shipped back home last week and made their transition through customs much easier.

In no time we were back home. Ty and Kim would start the weekend off getting settled into the old apartment. I dropped them off and then headed home. It had been a long day and I just felt completely worn out. I stopped at the light and waited for the green light to turn. The light went green and I proceeded through my turn.

"SLAM!"

Before I could even see what hit me, I could feel blood run down my face. The airbag had deployed and smashed my sunglasses into my forehead blurring my vision. I could feel a burning sensation like glass cutting my skin, and then I went black.

* * *

"Where is she?" I asked, "Where is my wife, Susan Walker? She was in a wreck."

"Honey she's in the ER the doctors are with her right now. Just a minute and I'll go get a nurse," the reception replied as she got up from the counter and went back into the hallway.

"Mr. Walker?" A female nurse asked as she walked towards me.

"Yes, I'm Chance Walker. How is she? How is my wife? Is she okay?" I asked.

"She's going to be just fine. She has only minor injuries and is resting comfortably."

"Thank GOD. Where is she? Can I see here now?"

"Yes just follow me," the nurse said as she walked back into the ER.

I followed close behind her not knowing what I would see or how I'd react to Susan's injuries, but the nurse said Susan was fine and that did relieve some anxiety. I picked up my cell phone and left a message on Ty and Kim's house phone since nobody picked up.

The nurse pulled the curtain back and my heart sank. Susan was lying on the ER bed her clothing covered in blood and a nurse wiping more blood from her beautiful face. It took all my strength to contain myself.

"Hey Chance," Kim spoke up as she reached for me, "I'm glad you're here. She's going to be okay."

"Yes that is what the RN told me, but she doesn't look okay. Why isn't she awake? How did you know she was here?"

"Susan is okay. The doctor gave her a shot for the pain. Her phone was on and I guess during the impact it dialed me, and I could hear her scream. I stayed on the phone until I hear someone's voice. I started yelling into the phone then a man's voice came on asking who I was, and if I knew the lady in the car that just got hit and told me the ambulance was there and they were taking her to the hospital," Kim explained.

"Her phone called you? Okay. Did she break anything?"

"Yes I guess I was the last person she spoke to on her cell phone and the force of the wreck must have activated it. She's not in too much pain and nothing is broken. The doctor gave her some mild medication for the cuts on her arm and face from the glass. She was alert when I got here, and she's just in and out right now. She has a mild concussion and Chance," Kim trailed off, "you'd best sit down."

I sat down waiting for the bad news.

"Chance, you're going to be a daddy," Kim said.

"What?" I asked.

"Susan is pregnant. She's been pregnant for a while according to Doctor Parker. Maybe, two full months or possibly into her third month already," Kim said.

"Susan's what? Really, does she know?" I asked.

"No I don't think she even knew and they haven't told her yet either. Doctor Parker feels she needs to rest first then we can break it to her later," Kim replied as she walked back to sit next to Susan and take her hand for comfort.

"Wow! I'm going to be a dad," I repeated as my heart jumped into a quick pace over the excitement and wonderful news.

"Yes looks that way. Chance there's more," Kim replied

"More? What?" I asked.

"Yes more," Kim said and giggled with her response, "plenty more."

"What the hell are you talking about Kim? Are you sure the doctor didn't give you a shot too?"

"No I'm right as rain. You my wonderful brother are going to be a daddy," she said as she continued with her childish giggle, "looks like you two are having twins."

"Twin what?" I asked then my eyes opened wide. I realized what she meant.

"Yep that's what Doctor Parker said. He did an ultrasound to make sure the baby was okay after the wreck, standard procedure and all, and well there were three heart beats," Kim said, "Susan's heartbeat and two more."

"That is incredible. Susan is going to flip out, Mom is going to flip out," I replied with such excitement that it brought Susan out of her mild slumber, "holy crap twins."

"Oh honey," Susan responded as her eyes slowly opened.

"Kim, will you go get the nurse?" I asked as I quickly took Susan's hand and gave her a soft kiss.

"I'm sorry. I don't know what happened. One second I was turning to go home and the next I was being hit, and then I blacked out," Susan said.

"It's okay. You're fine and that's all that matters now," I quietly replied as I stroked her hair, "I love you Susan."

She looked up at me and smiled raising her hand up to touch my face, and then she was out again. Why hadn't I noticed it before? She's as radiant as any pregnant woman I'd ever seen, and she's as beautiful as ever.

* * *

I woke up to the smell of roses and soft noise of familiar voices. I was okay and I was alive. I could feel his hand as his thumb caressed my cheek and my eyes slowly opened to see his face.

"Hi," I quietly spoke still feeling groggy.

"Hello beautiful," Chance said. "How are you feeling?"

I smiled and raised my hand to his face needing to feel him closer.

"I love you," I said.

"I love you too babe. Is everything okay?"

"Yes I'm fine now you're here, and I'll be fine," I replied.

His smiled returned to his face and a new glimmer of light danced in his eyes.

"What?" I asked.

"You look radiant," Chance replied as he bent over and kissed me.

I allowed a soft moan to escape as I savored the sweetness of his lips.

"I'm not so sure about radiant, but overall I do feel pretty good," I stated.

"That's good. Babe, I was wondering did you manage to hear my conversations with Kim when we were in the ER," Chance asked.

"No, I can't say I remember much of what I said to whom or what anyone else said to me, for that matter," I replied.

"So you feel pretty good right now?" Chance asked.

"Yes I feel fine. Why? What's wrong Chance? Is there something I need to know?" I asked feeling confused.

"Well what's the best way to put this," he replied as he pursed his lips.

"Is there something wrong with me?" I asked.

"I wouldn't say wrong. More like something incredible," he chuckled as he displayed a big cheesy grin.

"Incredible? How incredible?" I asked feeling less anxiety as I studied his emotions.

"Susan, you remember our "future idea" we've been working on?" Chance asked.

"Yes," I said. "Why?"

"Susan," he said as he took a deep breath and exhaled. "You're pregnant!"

"I'm what?" I asked as I shook my head in disbelief blinking my eyes trying to focus.

He began to laugh and then kissed me again.

"Babe, you and I are going to have twins," he said with pride and excitement.

"I'm pregnant are you sure and with twins?" I quickly asked and sat up in bed.

"Yes you are and yes with twins. Doctor Parker confirmed it with me about an hour ago. He did an ultrasound back in the ER to check your abdomen for any possible trauma and came up with three heart beats, yours and two more," Chance explained as his smile grew bigger and the flicker I saw in his eyes returned.

"Wow twins," I practically shouted then my emotions went all crazy again and I began to sob, "we're going to have twins," I repeated as tears of jubilation flowed freely. I looked up to Chance, and he was crying. I held my arms up for him to embrace me, and in no time we were kissing, laughing, and crying.

"Isn't this incredible?" Chance asked as he pulled away to study my reaction.

"Incredible doesn't being to describe it. I love you so much. This is amazing," I said as my voice cracked, tears streamed down my face, and my heart lifted up as it began to sing.

"I love you," he repeated between kisses, "I love you."

A knock at the door broke us from our joyful embrace.

"Hello. How's my girl?" Ty asked as he and Kim entered the room.

"Oh now you two stop it, you're going to get me crying again," Kim said.

"I'm sorry I can't help myself. This is the happiest day of my life," I replied as I gave her a hug.

"So mommy, how do you feel?" Kim asked.

"I feel wonderful," I responded and turned to kiss Chance once more.

"Congratulations sis," Ty said as he held his arms out for a hug.

"Thank you," I said as I accepted his hug.

"Today is the best day of my life," Chance expressed as he held my hand close to his heart and smiled, "just when I thought my life couldn't be more complete you give me this."

"I know the feeling and I feel it too," I replied.

"I'm going to be a dad. This is so cool," Chance said.

"Congratulations bro," Ty said as he patted Chance on the shoulder.

"Thanks man. I can't think of any other two people on this planet, we'd rather share this moment with," Chance replied as he turned back towards me and smiled.

"It is just amazing and twins no less," I quietly said as I placed Chance's hand on my stomach, "when I think how much I love you and how you, my wonderful husband, have filled my life with so much, I can't help but feel overwhelmed with excitement, and now this," I continued as I placed my hand over his and smiled.

"I know it is amazing, you are amazing, and I love you," he softly said as his lips offered a deeper kiss to allow me to understand his emotions, "you've given me everything I could have ever dreamt of and now the greatest gift of all."

His eyes met mine and my heart melted. My soul found solitude in his words. My lips found the greatest passion. I had the man of my dreams right before me, Chance. More than before and unlike any emotion I had ever felt in my life. I knew he was the one I had always been meant to be with, to share my life with, and to bare his children would be the greatest achievement of my life.

"I love you," I said as my soul found the rhythm of his.

"I love you," he replied as he leaned down to place his head on my stomach, "and I love you my beautiful babies."

Tears ran down my face again at the sight of this incredible man's display of never ending love.

"You know I've always wanted a big family," Chance said as his tender lips returned to mine.

"That sounds like a wonderful "future idea" to me," I replied.

Chapter XVII

Serenity

The months that followed were filled with baby showers, baby proofing our house, and setting up a nursery fit for two.

Chance was as wonderful and going overboard as usual.

"Good morning beautiful," Chance said as he touched my face.

"Good morning," I replied as his lips softly kissed mine.

I sighed taking in his tenderness his eyes were full of love and devotion. I felt as he ran his hand over my stomach.

"Good morning my beautiful babies," he whispered as his lips kissed my huge stomach.

He was so cute and excited about the arrival of our children.

"Only a few more days," I said as I ran my fingers through his soft hair.

He leaned up and kissed my hand.

"Yes I can hardly wait." Chance said. "How are you feeling today?"

"Actually I feel pretty good," I replied. "OH! Did you feel that?"

"No! What? Where?"

"Right here," I said as I placed his hand on the spot of my current movement and giggled.

"I felt that," Chance replied. "WOW!"

"Yes they've been kicking the crap out of my ribs all night," I said as I gasp from a much sharper pain that surged through my abdomen.

"Are you okay?" Chance asked.

"Yes, the natives are getting restless," I chuckled and smiled.

"That's my boys," Chance said.

"Boys? Are you sure? Don't you mean girls?" I asked.

"No I'm pretty confident they're boys," Chance declared.

"Well I guess we'll soon find out if we have one or the other. I have to say I'm happy we left that part a mystery. It makes for more excitement," I said. "Don't you think so?"

"Yes, but I still say boys," Chance said as he smiled and kissed my lips.

I moaned as my body reacted to the sweetness of his lips.

"You know I love your kisses," I said as my hand stroked his cheek.

"I can't help myself even seeing you nine months pregnant I'm still aroused and desire to feel your bare flesh against mine," Chance replied as he kissed me.

"I love you," I moaned as his lips continued their erotic tease of my flesh.

"And I love you even more than I thought could be possible," he quickly said as his lips found mine.

He was incredible even as pregnant as I was he still managed to bring forth that burning urge to give myself to him and allow him to take me.

"OH!" I shouted as I broke from our lustful kiss.

"What? Susan, what it is?"

"I think my water just broke," I replied as I felt the sudden gush of fluid leaving my body.

"Alright, stay calm. I'll call Jeff and the hospital," Chance said as he sprung from our bed.

"Okay. Yes, I think our children have decided today is their birthday," I replied as I began to gasp from the heavy contractions that followed.

"Jeff, her water just broke. What do I do?" Chance asked over the phone. "Okay we'll leave right now and see you at the hospital."

Chance hung up the phone and rushed to get my overnight bag.

"You'd better go tell mom, and she can help you get us ready," I said.

"Got it," he replied as he left the room yelling to my mom that it was time.

Mom had just flown in yesterday and would be staying with us for the next four weeks in preparation for the delivery and also to help out after the babies were born. We'd planned for a scheduled C-section in another week, but it doesn't look like our children can't wait.

I quickly picked up the phone and called Kim and Ty.

"Hi Ty it's time," I said.

"It's time for what?" Ty asked.

"My water just broke and we're leaving for the hospital right now," I said.

"Okay we'll meet you there. Be careful," Ty said as he hung up.

"Daisy's already in the car," Chance asked. "Are you ready to go?"

"That's great, but I don't think I have a choice at this point," I informed him as another contraction rocked through my body and I gasped.

"Okay. Breath and stay calm," he insisted as he took my arm helping me into the car.

"Oh my, these are getting closer together," I said as another contraction hit.

"Just hang in there babe we'll be at the hospital in a minute," Chance replied.

Chance pulled up to the hospital ER and rushed into get a nurse to help me inside.

Ty and Kim showed up first and waited with mom in the delivery waiting room until the rest of the family showed up.

Within a few minutes, I was being wheeled into the delivery room.

"Hello Susan. I see your children have decided they want out today," Doctor Gibbons spoke as he greeted us at the entrance of the delivery room.

"Hi. Yes they are as ready as I am," I replied and took in another deep breath.

Chance was at my side the entire time and never let me out of his sight.

I was transferred up to the delivery table and Doctor Gibbons proceeded with his examination of my abdomen with the ultrasound.

"Well Susan, we are ready to proceed with the C-section," Doctor Gibbons informed us.

"Okay let's do this," I replied as I squeezed Chance's hand.

The delivery room filled with various nursing staff and medical support for the procedure. I was draped and prepped for surgery. Chance sat quietly in a chair next to my face talking to me and keeping me focused on him as Doctor Gibbons began to cut my abdomen. I could feel pressure, but not much else. Chance began to stare intensely at the goings on as he held my left hand. His eyes grew wide as the first head emerged.

"Oh," Chance let out as his smile intensified.

All I could do was watch his face and his reaction as it allowed me to fill his joy and amazement.

"Okay we have a boy," Doctor Gibbons spoke loudly.

A small cry followed as the fluid was suctioned out of the baby boy's lungs.

"He's perfect and a full head of hair," Chance chuckled.

"Here Chance go ahead and cut the cord," Doctor Gibbons said.

Chance stood up and took the scissors and cut quickly. He was glowing.

"Mark the time 11:01 a.m. July 4th, it's a healthy baby boy," Doctor Gibbons stated.

The prenatal team cleaned him up, weighed him, measured him, wrapped him in a blanket, and then brought him to me to see for the first time.

My eyes filled with tears as my heart sang. He was beautiful.

"Tyler Robert Walker I love you," I spoke his name and placed a kiss on his forehead, and then I looked up to Chance as he smiled.

"He's beautiful," Chance replied as he leaned over and kissed Tyler.

I could feel more pressure as the next baby was removed. The crying was immediate with this one.

"Okay looks like we have another boy," Doctor Gibbons stated as he allowed a light chuckle.

"I knew it, I knew it, and I was right!" Chance spoke with happiness and kissed my forehead.

"Mark the time 11:04 a.m. July 4th, it's another healthy baby boy," Doctor Gibbons reported.

Chance cut the cord and the prenatal team took similar care of our next son.

"I love you," I said as Chance bent down and kissed me.

"I love you and this has to be the best day of my life," Chance replied.

"Thomas James Walker I love you," I spoke his name as the nurse placed my second son in my arms.

I kissed him and began to cry as my heart was overwhelmed with immense pride.

Both boys were perfect. We did it, we created two of the most beautiful little baby boys I'd ever seen.

The nurse gave Chance our son Tyler to hold as I held Thomas.

I was so in love with my little bundles of happiness. Just like their daddy they stole my heart and brought me calm as I studied their perfect faces.

"Congratulations Susan, you did great," Doctor Gibbons said as he smiled, "those boys are both perfectly healthy."

"Thank you Doc," I replied.

I kissed my babies one by one and allowed Chance to take them out to the waiting crowd to introduce our boys to the family. Doctor Gibbons continued with his surgery to remove the rest of the placenta and staple me up.

Chance and one of the nurses took our boys to the waiting room.

"Hello," Chance spoke up as every jumped to their feet, "I'd like you all to meet Tyler Robert and Thomas James Walker."

"Oh they are beautiful," Kim replied as she softly kissed each head.

"Son they are perfect and look at that they've got your light brown hair," Linda commented as she stroked Thomas's hair and kissed his cheek.

Chance handed Thomas to Linda and handed Tyler to Daisy.

"Congratulations man. We're happy for you both," Jeff said.

"Yea man this is great," Abe agreed.

"How's Susan doing?" Ty asked as he held Tyler gently just beamed at his nephew, "hi my little buddy Ty."

"So she named one after Ty and you?" Kim asked.

"Yes she said it was only appropriate that they be named after the first set of "twins," Chance chuckled, "Doctor Gibbons is finishing up with her as we speak, and she should be going to her room in a few minutes."

"That is wonderful," Daisy replied.

"Twin boys, only Aunt Sue and Uncle Chance could've been this lucky," Aaron said with a chuckle.

"They are perfect little angels," Daisy said.

"These boys are going to be so spoiled," Aaron said as he held Thomas in his arms and began to hum a lullaby.

"Well ladies and gentlemen it's time to give these boys a rest and get them back to their mother," the nurse spoke up.

"Yes, give us about twenty minutes to get settled into the room then everyone can come up to see us," Chance said. "Hey Kim, did you remember the camera?"

"Yes, I have it right here with fresh batteries it's ready to go," Kim replied.

"Okay then we'll see you all upstairs in a few minutes," Chance spoke as he turned to follow the nurse to our room.

I was already in my bed resting when Chance and a nurse came in carrying our babies.

Chance was beaming with happiness. His smile was regal as he entered my room.

"Look what we brought you?" He asked up as he walked towards me.

"My little angels are incredible," I said as I embraced Tyler.

"You did wonderful today," Chance responded as he leaned over my bed side and kissed me ever so softly.

He was holding Thomas in his arms. I could see the features of their profile.

"They both have your perfect nose, chin, ears, and hands," I said.

"I don't know about perfect," Chance smirked.

"Everything about them and you are perfect," I replied as I raised my hand to caress his face. "Thank You!"

"For what?" Chance asked.

"For loving me and never giving up on us," I quietly responded, "this is more wonderful than I could've ever dreamed it to be."

"Loving you was the easy part, and I would've waited as long as it took to win your heart. I'd never give up on you or us."

"I love you," I replied as tears ran down my face, and he began to kiss my lips tenderly.

"I love you Susan Walker. I will love you with my last breath."

The boys began cooing in unison as if they could feel the love between us.

"They are truly incredible," I said as I kissed each forehead and laid them back down into their beds. My eyes overflowing with tears as the gratification overwhelmed me, and I smiled.

"You're truly incredible," Chance replied as his arms wrapped around me and he pulled me closer to his body, "when I think my life can't be any better and my heart can't feel more loved. You give me serenity."

His lips finished explaining what words could not. I had never known a man to love me so much and devote himself so completely. I found myself kissing back with great eagerness as my soul felt whole again. Even now his kiss could turn me into mush.

He sat next to me at my bed side as we watched quietly over our children as they slept. My life was complete.

One by one our family members entered our room quietly and beaming with smiles.

"Hi honey," Mom spoke as she hugged me and kissed my forehead, "you did great today."

"Thank you. I couldn't have done it without Chance," I replied, "he was so calm and collected during the entire delivery. He kept me grounded and focused the entire time."

"He's a natural," Robert spoke up as he patted Chance on the shoulder, "the boys are beautiful."

"I know they're these incredible little bundles of mini-me's," Chance expressed as he put his finger in Tyler's tiny hand and then offered his other hand for Thomas.

Tyler and Thomas both responded by grasping his fingers and offered a sleepy smile.

"I never thought I'd see the day when I had twins," Chance chuckled.

"How do you think I felt? I didn't even know for almost two months I was even pregnant," I said as I smiled.

"Just more proof you're still clueless," Ty chimed in.

"Yes it seems I was. Walker men have that effect on me," I snorted and leaned into Chance.

"I can't argue with you there," Chance snickered and softly kissed my forehead.

"Okay guys let's get some family pictures," Kim stated as she held the camera up and snapped a picture of the boys holding Chance's fingers again.

For the next four days, I recovered from the delivery, and the boys remained in my room the entire stay. The boys were relatively healthy for twins. Each weighed in just over five pounds and showed no signs of any problems or complications of any kind. They'd managed to beat the odds and develop in the womb full term.

"Are you ready to go home and relax?" Chance asked as he entered the room.

"I don't know how much relaxation I'm going to get with two newborns, but I'm definitely ready to go home," I replied.

"Good I know Bruno is excited to meet his new playmates," Chance said.

"You keep Bruno away from our children until we've had time to adjust. Then we can introduce Bruno to the boys. I don't want to overload Bruno with too many new changes in the house," I replied.

"You're right. I'll keep him outside for a few days then we can slowly introduce him to each boy," Chance said.

A knock at the door interrupted our conversation.

"Okay Mrs. Walker you're good to go," Doctor Gibbons spoke up as he entered the room, "here are your discharge papers, and I'll see you back at my clinic next week."

"That sounds great thank you Doc for everything, and we'll see you next week," I replied.

A nurse had me ride in a wheelchair with the boys in my arms as Chance went out to the parking lot to get the car.

I was stunned when I saw Chance pull up in a large SUV.

"Who did you borrow that from?" I asked.

"Nobody it's ours," he stated as he opened a door. "So what do you think?"

"Nice and it's got plenty of room," I commented then smiled. "You did good babe!"

One at a time Chance placed each boy into their car seat and locked them in. He held his hand out to help me out of the chair and into the new vehicle.

It was a quiet and comfortable ride back home. I found myself looking over my shoulder ever few seconds to make sure the boys were okay.

We arrived home to a house full of guest waiting to welcome us home.

Everyone was there to greet us and take turns holding the boys as I went off to shower and change out of my hospital garb.

Chance was in our bedroom sitting on the bed as I walked out of the bathroom with nothing but a towel on.

"Hi. Are you taking advantage of the free time while you can?" I asked.

"Something like that," he replied as his evil grin appeared, and he raised his brow while pulling me into his arms, "our parents are taking care of the boys, so we could have some private time to relax and rest up."

"Mr. Walker what are you up to now?" I asked as he began to tug on my towel.

"Just taking a few minutes to wrap you in my arms and show you exactly how happy you've made me," Chance said.

"Then please show me," I whispered as his lips worked feverishly over my bare flesh, and my yearning peeked. I let out a soft moan as he took me into his arms.

We lay back on the bed as Chance managed to contain his libido settling for a tight embrace of my body in his strong arms. He was tender with his kisses and his firm hands caressed my skin relaxing me.

"I love you," I whispered as my mind shut down and as my body drifted off to sleep in his arms.

* * *

Beep. Beep. Beep.

I heard the sound as I slowly opened my eyes only to see them looking at me and snickering.

"Turn it off Ty!" I demanded.

"Wow that must have been some dream. You moaned Chance's name at least three times and even smiled once," Ty said snickering as he floated by.

Ty and Derek broke out into laughter.

I stuck my tongue out and closed my eyes trying to return to my dream.

"Commander it's time to send our report back to Earth," Ty said firmly.

I closed my eyes and stretched my arms out hoping to smack Ty.

"Fine," I declared in a raspy voice as I released my body for my cocoon. "Is everything ready?"

"Yes we're ready to do the final inspections and check lists before we blast off," Derek informed.

"Okay then boys let's get this orbiter off the lunar surface and go home," I joyfully spoke as I floated by and popped Ty hard on the back.

"Crap Susan, that's going to leave a bruise and Kim's going to kill me," Ty chuckled.

"I'm sure she'll understand. I love you Ty," I said as I giggled and made my way to the communication link control panel.

One hour later we began our communication with Earth and finished our checklist procedures for departure with mission control.

"Derek, you and Ty get strapped in," I instructed.

"Roger Commander," Derek replied.

"Ty, is everything strapped down and ready to go?" I asked.

"Yes everything is complete," Ty replied as he buckled himself into place.

"Houston this is lunar Freedom, over," I said.

"Lunar Freedom, we read you loud and clear. You're good for departure in ten minutes," Chief Banks replied.

"Roger that Houston, all systems go for departure," I responded.

I turned to check on my crew. Both men gave a nod to let me know everything was good. Then I proceeded with our departure protocol, and systems check.

"Lunar Freedom, all systems are go, sequences begin on my marks, and engines go," Chief Banks said.

"And Houston we have lift off," I replied.

"Roger, ground control has confirmation, orbiter has lift-off, and all system go," a female voice from ground control back on Earth informed.

"Houston, we are exiting the lunar gravity," I informed.

"Roger lunar Freedom, you are clear of the lunar surface, all systems engaged, tracking system is working properly, and orbiter course has been confirmed," the female voice stated.

"Roger Houston, our main thrusters have engaged, and we are on our way," I reported as the orbiter made its journey back home.

"Lunar Freedom, we'll see you back on Earth in a few hours. Great teamwork everyone," Chief Banks responded.

"Roger Houston, hey Chief, will you be so kind and tell my husband and my boys, I'll be home in time for the ball game and to have a pizza ready," I communicated.

"Roger lunar Freedom, will do, and you have a safe journey back. Houston over."

I would like to take this opportunity to give special thanks to the following individuals:

To: Stacy Cornish-Godsey for all your hours of proof reading, spell check, editing skills, for a wonderful poem for this novel, and keeping me on track. You have been my rock.

To: Amber Chaffin-Walters for all your hours of proof reading, editing skills, spell check, and encouragement throughout.

To: Aaron Pashka for granting permission for his name, likeness, and music to be published in this novel as well as his friendship and support.

To: South Jordan: Michael, Bobby, Mike, and Greg for granting permission for your names, likeness, and music to be published in this novel as well as your friendship and support.

To my wonderful sisters: Sandra, Charlotte, Nancy, and Debra for your unconditional love, support, and encouragement to believe in myself and to never give up on my dream.

Special Thanks to the following:

Barry Manilow
South Jordan
Aaron Pashka
John Nathaniel
Silvergun
J Minus (rock)
Boyce Avenue
Absence of Concern
Jon Robert
Out of Ether
Josh Golden
One Less Reason
Village Idiot
The Real You
Shorelines End
10 Years
Nickelback

Thank you to the artist and bands that inspired me during my long hours of writing this novel and for giving me a great play list. Your lyrics and music gave me the "muse" to write my novel while your dedication to your dreams helped inspire mine. For this I thank you all!

Follow the author A.S. Johnson on MySpace, Twitter, and Facebook.

CPSIA information can be obtained at www.ICGtesting.com
Printed in the USA
BVOW031013170113

310560BV00009B/60/P

9 781609 765453